Ellipsis…

Ellipsis

Kristy McGinnis

Glassy Lake Publishing

Copyright © Kristy McGinnis, 2020
First Edition 2021

Cover art by Cherie Fox

ASIN: B08TR715N3 (Amazon)
ISBN 978-1-7365367-0-4 (paperback)
Glassy Lake Publishing

You're the compass that ensures I am never lost. Dedicated to my east, south, and west... Patrick, Baylee, and Anabel. And to my eternal True North, Brian.

Part 1

1

*Once, on a family trip to Tucson, I witnessed a
blooming cereus cactus. The fragile snow-white flower
bloomed just one night a year, stretching greedily for
sun's rays it would never feel. I can't help but wonder
now, did it know about its short-lived fate, or did it
preen with clueless vanity under the haughty glow of
moonlight?*

*****

The first time we met, I was nude and shivering
on a gold tapestry covered settee. I spent most of the
hour with my eyes squeezed shut against the blinding
white lights overhead. No one ever protested; they

weren't interested in my eyes. The shadowy figures across the room existed in a hazy world I purposely distorted through the lash covered slits of my eyes. Wherever he sat in the room, I didn't recognize him as anything other than yet another silhouette I purposely obscured into otherness. I preferred to think of the strangers that worked my image with paintbrushes as anonymous entities, something not quite human, shadowy forms not quite aware of my own humanity. It was less embarrassing that way.

As I lay there, I pretended I was rich; I was Onassis rich, soaking sun from a yacht deck somewhere in the Mediterranean. If they'd turned the heat up just a little, the fantasy might have been more believable. A cramp had screamed in earnest from some meaty place in the center of my back and I felt a small tickle that threatened to bloom into a full itch on the back of my scalp. I fought the distractions and remained immobile. Financially, I needed the gig to work out. Relief came only when the professor announced the session was complete for the day.

The eight students who had spent the previous hour studying me intimately were suddenly disinterested, as if they were oblivious to my existence. In an instant, I'd gone from observed to observer. I sat upright, draped myself in a large robe and watched them pack up their supplies. Small bits of casual conversation drifted to me as they made their way to the door. This was how these sessions always seemed to end. I was significant for 90 minutes, and then I was nothing again.

I was gathering my belongings, still shrouded in a large man's robe, when he ran back into the room. We'd almost collided as I walked past the doorway toward the changing curtain, and he stopped abruptly.

The thing I remember most about that moment was the way our eyes locked, and his expression changed to one of surprise. It was as if he'd never seen me before, never stared at my completely exposed body replicating it in some form on a canvas now stored in the back of the room. Then the moment passed, and I saw the recognition flicker.

"Oops, hello," I said with as much faux cheer as I could muster.

He nodded seriously, and our eyes met again. I felt it, a tiny warning bell. I knew I could get lost in their dark depths. He broke the gaze first and stepped aside, motioning further into the classroom and explained, "I forgot my jacket."

He had an accent, one I couldn't really place. It was vaguely Russian perhaps, but with a deeper, warmer subtext that hinted at Hebrew and French influences. He was becoming more interesting by the moment. I chuckled nervously. "You don't want to do that; it's a cold one."

That earned me a quizzical look. I'd later realize just how many common American colloquialisms Narek didn't understand. His English was quite good, but commonly used expressions and turns of phrase sometimes escaped him. It was one trait that somehow stayed endearing, even when everything else became contemptible. This was before that though; this was when everything about him, from his black curly hair and his deep brown eyes to his paint-splattered t-shirt, drew me in. I wanted to touch the tiny delicate feathers of paint on his arm. Woah girl, I told myself, slow down.

"Sorry, what is your name again?" he asked.

"Nell. How about you?"

"Narek," he replied simply. The brief silence that followed felt a bit awkward and stilted, it was a moment where the most natural thing in the world would have been to nod and step aside, but I couldn't just let the moment pass, I needed to know more about him.

He glanced toward a jacket hanging on the back of a chair as if he were about to grab it and go, but I didn't want him to walk away yet. I wanted to know more about him, and I was still brave and unbroken then. On impulse, I asked if he wanted to grab a cup of coffee at The Bean Shack. That he might actually say no hadn't really crossed my mind.

He'd tilted his head and looked at me curiously as if I were a cake on display. He was judging me, trying to decide if I might be worth the calories.

Finally, he said, "I will like that."

I smiled broadly and told him I would get dressed and be right back. At that, he averted his eyes as if he were suddenly aware of my state of undress beneath the robe and the fact he'd already seen it all. Somehow, that made him all the more endearing.

I went behind the curtain in the back of the room and slipped into my comfortable yoga pants and t-shirt, then leaned over the sink to peer into the mirror. I'd blown out my long, golden-brown hair that morning, and it still shined with the healthy post-heat glow. As was the custom at the art school, I wore no make-up for the session, so I took a moment to run mascara through my lashes, and the slightest hint of bronzer over my cheeks. Assessing myself frankly, I wasn't displeased. If I'd only been blessed with another four to five inches in height, I might have had a shot at modeling with an actual agency instead of at an art school. Narek was the personification of tall, dark, and handsome, but I would be a worthy companion, I mused.

Over coffee, we hit the basics. To my surprise, he was 22, only three years older than me. He seemed so much older than most of the college boys I usually met. His serious nature presented as maturity, and I bit back my normal playful banter in response. When I asked where he was from and he answered Armenia, I leaned in across the table to learn more.

"Okay, I will admit I know pretty much nothing about Armenia. It's in the Middle East, right?"

Finally, he rewarded me with a grin. "You start with a hard question. Armenia is perhaps Caucasus. Maybe European. Maybe Asian. Some Armenians would say we are Middle Eastern, but most would say we are not. We are white, even if some of us are perhaps more brown. We are Christian, we were the very first nation to establish Christianity as our national religion, in fact. This is what they will say."

He shrugged, as if what others said was not really important to him. I was intrigued.

"So, everyone has an opinion? It sounds a little like asking anyone you meet in Virginia if they are Southern. The guy from Arlington probably has a very different answer than someone from Lynchburg."

He waved a hand slowly and said, "Maybe a little, but it is more complicated, I think."

I was fascinated by his accent and by his mouth as he formed each word. I prodded him with more questions to keep him talking. He'd landed in Richmond, almost by default. He'd applied to art schools in several major cities, with the ultimate dream of studying in New York. None of the New York schools had come through with funding, so when the Richmond School of Art and Design offered him an impressive grant, he'd reluctantly accepted it. But Richmond seemed to suit him just fine. The city had enough of a unique vibe to keep him interested, he was enjoying the caliber of the school itself, and as he told me with another grin, Virginia women had quickly become his favorite.

I felt a quick thrill of pleasure at those words and winked at him before replying, "Too bad I'm a Michigan girl."

Now he looked eager to hear my own story, so I smiled and explained, "I'm the all-American girl. Raised in northern Michigan, Dad's in manufacturing, Mom's a housewife, sister's a brat. My family is Lutheran; they all drive American made cars. I hate the cold and wanted to be somewhere more exciting, so here I am. I'm studying English now over at VCU but will ultimately go to law school. That's the short and short of it."

The truth was I sometimes felt almost embarrassed about my childhood and family. It was idyllic in a lot of ways. We lived in a world where conflict was recognized as character building, but my conflict had been limited to a somewhat rocky relationship with my younger sister and a few pouty breakups in high school. I'd been a voracious reader my whole life and the heroines in my books had such interesting lives compared to my own. Not very secretly, I'd yearned for more drama, more adventure. Finally, after 18 years in the same house, I'd set out to find it some 900 miles away from home. Now, I thought as I eyed the handsome man across from me, it seemed like things might finally become very interesting.

As we shared the stories of our own journeys to Richmond, he revealed that his had been launched with considerably less support than my own. As the youngest child of four and the only son, Narek had been doted on by both his parents and his grandmother, who lived in their household. Neither of his parents were thrilled he was pursuing an actual career in art, but they'd found some measure of acceptance because he was, after all, the baby of the family. That support had eroded considerably when he announced he wanted to study in America. They were devastated that he would go so far away, and only his promise of return after graduation gave them any solace.

It had only been a few hours since we'd first spoken, yet his mention of returning to the place he called home made me feel unreasonably unhappy.

I tried to keep my voice light and cool. "So that's it? Finish your last year and a half here, then pack up and head back?"

His jaw clenched and he shifted uncomfortably. "No. I just haven't found the way to tell them yet that I plan to stay in America." At my raised eyebrow, he continued, "There is much more than I can explain right now, but this is not an easy thing for them. I will wait until it is a right time."

As I finished the last sip of my second large coffee, I felt a pang of regret and wished it had taken more time. As if reading my mind, Narek asked, "Would you like to have dinner?"

Our formality had dissipated over the caffeine and sugar, and dinner was a more relaxed affair. As our conversation bounced around a myriad of casual topics, we discovered the commonalities. By the time the check came, we'd discovered mutual enjoyment of strong coffee at odd hours, pistachio ice cream, David Bowie, and riding trains. With each new revelation, I felt my excitement grow. I exclaimed, "Oh my God, me too!" more than once.

Almost more important than our mutual enjoyment of certain life pleasures was our shared dislike of winter. My top priorities in life were to breeze through college and then law school, and to avoid winter at all costs, and not necessarily in that order. He laughed as I described the arctic hell that was Northern Michigan in January and agreed vehemently that if there was a hell, it was likely filled with snow, not fire. This led to a more serious conversation, where he confessed that while his family was very religious, he identified as Agnostic. This was something else we had in common, yet another confirmation that our mutual attraction made sense.

As he walked me back to my campus, I glanced up to see the silhouette of his handsome face in the subtle lighting along the sidewalk. I was suddenly very thankful I had a single dorm room. When we reached my building, we paused and he leaned in for the kiss I'd fully expected.

Afterward, as I stood only a few inches from him, I asked softly, "Do you want to come up?"

He grinned and said, "I love American girls." and then followed me up the stairs.

2

My body adapted to his at an almost frantic pace. Each date ended in a sweaty tangle, either in his tiny apartment or my even tinier dorm room. Whatever I thought I knew about intimacy had been based on the awkward fumblings of teenage boys fueled by the beer we'd sneak from our parents' refrigerators. If I'd naively believed I understood what my body was capable of, Narek shattered that understanding. With the patient, skilled caress of his hands and mouth, he coaxed out that dormant part of me always lying in wait. When I'd awaken in the morning, he would often still be there, tangled in my cream-colored linen sheets. I'd stare at his sleeping form; our previous roles would be reversed. I studied him and painted him in my own mind's canvas.

We weren't just discovering each other in the dark, we spent hours talking in the light of day. Narek had revealed who he really was, and that person was more complicated than I'd originally thought. He was indeed Armenian, but he'd actually been born in Azerbaijan. His father, a chemical engineer, had emigrated there in the 70s as part of the Soviet attempt to better exploit the oil fields in the Caspian Sea. It was in the ethnic Armenian community of Baku he met Narek's mother. They'd married fairly quickly and the babies began to come. Narek, the final child, was born in 1982.

Narek remembered his early childhood as normal and happy enough. For almost eight years, Azerbaijan was his physical home, although he was raised to always remember he was Armenian. He would understand later that events were happening around them all of the time, but his father's position of relative privilege and his mother's large protective family had insulated him from the growing tensions. When things did finally explode in January of 1990, his own innocence would be shattered.

"The pogrom was really only a week long, but I was eight years old, so it felt like a lifetime," he explained.

"Pogrom?" I asked. The word sounded both vaguely familiar and very foreign all at once.

"Yes. It is a, I don't know the word to use. It is like a riot but worse. They drag people, Armenian people, into the streets and beat them. Some are killed. They break into homes and take the things Armenians have worked hard for and created. Even my father, who is respected by the Azerbaijani, is scared."

As he told me the story, his calm voice and still face suggested he was reciting someone else's tale. A stranger who listened to him, would have thought he was utterly unaffected by the horror he described. By that point, though, I was no longer a stranger. No matter how matter of fact his voice might sound, I could see his clenched hands. His nails were trimmed and tidy, had they not been, I knew they would have drawn blood from his palms.

"On the fourth day of the pogrom, they took our neighbors. He was a well-respected computer scientist. She used to give me freshly baked lavash. It would be still hot from her oven, and covered with honey. But after that day we never saw them again. Then on the fifth day, my oldest sister Mariam disobeyed my father and snuck out to visit her friend. She was caught by three men."

My eyes wide, I put my hand over my mouth. I was afraid to ask but had to.

"Was she, is she alive?"

He nodded, "Yes. My parents said she was robbed and then saved by a passing Azerbaijani who knew my father. Of course, she wasn't just robbed, but it is what we said to protect her honor."

I didn't bother to wipe the tears; everything he described was so horrible, so beyond the scope of my naive American experience.

"Where is she today?"

"Armenia. We all fled there immediately afterward, my parents, my mother's mother, her sister's family, we all went to my father's family in Yerevan and then life was normal and happy enough again. Mariam is married now and has two children; she is a physician's assistant. We do not speak of our time in Azerbaijan, none of us do. Not with each other anyway. I'm surprised to speak of it with you if I am truthful."

I struggled with how to respond and finally settled on, "I'm so sorry that happened to all of you. How do you get over something like that?"

He shrugged and said simply, "My life has been a good one so far. It was just a week."

Part of me understood that the kind of childhood trauma he described wasn't something you just got over. It had branded some hidden place in him, a place he kept carefully compartmentalized and rarely opened. It was tragic and dark enough, though; I didn't want it to become a part of us. Selfishly, I was relieved when he changed the subject to something lighter. If I perhaps craved a little drama, I certainly didn't want the kind that might threaten happiness.

What I didn't really understand at the time was how many locked away spaces Narek housed. When faced with grief, or trauma, or dread, or shame, or fear, Narek had the uncanny ability to pack it all up and stuff it into one of those spaces. I was a talker, a yeller; I needed to face those emotions and then force myself to work through them. But he would turn and walk away from them.

When the initial exploration of private closets was satisfied, we moved onto a safer, more comfortable pattern. In the months that followed, we greedily shared whatever free time we could, although free time was a luxury we had little of. It was the second semester of my sophomore year at VCU; I needed to keep a high GPA in my pre-law tract if I wanted a shot at a decent law school. On top of my own study hours, Narek's class schedule and studio time were ambitious. Work kept us busy too. We both had evening jobs, he waited tables at an Armenian restaurant, and I served drinks at a dive bar on the outskirts of the city. Somehow despite our schedules, though, we found the time to fall in love.

Twice a week, we found a secret respite, I'd lay posing in the studio, and would squint my eyes against the bright lights to find his across the room. The anonymous, disinterested faces in the class were unaware we were dating, and that only added to the excitement of our game. After enduring over an hour of public foreplay with his brush and my eyes, we'd sneak off for an urgent lovemaking session. Physically, we had been a match from the very start. We didn't have sparks, or kindle a slow burn; we'd just jumped right into the fully engulfed incinerator. That physical connection pushed us to discover something deeper and more meaningful.

The golden spring morphed into a white-hot summer. Our schedules were more relaxed and together we explored the city. Whether we were rafting on the James River or riding bikes along the Capital Trail, we had become children of the summer and I read so much promise in that. We were serious enough by then that I was introducing him to friends and coworkers as my boyfriend, and it was generally known we were an exclusive couple. We were established.

In July, we bought plane tickets, and he accompanied me home to Northern Michigan to meet my family. Mom liked him immediately; she was suckered into those big brown eyes as quickly as I had been. I'd known she'd love him; he was exactly the kind of young man that middle-aged women were charmed by. He wore his shy smile and a deferential head nod like a crown.

"He's a hunk!" she whispered as we cleaned up the dishes after that first night's meal.

I rolled my eyes at both her word of choice and the fact she'd actually said it out loud, but then conceded with a nod. Yep, Narek was a hunk.

Dad was indifferent, but this, too, had not been unexpected. My father was indifferent about every boy I'd ever brought home, and to be fair, there had been enough of them he had no reason to expect it might be safe to get attached. Still, he was friendly enough with Narek, before disappearing into his garage to do whatever it was, he seemed to spend hours doing out there.

My only sibling, Sarah, deemed him "hot" but was quickly bored by our public displays of affection and disappeared for most of our visit with her friends. Sarah and I had always had a somewhat strained relationship. She was four years younger than me, but it wasn't just age we didn't have in common. As children, I'd always been the responsible one. Sarah would toss a deck of cards in the air, and I'd clean them up. I expected I'd always be cleaning up Sarah's playing cards. Like me, she was a talker; but unlike me, she had no filter for what came out of her mouth. More than one family or neighborhood drama had been exasperated by Sarah's big mouth.

When our visit home ended, Sarah dutifully leaned in for a quick, perfunctory hug and then commented, "Well, if we don't see you again, it was nice to meet you, Narek."

He laughed at that and assured her it had been mutual, then accepted the much warmer goodbye from my mother and a respectful handshake from my father. I felt proud as we walked into the airport. I knew my family had watched us walk through the door, and I knew they had judged that I'd chosen well.

There's a natural shift that happens to a relationship when a girl brings her lover home to meet the family and after returning to Richmond, it felt like the most natural thing in the world to suggest it was time to share his apartment. I was eager to leave student housing, I quickly moved my meager belongings in, and we played house in earnest. When I called home to tell my parents, I could hear the concern in my mother's voice. She'd attempted to temper it with a false cheerful note, but I'd spent 18 years with her before heading to college and I heard it.

"That sounds wonderful," she'd said dutifully.

"Mom... you don't sound convinced."

It took prodding, but she finally admitted she was worried. She liked Narek a lot, but would this move derail my own plans? I assured her that wouldn't happen. I'd dreamed of being a lawyer since girlhood, and I'd worked far too hard to make it happen to give it all up now. In two years, I'd graduate VCU with my English degree; I'd get into the College of William & Mary School of Law, I'd make the law review staff, would intern for a supreme court justice, and would ultimately practice constitutional law. I had every step planned; I was meticulous about checking off every necessary box. My parents had a lot riding on my academic success; we were a modest, middle-class family from rural Michigan, and they'd worked hard to give me the out-of-state education I'd dreamed of. With the absurd aplomb of youth, I was certain I wouldn't let them down.

Moving in together jettisoned our relationship to another level. I'd underestimated just how deeply under my skin he would burrow and just how quickly it would happen. Before cohabitation, I had wanted Narek. After moving in, though, I found I actually needed him. Very quickly, I admitted I was in love with him. I loved how every morning he awoke with the softest fringe of tiny black hairs across his jawline. I loved how his shirts were all speckled with the tiniest of paint splatters. I loved the spicy smell of the deodorant he wore. I loved how thick the dark thatch of hair was at his groin. I loved how he sometimes reversed his adjectives and nouns. I loved how excited he got whenever he saw a stray cat in the city. I loved how he slept perfectly still on his back, as if nothing ever troubled him in his dreams. Most of all, I loved his eyes. They were deep brown pools that held secrets I longed to uncover.

Narek wasn't as demonstrative as me, but I was confident that he loved me in return. Sometimes in the evening, I'd lay on my back and allow him to explore my body. It wasn't a sexual exploration; it was the careful caress of an artist appreciating curves, valleys, dimples. His fingertips would move lightly along the hollow of my cheek, as his mind recorded the shape. Later, he would replicate the shadows on canvas. The words he couldn't quite say out loud, would spill out in amber, copper, and red from the mouth of his brush. His paintings said I love you. I love you and I won't leave you.

As much as I loved Narek, though, I didn't lose myself in him. Not completely. I was still firmly dedicated to my plans, still determined to reach my own goals. Loving Narek was necessary by that point, but I knew my plans would have to come first.

With autumn came the start of my junior year and Narek's final year at RSAD, and the first fine cracks began to appear in the beautiful glass house we'd built. His senior thesis would have him traveling abroad to Florence for six weeks, where he'd study in a space the true masters had once studied. I felt insanely jealous about the opportunity. Along with my envy of his ability to travel to a place so storied and beautiful, a heavy sense of dread filled me at the thought of his absence. Six weeks sounded like a lifetime, and everyone knows a lot happens in a lifetime. I had never suffered from a lack of self-esteem, but I drove myself half-crazy imagining the Italian beauties he'd meet. I was also worried because Italy was a lot closer to Armenia than Virginia. What if he got there and decided to just stay?

Part of the deal I'd made with the forces that had allowed Narek to love me back at least a little had been my quiet promise to hide any hint of fragility. I tried not to let him see me needing him too much, but on at least one occasion, my resolve wavered.

"You could have chosen Washington, DC, instead, right?"

"Yes, but that would have been terrible. Maybe okay for someone who is more interested in being a curator, not for a serious painter. Besides, it's Italy," he replied shrugging.

"Maybe I should have taken the semester off and joined you…"

His facial expression made it quite clear that notion was ridiculous. "Why would you do that? I will be busy and you wouldn't graduate on time then. John and Nancy wouldn't be okay with that."

I rolled my eyes; since when did we concern ourselves with what my parents might think?

"It's just… I'll miss you," I said softly.

He'd pulled me close and nuzzled the top of my head with his chin before promising, "I'll miss you too, it will go fast, though."

I kept further fears to myself, unwilling to look weak and unreasonable. When drop off day arrived, I played it cool. I gave him a goodbye kiss and told him I'd see him soon. I resolved to myself that I'd fill every moment of the next six weeks when not in class or at work, studying for LSATs. Refocusing on The Plan would give me purpose and help time pass more quickly. That singular vision got me through the first three lonely weeks of his absence.

Despite my best efforts to pretend life had gone on, the apartment was too quiet, the bed too empty, and the phone calls too infrequent. We would go days without speaking to each other. Between the time difference, my overloaded work schedule, and Narek's weekend forays around Italy with his new friends, I felt deserted. For his benefit, though, I continued the illusion of "cool girlfriend" whenever he'd call. If he casually mentioned drinks after class, I'd resist the urge to demand his companions' names. If he mentioned being tired, I stilted the desire to ask what had kept him so busy the night before. When occasionally I heard female laughter in the background, I pushed the ugly accusations far from my lips. I knew they could never be uttered.

Narek had never given me reason to question his loyalty. The only women he looked at were models in his classes, and I knew from experience he didn't actually see them when they were on that display. He wasn't a flirt; he didn't even flirt with me, really. He was guarded and kept his internal thoughts hidden well. And that was actually the real problem. Even as I gave everything to him, I'd felt the reserve. I knew he had yet to truly open up to me. This trait felt survivable when we were spending every free moment together. With his physical distance, though, the emotional distance became exaggerated and unbearable.

It was at the end of his fourth week that my facade finally slipped. We'd preplanned a phone call, and when the call never came, I felt uneasy and frustrated. The next day, my anxiety continued to climb, and I took the ridiculous action of calling in sick to work so I could wait by the phone. I stared at it beseechingly and willed it to ring but was only rewarded with silence. By evening despair had overtaken me.

I found myself balled up in bed, sobbing into his pillow, imagining the worst things possible. I pictured him lying on his back naked, a dark-haired woman riding him, breasts bouncing, head tilted back. I pictured his hands clinging to her hips, then moving across the peaks and valleys of her body. She changed; she was blonde, she was fat; she had short hair, she had tiny breasts, she had long red curls. I pictured him fucking every single woman in Italy. Now I was sobbing into the damp pillow. Finally, I couldn't take one more image, and I knew that I was going to vomit. I ran to the bathroom and emptied the contents of my stomach.

After showering, I felt calmer and saner, more like my normal self. I slipped my invisible cloak of cool, impervious confidence over my shoulders. I made myself tea and poured a little whiskey into the mug, and sat down to consider my extreme reaction. I was worried. I'd never been the jealous type, and I certainly wasn't the sob into a pillow kind of girl. I felt emotionally fragile, and it was a disturbing feeling. What was wrong with me? Where was the old Nell? As I ticked through a mental list of all that could be broken within me, the thought occurred there could be a chemical component to this. Perhaps this could be as simple as an extreme case of PMS. Perhaps my body was sabotaging my peace of mind with an assault of hormones.

As if a thousand angry ice pellets were assaulting me at cosmic speed, a different realization hit me. My period. Where was my period? I ran for the kitchen; we kept a wall calendar hanging in there. I'd never tracked my cycle in writing, but I needed a visual aid to count back. He'd been gone for four weeks. Before that, how long was it before that? I tried frantically to piece together our hectic lives of a month ago. It hadn't come the week before he left; I was sure of that. Two weeks before we'd gone to Virginia Beach, I'd remember if I'd needed tampons. I felt cold; it had to have been at least six weeks. Maybe more.

After walking to the CVS and buying a small cache of pregnancy tests, I sat on the 20-year-old floral sofa he'd rescued from a street corner the year before I moved in with him. I gulped water, so much water I thought I'd burst. And then, when my bladder threatened to do just that, I forced my legs to move to the bathroom. My stream was heavy enough to time out two different test sticks. Another sat unused for the moment. I expected to wait five minutes then see a result, like they do in the movies. What actually happened was I watched a second line in the "pregnant" window appear immediately on the first test. The second test turned pink twenty seconds after it started processing my urine. Numbly, I looked at the remaining test and knew it was pointless.

I would like to say I was suddenly filled with an indescribable joy and that I tenderly rubbed my still flat belly and imagined the baby within. I'd like to say I handled it gracefully and celebrated the moment with a prayer of gratitude. I'd like to say I felt even a hint of happiness. I'd like to say my first instinct wasn't a panicked, "How do I get rid of it?"

In actuality, escape was all I could think of. How does one escape a prison growing within one's own womb? I pictured my entire future during those bleak early hours. Narek would leave me. He'd stay in Italy. I'd get fat. I'd have to leave college, forget law school. I wouldn't even complete undergrad. I'd have to go back to Michigan in shame. I'd have a screaming, ungrateful infant who would demand every ounce of my soul. I'd never be a lawyer. I'd mooch off my parents until I met some local older man who'd already been married and divorced twice. We'd live in a trailer, and my child would perpetuate the cycle. Narek would never know her.

I know, of course, that I was being ridiculous. I had options. It was 2004, after all, not 1884. There was the obvious choice, the one I immediately was leaning toward. A clinical procedure. I avoided using the "a" word, even in my own head. It would be a medical procedure. An evacuation of my body. A minor surgical event. I'd feel a little emotional afterward, bleed a few weeks, and then get back to my real life. I'd known girls who had been through this, and it certainly seemed they'd emerged on the other side none the worse for having made that choice. There was also adoption. I wasn't inclined to think about that one seriously; I didn't just not want a baby. I didn't want a pregnancy at all! I wanted it to be over as soon as possible. I certainly didn't want to explain myself to my family and friends, I couldn't afford to miss work if the pregnancy was complicated, and if Narek came back, I wasn't sure he'd go along with that at all.

Narek. The other option was to pick up the phone and call the emergency number he'd left for his housing community. Have them hunt him down and get him on the phone. Tell him the truth. Why shouldn't he suffer the burden of this choice alongside me? In the most unliberated moment of my young feminist life, another thought suddenly occurred to me. If I called Narek and told him, maybe guilt would force him to come back to me. Maybe he'd feel obligated to take care of the baby and me, to stay with us forever. Maybe if he knew, we could actually live happily ever after.

I chose none of the above. I did seek crisis pregnancy centers, collecting phone numbers and addresses, but delayed acting on the impulse. When I looked at the carefully lettered list of addresses, I felt frozen with indecision. Unable to commit without him, I resolved to wait for Narek's hopeful return. When Narek finally called a day later, I once again forced the fake cheery facade. I once again chose not to press him with questions. I shared no hint of the life-altering thing that had happened to us. That he didn't notice the hint of sadness and fear in my voice troubled me more than I wanted to admit, but I reveled in the fact he still spoke of "When I get home."

He did, in fact, return. When he entered our apartment, he pulled me against his chest. Inhaling the scent of him, relief washed over me. It was still him. Pulling back, I met his gaze. The pregnancy was on the tip of my tongue, but first, I had to know something else. I hadn't planned to speak of my immature fears and insecurities, but I needed to know. I needed to hear assurances before I shared my condition with him.

"Was there anyone else?" I asked as calmly as possible.

His eyes. I watched his eyes, and I knew what I saw. They darted quickly to the left. It was just for a nanosecond, but I saw it. He shrugged and shook his head.

"Don't be ridiculous. You're the only one; I came back, no? I don't really think we should talk about it. Is a stupid question. I don't ask you, is there another man, no?"

His annoyance made me feel small. If he'd asked me if there had been anyone else, I would have laughed. It was such a preposterous question; I'd have asked if he had just smoked a joint. If he seemed very sincere and worried, I would have just held his hand and looked into his eyes and professed my love and reassured him of my faithfulness. Maybe if he asked ten times or a hundred times, I'd be annoyed. But it wasn't such an outrageous question to ask after six weeks apart, just once.

It was spoiled. I felt ridiculous thinking it, but everything was spoiled. I'd convinced myself that my fears were ridiculous and strictly hormonally driven, but at that moment, I felt a sudden clarity. There had been someone else. Maybe more than one. I understood he came back to me, to our life here, because this was where he wanted to be. I understood he loved me. I understood he wouldn't purposely hurt me. I understood he would never confess a thing to me. I understood I had to accept this and move on with him or without him.

In the end, I chose not to give my thoughts the power of my voice. I chose to dutifully follow him into our bedroom and make love. Afterward, I lay by his side. I stared at the ceiling for a while and then finally said the words. "I'm pregnant."

He didn't reply. He lay perfectly still, and I wondered if he'd fallen asleep. Then I felt his hand creep over my torso and eventually come to rest protectively over my lower belly. Silent tears ran down my face in the dark, tears of both anguish and relief.

3

Some women are filled with joy when they first feel the
infant within move. It was a strange fluttery feeling that
felt more like tiny gas bubbles than the more violent,
insistent kicks that would come later. They call that
first feeling "the quickening," and liken it to something
miraculous and beautiful. When I felt it, all I could
imagine was the birth scene from Alien. There was a
creature inside me. I'd always been mildly
claustrophobic, and just imagining this from the
infant's viewpoint gave me a slightly panicked feeling.
It was trapped, and so was I.

 My belly was slow to show anything. My
obstetrician confirmed I had a healthy pregnancy, but
with only the most subtle rounding of my belly, I'd
convinced myself there was still the tiny possibility this

was all some huge mistake. I had some strange disorder that made me secrete pregnancy hormones for false-positive tests. My indigestion just happened to sound like a fetal heartbeat on the monitor. My breasts were so sore because I had the world's worst case of extended PMS. The quickening had changed all of that.

I knew I couldn't indulge in fantasy much longer. I also knew my parents would need time to adjust to this news, and the window of appropriate time was quickly closing in. We'd flown to Michigan a few weeks prior for Christmas; that would have been the ideal time to tell them, but I'd convinced myself it was kinder not to ruin their holidays. I wore a fake smile, fake enough my mother had pulled me aside and asked if everything was okay. I told her I was stressed over waiting for grades to post from my finals and had probably been working too hard. I skipped the spiked eggnog without fanfare and made it through Christmas Eve services without spontaneously bursting into flames.

Narek had wanted me to tell them then, he liked my parents, and they liked him. He was optimistic they would welcome the news. Most of what Narek knew of American culture came from movies and television shows. In modern pop culture, this stuff happened all the time. Pregnant women didn't become pariahs, grandparents quickly jumped on board to be supportive; everyone lived happily ever after. He had an annoying tendency to swing from criticizing American culture to idealizing it. For what felt like the thousandth time, I explained I wasn't afraid of being cast away. I was afraid of disappointing them.

"You don't understand. This isn't supposed to happen to me. I am the one they never worried about because I always had a plan. They always knew I'd stay out of trouble, not because I'm particularly good, but because I'm particularly smart! This will crush them."

"Just call them. You make this too hard. Maybe John and Nancy are happier than you think about baby."

I didn't fail to notice that while he pushed me to call my parents, he refused to even discuss when or how he'd tell his own family. Not only had they never met me, they didn't even know *about* me. I had some minor resentment toward that, but it was tempered by a fair amount of sympathy for a family that had been through so much and an understanding of how significant our cultural differences were.

He had once explained, "To be Armenian is not like being American or French or Chinese. We are a small ethnicity, over a million and half of us were wiped out in genocide, we have not yet recovered from that. For my parents, it is important I marry an Armenian woman, carry on our family name, but also important is to carry on our culture. When I came here, it was with the promise I would someday return. It will take time to let them understand I will stay. You must be patient and understand this cannot be rushed."

I reminded him of that conversation. "My family may seem less complicated, but you know that we both have a religious problem. Your church may be older and more conservative, but John and Nancy are good Lutherans and they're no happier about my distance from the church than your family is about yours."

"Yes, but is still different. Your parents' church is a choice. My parents' church is national identity. All good Armenians are Apostic, it is not just a religion, it's part of us. Here in America, I can be Agnostic, but when I am home, I still go to church, not because of religion, but because I am Armenian. You don't go to church in your own country and is okay. No one thinks this is strange."

"Narek, you know every time I go home to Michigan, I go to church with my family. It's the same thing. My parents really believe every word in the bible, and I'm telling you, they will expect that we marry."

He looked away uncomfortably, and I sighed. "Jesus, Narek, I'm not saying I want to get married, relax. You know I am fine with the way we live. I'm just saying for my parents it will be an issue. And that's not even touching on their reaction when they realize how much this will affect my education and future. You're not the only one who is complicated."

The truth was I was happy not to have to deal with his meddling family, and the descriptions he gave had assured me they would be meddling. If Narek never mentioned me to them, maybe that would actually be a blessing. But considering how understanding I had been, it felt hypocritical for him to push me when I was giving him so much grace.

As the second trimester of my pregnancy ended, I realized I could no longer button a single pair of pants I owned. I switched to leggings and track pants with loose-fitting shirts and felt conspicuous on campus. There was no hiding my condition anymore. I needed my parents to know before the casual acquaintances and complete strangers of my Richmond world, so finally, on a cold January day, I summoned the courage to pick up my phone and selected my mother from the contact list.

She sounded breathless and happy. She'd just returned from taking my sister out for prom dress shopping. They'd found the perfect dress; it was pink, of course. They'd have to go to McAllister's for shoes later in the week and…

I couldn't handle one more word. The image of my fresh-faced sister, pure and virtuous in a pink gown with her whole life ahead of her, was too much at that moment. I interrupted.

"Mom. I have to tell you something."

It came out louder than I planned, but it did the trick. She stopped talking. I took a deep breath and then vomited the words in a rush. Pregnant. Due in May. Sorry. So sorry. Spring semester would not happen. Narek being supportive. No, not discussing marriage. Staying in Richmond. Not sure what next. Sorry.

My mother, to her credit, didn't cry. She didn't yell, and she didn't ask me anything stupid like how could this happen to us? Narek was wrong about one thing, though; John and Nancy most certainly were not happier than I thought about baby. I heard the strain in her voice even as she attempted to sound balanced and supportive. The word "congratulations" was never uttered. She reassured me they loved me and would support me in whatever way they could. I reassured her I was fine, the baby was fine, Narek was fine, everything and everyone was fine. Fine. And then we said goodbye.

I wasn't fine. I'd turned in my medical leave forms at school, and it felt as if my dreams were slipping away. No matter how often I told myself this was just a delay, not an end, I felt like a failure. I was still waitressing but had stopped modeling at the art school for obvious reasons. Working on my feet all night as the alien in my belly absorbed all my nutrients left me depleted the next day. I lived in the permanent fog of exhaustion.

Things weren't going well at home either. Narek was growing increasingly distant. I wasn't sure if it was my obviously pregnant body or my sour mood he was attempting to escape from, but he was spending more hours at his studio than he ever had before. Sometimes he would lie next to me and cup my enormous belly, taking delight when he'd feel the baby kick. Other times, he'd ignore me, losing himself in one of the endless series of American movies he was obsessed with. We argued over small, petty things. We stopped making love.

The biggest elephant in the room was the question of what happened next. Early in the pregnancy, I'd shared my belief that a baby was a foolish reason to marry. I had meant it at the time. I'd heard enough horror stories of couples forced to marry who later regretted it and the ugly divorces that followed to know it was a bad idea. Yet as unreasonable as I knew I was being, the fact Narek so readily agreed and never perused the subject again hurt me. The baby would be here in less than three months, and I was worried about the permeance of anything. Narek's parents still didn't know about the baby, and I felt dread in the pit of my stomach whenever I thought of that and what it might mean about Narek's long-term intentions.

The apartment wasn't ready, either. My parents had sent a bassinet, and we'd set it up in the corner of our bedroom. That was the sum total of our preparations. I knew the girls at work would likely throw me a shower and that my family would flood us with gifts when the time came. I was confident the infant wouldn't go naked or hungry. I was lost in my own anxiety, though, and unable to muster the excitement to actually do any shopping myself.

Most of my anxiety was rooted firmly in my complete lack of certainty over my educational and career future. Part of me still clung to the ridiculous notion I could pick up in September, less than five months after the baby was born, where I'd left off. I'd somehow find affordable childcare and learn to function without sleep, and I'd make it through a year and a half of undergrad and another three years of a demanding law school. Narek would step up and help me make it work. This fantasy sounded both ideal and hopelessly unrealistic. I knew I'd never be satisfied playing the housewife long term. That had worked for my mother, but she'd raised me to think much bigger. There was also the not so small matter of money. We earned a pittance through our regular jobs; Narek's pieces had recently begun selling, but that income was hardly guaranteed. I'd eventually need a real job and a real job would likely require me to complete my degree.

My 36th week of pregnancy passed, and I went into full panic mode. Where just a few weeks before I'd still been hoping I could somehow pretend and ignore reality away, I suddenly felt frantic to be properly prepared. My baby shower, a really humiliating and agonizing affair that involved smelling baby food blobs in diapers and drinking mocktails with cutesy baby names, had netted us a fairly full layette in neutral colors. Boxes full of baby clothing and gear filled our apartment. Our much too small apartment, I'd concluded. The vision of a baby sleeping quietly in the corner of our bedroom was disrupted by the reality of baby gear taking over every corner of the apartment.

Narek loved living in the city. He loved being able to walk or bike everywhere; he thrived on the surrounding energy, admired the urban art, and appreciated the many ethnic food choices. I thought I loved it too, but suddenly I wasn't sure it was the best place to raise a child. Maybe a little house in a neighborhood away from the center of the city would be the better choice. When I broached the subject with Narek, we had one of our worst arguments.

"How do I go to studio? We have one car," he'd replied stubbornly.

I shrugged and said, "I don't know, maybe buy another car. Or work our schedules so that only one of us needs a car at a time."

His facial expression was unreadable, and he finally replied, "No. Staying in city."

Furious that he was just blowing off every great point I'd been making, I started yelling. The baby would need space. The baby couldn't sleep in our room forever. We would get sick of carrying the baby up and down the stairs. He was selfish; it was all about Narek's needs. He didn't care about the baby. He didn't care about me. If he cared so much, then why didn't he tell his parents? Why did he complain every time we went to a Lamaze class? Why hadn't he painted a single painting of me pregnant? Why was he always leaving? The baby deserved better.

In the course of our year and a half long relationship, Narek had never yelled. I was a yeller by nature, although I tried to mask and temper that around him because he was so calm. Narek could be a sulker and a disappearer, but never a yeller. Now suddenly, he was yelling.

"The baby, always the baby! I didn't ask for baby! I didn't come here to make baby, I come here to make art!"

Well, there it was. He resented me and the baby; he didn't want us. I started crying and ran for the bedroom. Laying in the fetal position, I started mentally packing. Going home to Michigan seemed my only real option. I was ticking through the pros and cons of trying to do it before the baby's arrival when he entered the room. He sat on the edge of the bed next to me, silent for a moment. Finally, he spoke.

"I'm sorry. I want you and baby; I just don't want to move from city. It's true, this is too small. Let's find a bigger apartment, one with other bedroom for baby."

I threw myself into his arms and commanded the small siren of alarm that seemingly grew louder every day in my head to be silent. I could choose to acknowledge my wildly surging emotions as the normal games late pregnancy hormones play. I could choose to ignore the cautionary voices in my head. I could choose to be happy. As his arms wrapped protectively around me, I surrendered my fears and accepted his love. I let myself believe fully the lie we all tell ourselves from time to time. I really could live happily ever after.

4

Precariously, I lay on my side on the golden settee, my giant belly threatening to pull me over the edge completely. I was a goddess. A giant goddess, a beautiful-ugly thing like Medusa. He stopped his brush strokes periodically to smile at me. I didn't bother stifling my giggles every time he did. I felt ridiculous posing in this condition, but this was the happiest I'd felt since the pregnancy began.

In the weeks following the big fight, we'd clung to each other with a renewed commitment. We'd researched apartments; we wouldn't make that move until after the baby was born, but we wanted to do it as quickly as possible. He'd been more attentive, spending less time away at his studio. I was making an effort too. I was stifling my hormonal urges to snap every time he cleared his throat. I ignored the dirty dishes he piled in the sink. I stopped pressing him to tell his parents.

It was an affirmation when he'd asked me to replicate the pose that had first brought us together. I hadn't been his model in a long time, something that bothered me a lot. I knew that Narek loved me, but he loved painting even more. Honoring me on canvas was the ultimate declaration of devotion. I'd eagerly agreed and found myself back in the old studio, where he now taught.

That my water would break as I lay on the settee where our story had begun was appropriate. Childbirth classes had made it clear this wasn't an emergency. Without having experienced a single contraction, I had hours, if not days, before active labor would start. Every ounce of preparation and knowledge flew out the window, though, as soon as I realized what was happening. With eyes wide, I'd stammered to Narek, "I, it's, well, my water broke."

He sprang into action, telling me to dress. He said he'd run the four blocks back to the apartment to grab the overnight bag I'd kept packed and waiting by the door and to retrieve the car. He returned, out of breath, and helped me down the steps into the waiting car. As he held the door open for me, I glanced up at him. He looked worried but flashed me a smile anyway.

I'd studied childbirth as meticulously as I'd once poured over LSAT guides. I'd carefully memorized what to expect throughout the whole process, stage by stage. I knew that first labors were usually about eight hours long, once the real contraction kick in. I didn't feel the first one until we reached the hospital. It was a strange feeling, more pressure than pain, and I naively practiced the breathing technique we'd learned in class as Narek signed me in with the desk clerk. I hadn't understood I should have enjoyed my normal breathing then, for as long as possible. All too soon, I'd need those techniques for real.

We'd meticulously preplanned my labor, in the same way I planned my entire life. I'd decided to experience childbirth without drugs. Narek had been no small influence in that decision-making process; the lesson he learned while eavesdropping on his female relatives was that drugs were dangerous to newborn babies. Medicating childbirth simply wasn't an option for them. When he'd expressed those thoughts to me, I'd done my own research and concluded there were enough arguments against drugs. I'd go with his suggestion.

If I'd been willing to concede there, one area I was not willing to give an inch on was the idea of laboring without him. After reading an article about Armenian childbirth practices, I'd angrily confronted him and demanded to know if he planned to be there. He'd smiled and put his hands on either side of my face before saying, "I would not miss it. We will do this like Americans. This is not an Armenian birth. It is the birth of an Armenian in America."

As we settled into my private room, I anxiously eyed the clock. I wasn't timing the contractions, the fetal monitor I wore around my belly could do that. I was watching the time. Eight hours, the books said I had eight hours. And so, it was with surprise, that around the two-hour mark, the previously minor menstrual-like cramps had morphed into something much more intense. My pain scale leaped from a 2-3 out of 10, to a solid 8 out of 10. Rapidly it climbed, 9 out of 10. Then screaming, I told the nurse it was a solid 10.

The labor nurse checked and pronounced my cervix was almost fully open and a doctor was called.

She commented, "Baby is in a rush to get here! You're one of the lucky ones, nice short first labor."

Lucky ones? I didn't feel lucky; I felt like my entire midsection was about to tear in half. I was yelling at her when the doctor finally entered. After a quick check, he confirmed the nurse's assertion, and the pushing could begin.

Sweating, face contorted, pushing. From somewhere in the blinding white pain, I heard Narek's voice. He sounded anxious; I thought deliriously. I clawed at his arm, desperately. Save me. His huge brown eyes were filled with tears. "Please push baby, Nell," he implored.

The nurse reassured him I was doing fine. I wanted to scream at her. I wasn't doing fine at all, but another contraction hit, even more intense than the last. I screamed in earnest at this and pushed again. Oh, dear God, burning now in my crotch. I feared I was ripping from end to end. "Narek!" I cried out in terror, and he leaned over my chest, his tears soaking the thin gown I wore.

"Again! One more, Nell, you're doing great!" the nurse encouraged cheerfully. I kicked one leg, hoping to make contact with her face, but she was quicker than me.

Another one. Push, push, push. Then suddenly, relief.

"Heads out, stop pushing now," the doctor instructed from somewhere between my legs. He said this so calmly, as if just stopping pushing was the easiest thing in the world. Another wave hit. I screamed. "Push, gently, gently..." he instructed, and then I felt the slippery thing escape from my body.

Almost immediately, an infant's cry filled the room. An angry protest of a cry. The nurse smiled and took the screaming, red thing from the doctor and brought it to me. "A boy! You have a son!"

Narek's face broke into a huge smile even as tears continued to stream down his cheeks, and as she placed the squalling infant on my chest, I felt my entire world shift. A son. I had a son.

We went about the business of checking a baby into the world. I labored on to deliver the placenta as the medical team weighed and cleaned the baby before wrapping him into a little cocoon and placing a tiny cap on his head. They handed him to Narek, who looked terrified he might drop the tiny 7-pound bundle. Watching him, my heart swelled.

The nurse smiled too, and asked, "What's his name going to be?"

We'd discussed and chosen names, but until this moment, we had never shared them with anyone else. I glanced at Narek as he held the well-wrapped bundle to his chest and answered, "Charles. Charles Vazgen Buyukian."

It was as if I'd spoken an incantation. I felt the magic of the name; a golden-clad spirit spun invisibly about the room, ready to fight to the death to protect my son. My son.

"Baby is very small. He is healthy?" Narek asked. I could see the sheer tininess of his son overwhelmed him.

The nurse smiled again and assured him Baby was just fine. Baby must have realized he was the center of attention because he suddenly wailed again. I motioned for Narek to bring me the bundle and put him hesitantly to my breast. We needed a little assistance, but soon he was correctly latched, and I had the slightest inkling about just how much my life was about to change.

We were released in the morning. Our impossibly small baby was placed gently into the bucket-like car seat. Straps, clips, bumper cushions held him in and promised to keep him as secure as a plastic toy being shipped from China. Still, both Narek and I felt slightly panicked, strapping him into the waiting car and during the drive back to the apartment. It was an awesome responsibility to be told you have a human being whose survival depended completely on you. It wasn't as if either of us hadn't failed at some relatively simple tasks in the past; there was no room for failure with this one.

If our small apartment had seemed cramped before, it was suddenly impossibly minuscule. The baby gear was everywhere; it sat stacked on every horizontal surface, and then within a day, my parents had arrived with even more. They were, of course, enamoured with their grandson. Whatever disappointment they may have felt over my derailed plans had dissipated into the sheer joy of smelling the magical elixir of a newborn baby's head. It had taken a while, but Narek was finally right, John and Nancy were happy.

As we stepped over the diaper bags and laundry baskets and suitcases, it became clear we needed to make our move as quickly as possible. For two terrifying hours, we left Charlie with his grandparents as we toured several two-bedroom apartments in the area. I found it difficult to focus on the units we toured; I trusted my parents implicitly, but anything could happen while we were gone. I pictured home invaders breaking in, a fire starting in the apartment next door, the boiler exploding (did our building even have a boiler?), the gas leaking from the stove, and a dozen other potential calamities. My parents had successfully kept both my sister and me alive to adulthood, they'd clearly proven they were capable, but I had that ominous but classic maternal instinct that only I could truly keep Charlie safe.

We did find a suitable apartment, although we wouldn't make the move until the end of the month. My father voiced his concern over our making the move alone, but we assured him we'd have plenty of friends who could help. He looked unconvinced, but with his own work schedule, he couldn't afford to stay any longer. As my parents' visit was coming to an end, my mother and I enjoyed a little alone time with Charlie.

"He really is perfect, Nell," she said with a smile as she touched the tiny, silky black curls on his head.

"I know. I can't believe we get to keep him."

She laughed at that but then turned serious. "Motherhood is a great gift and responsibility. I know you're going to do a wonderful job Nell, but I want you to seriously consider finding a church here and having him baptized." As if sensing the rising rebuttal in me, she threw a hand up and continued, "I know you're not big on church attendance but just think about it."

I murmured an acknowledgement that neither challenged her or indicated agreement, but I knew I hadn't fooled her. She sighed, and because apparently, my religious animosity wasn't a controversial enough subject, she plowed right ahead to another.

"So, have you and Narek discussed a date yet?"

"A date?" I asked, sincerely confused.

"For a wedding," she said cheerfully.

"Oh my god, Mom, of course not. I told you we have no plans to marry!"

My raised voice disturbed the baby and he made little angry sounds. Raising him to my breast, I looked at my mother accusingly.

She said, "I'm not trying to push, but what you actually said was you weren't planning on getting married at this time. And that was three months ago, so I wondered if maybe it was time yet.

"No. No, no, no. I will let you know if we change our minds, but you have to let that old fashioned expectation go already. We don't need a piece of paper to show our love; we don't need a piece of paper to be a family."

Her raised eyebrows and pursed lips told me she didn't buy a word of that, but she sighed and said, "Okay, I'll try to be patient. You know I love you, and I've already fallen madly in love with this little boy. Narek's a good man; he'll be a good father. I just want you all to be happy."

We tacitly moved on to more casual conversation, and when my parents left the next day, she hugged me tightly. I wiped the tears as we drove home and smiled at Narek. Now it was our turn. Without the buffer of my parents, the three of us began the fantasy of playing house in earnest. For a short period of time, I believed the fantasy was real. For a golden moment, I believed we would all live happily ever after.

5

Narek was distancing himself again. He'd hired on at a local gallery, and between that and his personal studio time, I found myself alone with Charlie most days and often in the evening as well. I had joined several mommy groups on the internet and found it wasn't unusual for fathers to take on extra work hours to lighten their own parenting load. This frustrated most of the posters and intellectually, I understood their feelings. It was 2005, we were an enlightened society. We acknowledged raising children was no longer "women's work," and our men had promised to be active modern fathers. The truth I couldn't admit in those online communities, though, was that I didn't resent Narek for leaving the majority of parenting to me. I secretly relished the fact that I had Charlie all to myself for much of the day.

On those same internet groups, I read about babies that never slept, babies always crying, exhausted moms, moms dealing with postpartum depression, moms with cracked nipples. They made me feel like the luckiest mom in the world. I kept my joy secret; I didn't want to make those facing more challenging parenting journeys feel bad. In the privacy of my own home, I'd squeeze Charlie gleefully against my torso and admire his perfect little head of black hair and whisper to him, "I won!"

At age three months, Charlie was preternaturally curious about the world around him. He'd sit quietly in his infant carrier in the front of my shopping cart, eyes wide open, staring at the world around us. People would often stop to comment about how alert and serious he was. They were drawn to his big, dark blue eyes clearly turning brown. Narek's eyes. He wasn't always serious, of course. When he did gift a recipient with his adorable, cheeky smile, the effect was contagious. The positive attention he garnered every time we went into public left me feeling embarrassingly proud.

At home, when it was just the two of us, I'd stretch out on the bed next to him and stare into his eyes. Baby talk felt awkward with Charlie, so almost from the very beginning, I spoke to him as if he were a fully developed, cognizant human being. I'd describe my idyllic childhood to him, filling his tiny head with visions of long summers spent playing on the beaches of Grand Traverse Bay. I told him about how astonishingly beautiful fall was when the sugar maples could blind you with their fiery-orange foliage. I chuckled as I explained how mild Virginia winters were compared to home; we measured snow here in inches instead of feet, and the locals still couldn't drive in it.

I also talked about Narek, a lot. I shared how we met; I talked about how talented he was, how big his dreams were. I confided about the future I envisioned for the three of us. Often, when I spoke about Narek, though, it was as if I were speaking of someone long ago. He felt so absent from our lives. The man in my stories sounded like someone who existed only in memory. Whenever I realized I was doing that, I'd feel uneasy. It was as if I sensed how precarious we really were.

It was shortly after Charlie's three-month birthday I made the big mistake. The gallery had hosted a special evening event, one of those sip champagne and gaze at paintings and pretend to be moved affairs I no longer attended. Narek had returned after midnight, and I happened to be up feeding Charlie. We had a friendly enough exchange, and then he headed into the shower. After carefully transporting Charlie back to his crib, I returned to the bedroom in time to hear a buzzing sound. I traced it to Narek's phone on the dresser, and without thinking, I picked it up.

The name on the screen was written in Armenian script; I had no clue what it was. It shouldn't have mattered, though. We had an unspoken agreement in our home to never touch your partner's phone. We were too cool and liberated for those kinds of sneaky games. For two years, this understanding had worked well for us. The thing was, normally, no one ever called after midnight, and considering our recent distance, my mind immediately went to the worst place. What if he were purposely hiding contacts in Armenian? What if it were another woman? I could not resist hitting the answer button.

It was another woman, albeit not the kind I feared. I said hello, and I heard a voice reply back through static, "Allo?"

I replied with yet another hello and was rewarded with a stream of Armenian in a voice I could only describe as annoyed. When I failed to comprehend or reply, the voice switched over to almost English.

"Allo? Where Narek?" she demanded.

"In the shower," I explained. "Who should I say is calling?"

"Shower? He bathes now? Who is this?"

I felt my stomach tighten; the woman sounded older. I had a sinking feeling I knew exactly who she was. She must be the woman I'd somehow avoided for over two years now. Whenever I allowed myself to think about it, I knew how insane our arrangement was. I'd always known at some point, there would be a reckoning. The truth would have to come out and the longer it took for that to happen, the more awkward it would be. Until then, though, we'd somehow pretended we could keep our lives separate and secret from Armenia forever. His parents weren't just unaware we lived together, they didn't know I existed at all. The call was a disaster.

Feeling desperate to fix it before Narek came out of the shower, I stuttered, "I think you have the wrong number," and hung up abruptly. I knew, of course, it was a mistake as soon as I did it. If she had a modern cell phone, and I assumed they had those in Armenia, she could confirm she had dialed exactly the right number.

Narek walked out of the bathroom with a towel wrapped around his waist at exactly the moment the phone rang again. I said, "Narek…" trying to warn him before he answered, but I was too late.

He answered as he left the room, sounding casual at first. His voice became more animated. He was speaking in Armenian, and I didn't know a word he was saying, but I understood it all nonetheless. His voice eventually dropped, and he was giving short, quiet answers. I didn't understand most of what he said, but I did understand when my name was mentioned. They continued speaking for twenty more minutes before I heard something else I recognized. Charles, Charlie Vazgen. More angry talk, then the contrite voice. Then a few quiet words, and then the speaking ended completely.

When he reentered our bedroom, I looked at him nervously. "I'm sorry," I said, meaning it. The look on his face was horrible, a look of total devastation. Whatever brief fantasy I might have indulged of this call perhaps being a good thing, in the end, was dashed.

He walked purposely toward his dresser and pulled out pants and a shirt, then slammed the drawer shut. Charlie began to shriek from his room next door, and I felt torn. I needed to get to my baby, and I also needed to stop Narek from dressing. I was certain of that. I looked at him beseechingly, but he refused to meet my eyes. "Charlie's crying," I said desperately.

He ignored me and began to dress, and I grabbed his arm, desperate to stop him. He yanked it away, and I pleaded with him to stop and just listen. His normally placid face was tight with anger, and for a moment, I thought he might actually reach out and strike me. Still hearing Charlie's wails, I turned and ran from the room to grab my son. Charlie's little face was bright red with outrage at the disturbance. I pulled him tight against my chest, as if he were a talisman, and stepped into the living room to confront a now fully dressed Narek.

"Please, I'm sorry, Narek. It was a horrible accident; I wasn't thinking. I just answered it on instinct, and then I panicked."

He finally looked at me and then said in the coldest voice I'd ever heard him use, "I won't talk with you. You don't know what is done."

He didn't slam the front door. Somehow, I felt as if the soft "click" of the latch was a thousand times worse than a reverberating slam might have been. It felt so much colder. I rocked a perfectly content looking Charlie in my arms, trying to spare him the shower of my tears.

Narek didn't return the next day. I walked dully around the apartment, shifting attention from Charlie to the book I was reading to the endless litany of chick flicks I kept popping into the DVR. I ordered Chinese for dinner, enough for both Narek and me, but still, he didn't return. He answered none of my calls, and I fought the urge to visit his studio and gallery to hunt him down. For the second night in a row, I slept with the warm, comforting presence of Charlie next to me.

On the third day, I finally heard the familiar, comforting jingle of his keys as he struggled to open the always glitchy door lock. Charlie lay cooing happily on his clowny blanket in the middle of the living room floor and Narek's eyes went to him first. I could see the softening in those eyes when he made contact with his son. Then he looked at me. There was still anger there. I could sense it in the same way I could often sense a coming storm from the mild ache in my knees. There was a hint of affection there too, though, and it battled valiantly with the darker emotion.

I'd spent days alternating between crying, raging privately to myself, and fighting the growing panic of trying to imagine how I'd support Charlie and myself if he didn't return. At that moment, though, every bit of angst and doubt fled, and I wanted nothing more than to throw myself into his arms. He stood with his back rigid, his legs slightly apart and his hands balled tightly at his side and I sensed physical contact would be a mistake. I knew there needed to be a difficult conversation before there could be any physical affection.

"Narek… I'm so sorry," I said once again, quietly.

This time he seemed ready to hear the words. He didn't rage or turn and run; he nodded slowly.

"I was angry, you don't understand what they are like. They are not like John and Nancy."

We'd had very few in-depth conversations about his family. He'd made it clear from the very beginning his relationship with them was complicated, and he didn't like discussing it. I knew they were a very traditional family; they thought of his time in America as temporary, and they were not happy about it. He dutifully called them once a week, and sometimes a package would show up, but until now, they'd been removed from our lives. I'd been only too content with that arrangement. I loved Narek as he was. We'd formed our own unit, immune to the pressures and expectations his extended family might have introduced.

"I know, but truly it was an accident. People make mistakes, they argue, you can't just leave over that. You have a son now; he needs both of us here every day."

Narek walked across the room and sat on the sofa; I breathed a sigh of relief. He was staying, for now at least. Needing to know, I prodded. "Your mother, what did you tell her about me?"

He closed his eyes and shook his head. "I try to explain, is different here. Not everyone marries, is okay to share apartment. I tell her you're not *pjatsadz*, you are just normal American woman. She doesn't understand, though, in Armenia this is not normal. She says *amot eh*, it means this is a thing of how do you say it?"

I wasn't sure what word he was grappling with, but I had the distinct feeling I wouldn't like it.

Finally, the word came to him. "Shame! Shame on me. Shame on you. That is what she says," he finally finished.

My cheeks burned; I understood the context even if I didn't quite understand the words. She thought I was a whore. "And Charlie? What does she say about her own grandson?"

His jaw clenched and unclenched. "He brings her *amot* too. I think this is mostly because she hasn't seen him. In Armenia, family is very important. If we were married and living there. We'd live in my parents' home. Charlie would be taken very good care of. But now we deny them that because we are here in America and we don't marry. She says she will not recognize Charlie because we do not bring him to her."

My stomach turned at the thought. I don't know how I was so certain, but my every instinct warned if Narek ever returned to Armenia he would never leave again. Charlie and I would feel bound to him, and we'd be there too, living in his parent's house. That horrible thought coupled with the worry and guilt that had led to three sleepless nights flipped a switch for me. I remembered how to be angry.

"Our son is not a shame! You've done just fine here without her or any of them in your life for years now. We are a family; we don't need them and as far as I'm concerned, she will never meet him now!"

He looked surprised by my outburst but not angered. "Maybe someday she changes her mind, but we will not bring him to her now."

That night we found each other again in bed, not through lovemaking, but by book-ending our sweet-smelling son. I lay on my side, listening to the sounds of Charlie and Narek breathing in concert. It had been a difficult week, and things had been said and done that couldn't be taken back, but as I drifted off to sleep, I tried to convince myself it was safe now. The bad time had passed. Finally, the soft lie lulled me into dreams.

6

Hope was a fleeting thing. We pretended for a while, but something had been broken and it couldn't be glued back together. It wasn't just the fact I'd broken our rules and answered the call, or even the fact that his mother had put such a horrible cloud over the legitimacy of our little family; we might have gotten past that. Narek's abandonment of Charlie and me was the real problem. He'd come back physically, but part of him I couldn't see really never returned to the apartment.

As he continued living his separate life away from us most days, my Spidey-Sense tingled. The less often he was home, the fewer times we made love each week, the more convinced I became he was checking out. I wasn't a foolish woman; I'd known heartache before and I knew when a breakup was coming toward you like a stealth fighter. This time would differ from past breakups though, this time, I couldn't just dust myself off, buy a new dress and stick pins in a doll with my girlfriends. When I looked at Charlie's cherubic face, I felt panicked. He was depending on me to somehow hold it together.

We depended completely on Narek financially. His art was selling well, he earned a decent salary at the gallery, and he had taken on the adjunct position at the art school. We certainly weren't uncomfortable or struggling, but I knew that could change in an instant if and when he left. I began sending resumes and filling out applications at daycare centers around the city. It seemed like the best way to earn a paycheck and avoid having to pay out for daycare for my own child. When I was finally hired at The Kid Garden, it was with great relief.

Next, I turned to my future prospects because I knew a daycare salary would only stretch so far and enrolled in my first night classes at VCU. I was determined to get the degree I'd walked away from earlier in the year. My plan might have changed, but I knew it was imperative there always be some version of it in place.

For the next six months, we maintained a careful, respectful balance of work, school, and shared childcare duties. On the surface, we presented the image of the perfect young urban couple to our friends. We still hosted the occasional dinner party in our small apartment. We had a trusted sitter by that point and would occasionally make the pub rounds with the old crowd, Narek still slung an arm casually around me when we walked into a party.

The truth, though, was that we barely talked anymore other than to exchange casual pleasantries or pass longer Charlie updates as we swapped off. And as for Charlie, he was blissfully unaware of the underlying tension. He grew and thrived under our shared care and the watchful eyes of my coworkers at Kid Garden.

At Kid Garden, they assigned me to the three- and four-year-old "Daffodil Room" while Charlie was safely ensconced in the 12-18 month "Rosebud Room." I enjoyed working with the slightly older children, the part of me that had naturally eschewed baby talk with my own son, enjoyed children who were of an age to reason at least a bit. Also, I knew that while it might have been nice to spend all of my time with my own son, that probably wouldn't have been fair to the other children. It felt like the best of both worlds, Charlie and I could both benefit from a little separation, yet I was just two doorways away from him at any time.

It was my normal practice to spend my lunch hour with Charlie and the other Rosebuds. On that fateful May day, I'd sat on the thick-carpeted floor, chatting with the care provider, periodically glancing at the toy shelf to watch Charlie. He'd been pulling himself up for some time by then, and you never knew what he might start grabbing and tossing. It had become his new favorite game. On that day, though, he turned to look at me and then, with a huge smile, let go of the shelf and awkwardly stepped toward me. One step, two steps, three steps, before he fell with an outraged little "oomph!" onto his bum.

I was so proud and so excited; Charlie might well have been the only human being in history to have figured out how to stand up on two legs. Coworkers ooh and aahed appropriately, yet didn't seem to quite understand just how incredible a feat Charlie had just accomplished. My child could walk! I wanted to share that moment with the only other person in the world who might be as impressed as I was.

I knew Narek wouldn't be home until several hours after me, and I just couldn't wait to show him what his son could do now, so we headed straight for his gallery after my workday ended. As we rounded the street corner, I could see the back of Narek's head through the large windows. He was deep in conversation with a woman I didn't recognize. That alone didn't concern me, the art world was full of women, and this one was standing in the middle of an open gallery after all. What gave me a funny feeling, though, was the look on her face. She was gazing up at him, smiling, and the smile seemed very personal. Then I saw her hand reach out, and she was touching his forehead. Although I could only see what was happening from the perspective of the back of his head, I recognized the gesture. I'd done it a thousand times, she was pushing one of his stray curls out of his eye. It was an intimate gesture, not something a stranger or casual acquaintance would have done.

My heart beating rapidly, I quickly said to Charlie in a sickly-sweet mom voice, "Want a cookie? Let's go to the coffee shop."

"Cookie!" he cried happily, blissfully unaware of the fact that I felt as if I might drop dead from a heart attack at any second.

We sat in the coffee shop across from the gallery for 40 minutes, where I continued to feed my toddler a steady train of cookies as I watched the gallery door. The slightly annoyed looking barista came to our crumb covered table multiple times to ask if we needed anything else, and I impatiently waved her away each time, turning back to the window. When the lights went off in the gallery across the street, I continued waiting. When no one exited a full 15 minutes later, I reluctantly put Charlie back into his umbrella stroller and made my way across the street. Peering in the windows, I saw no one. Had they somehow snuck out at some random moment I'd been looking away?

I fumbled with my keychain; it was still there. Narek kept the spare gallery key on my ring in case of emergency. I'd never used it before, but it struck me that this felt an awful lot like an actual emergency. I opened the door carefully and remembered the alarm after the fact. It was with immense relief I read the "unarmed" on the nearby wall panel. We stopped and listened. I could hear no one. I really must have missed them leaving. I was about to turn around and leave myself when I saw the painting on display in the center of the room.

I walked slowly toward it. I hadn't been to the gallery in several months, and I'd never seen this painting before. I recognized it immediately, though, for what it was. The gold settee; I felt a hysterical laugh build up inside me. He had recycled the same damned gold settee for his current students. This time the nude body on it wasn't my own, though; it was the blonde-haired woman I'd spied through the window earlier. Familiar with the original painting, which hung in our bedroom, Charlie cried out, "Mum!" helpfully.

A sudden ray of light spread across the floor as a door toward the back of the gallery opened. The office. I'd forgotten about that. He stood in the doorway, his face difficult to read because the light was behind him. We could only see Narek, but I knew he wasn't alone. She was in that office behind him; I was certain of it.

"He walked today," I explained casually.

Narek shut the door behind him and approached us. Even in the waning light, the distress was clear on his face. "I didn't expect you; you should have called."

Yes, I was certain he wished I would have called. I didn't reply to that comment. I walked up to him until I stood so close, I could smell her on his face. He looked a little fearful, and I wondered what he was more scared of, that I'd accuse him or that I'd try to kiss him. I reached a hand up and mirrored the exact gesture I'd seen the woman made just over an hour earlier; I moved the curl from his eye. His recoil made it clear I might as well have slapped him.

"I think it would be best if you stay... someplace else... tonight," I said softly, and after a moment of hesitation, he nodded.

Narek snuck in and removed most of his personal belongings while I was at work a few days later. I'd known what we had was over, but the cowardly way he'd walked away stung. When I returned home that evening and saw that his things were truly gone, I sat down on my bed and indulged in ten minutes of crying. I'd felt this coming for a long time, but I still mourned the loss of what we'd once had and what I'd once imagined we would have in the future. After blowing my nose, I took a deep breath and undertook the next difficult step.

Calling my parents wasn't easy, but I didn't want to prolong a fantasy life every time we spoke, and since we spoke daily, it seemed prudent to just get it over with.

"Hey, Mom…"

"Oh, hi honey, how's the baby?"

"He's good. I didn't call to just chat though; I needed to tell you something."

She was quiet, and I knew she was running every possible scenario through her mind. I put her out of her misery quickly.

"So, remember the time I called and told you I was knocked up and dropping out of college?"

She gasped and said, "You're pregnant! I knew it!"

"God no. What I was trying to say is keep that in perspective because I know you'll be disappointed and worried, but the important thing to remember is, I'm not knocked up and dropping out of college."

"Okay," she said in a way that made me certain she was on the brink of hysteria.

"Narek's moved out. But again, at least I'm not knocked up and dropping out of college!"

She was stunned. I knew how much she loved Narek; she'd held on to the dream we'd marry eventually and perhaps have more babies. She'd wanted for me what she had with my father. The kind of enduring, dependable love you knew would see you through old age. Even though I was the injured party in all of this, I felt unreasonably guilty for dashing her hopes. I declined to give her all of the gritty details but confirmed that I was quite certain and it was quite final.

She put me on speakerphone eventually so my father could participate, and in the unnerving way only a couple who had been married for almost thirty years could pull off; they were immediately on the same page with their advice. It was time to pack up Charlie and move home to Michigan. They pledged their full support during the transition, and I knew they were sincere, but that wasn't an option for me.

I was adamant about this. I wouldn't quit again; I would finish my night program at VCU. There was also Charlie to think about. While having my parents nearby would no doubt be of benefit to him, moving away from his father would be much more detrimental. He needed Narek in his life. I did finally agree to accept my father's generous offer to fund an attorney; Charlie would need more than just what I could provide. That seemed to make them feel at least a little better and we all began the business of accepting my new single status.

In the end, the end of Narek and I, he agreed to pay child support, and we created a visitation schedule I knew he would never keep. If he was entirely undependable as a boyfriend and father, he at least proved to be fairly consistent with his support checks. I clocked in 40 hours a week at the daycare, took classes every night, and soldiered through Charlie's first three years alone. Narek showed up once in a while, we might go months without hearing from him, and then there'd be a knock on the door. We maintained a veneer of civility, a distant politeness that belied the fact we'd ever shared the most intimate of moments. How foreign the once familiar landscape of a former lover's body could become, and it happened so fast.

7

My life wasn't shattered when Narek left; it was merely broken into a handful of sharp-edged pieces. I carefully picked up the shards and attempted to glue them back together with hard work, a whole lot of studying, and very little sleep. My goal was basic; I would build a life I could be proud of and become a woman worthy of my son's pride.

In late May, my parents flew into Richmond and held Charlie on their laps in the crowded Seigel Center. At just three years of age, he didn't quite understand the fuss, but Mom told me later that he had clapped his little hands together jubilantly when I'd walked across the stage to receive my diploma. We'd stopped outside to indulge in a photo op, and as a stranger snapped a shot of Charlie and I between my two beaming parents, I allowed myself to indulge just a bit in the warm glow of gratification that only someone who had failed and then recovered can understand. I'd done it. I'd bucked all of the odds and had finished my degree.

With my old dreams of law school swept aside, I focused on creating a new, more realistic plan. I would pursue my Master's degree and teaching licence next. One of the more unexpected revelations that life had given me when it blessed me with Charlie was the interesting fact, I was actually good with children. I enjoyed their company far more than I'd ever have guessed from the babysitting days of my youth. Their undiluted joy was contagious; their willingness to embrace life filled me with hope and inspiration. Even better yet, children seemed to like me in return. Teaching felt like a natural evolution from my daycare experience; it was an attainable and realistic plan.

If my professional life was finally taking shape, my personal life had flatlined. Charlie was the only man in my life in those early years. I'd been asked out plenty, but I had no desire to pursue anything new, not yet. Although I'd never have admitted it to even my closest friends, part of me was still tender from the wound Narek had left. I wasn't sure if it would ever completely heal, and it seemed foolish to consider courting a potential reinjury from anyone else. Not that I really believed that anyone else would be able to reach in deep enough to touch my bruised heart. Not really. Narek had been the love of my life, and the only reason I was able to wake up each day and move forward happily was the indelible gift he'd left me. Charlie. Charlie was the center of my world.

After the breakup, I had decided to stay in our apartment for a while and save what money I could, hoping I'd eventually be able to buy my own home. Slowly, surely, Narek's footprints disappeared from that apartment, and it became just mine and Charlie's. I boxed up the clothes he had missed during his first pack out and handed them over when he finally managed to stop by for a visit with his son. I tossed the spice jars his mother had sent, intended for dishes Narek had never bothered cooking. The books and movies he'd decided he didn't really want went to Goodwill. The paintings were what I struggled with most.

Narek had always kept most of his work at the gallery. We had a few smaller oil paintings on the living room wall, though, and those came down quickly. Begrudgingly he accepted them back and took them to display in his new life. Much more difficult to part with were the two most personal works, the portraits of myself on the gold settee. I certainly couldn't just donate nude paintings of myself, and I didn't really want Narek to possess them either. He'd lost all rights to look at my body. Cutting them to shreds also wasn't an option. I couldn't bear the thought of destroying Narek's golden interpretation of my pregnant image. Beyond being a visual reminder of the most important night of my life, it was proof that at some point in our relationship, Narek had loved me as fiercely as I loved him. That love was evident in every brushstroke. The earlier painting was perhaps less sentimental, but I still felt fondness for the young, carefree girl on the canvas. Ultimately frozen with indecision, I decided to pay for a small climate-controlled storage locker and moved them there for safekeeping.

The next two years were among the most exhausting but rewarding years of my life. I worked feverishly through grad school and student teaching, as focused on my new The Plan as I'd once been on the old one. When not busy with work or school, I spent all my time and energy on developing the amazing human being that was my son. Charlie saw the world through lenses filled with magic and beauty. He discovered joy everywhere, from the dead crickets I'd pick out of his pockets to the garbage truck he gleefully ran to greet twice a week. Walking around the city with him was like exploring an amusement park every day. Some new, unexpected thrill existed around each corner and Charlie was determined to find them all.

As his little body grew leaner and older, his resemblance to Narek only increased. He'd also displayed some of his father's artistic talents. When his little preschool class held their art fair, his own drawings and paintings looked different from the other children's work. They were better composed, used up more of the white space, were bolder in color and in the decision to deviate from whatever the class example had been. He'd inherited his father's best features, and I was thankful for that. He wasn't all Narek's son, though. His early love of reading, the way he doggedly pursued whatever task he was intent on, his outgoing nature; those traits were all me.

With time came more substantial changes. In May of 2010, I completed graduate school and received my provisional teaching licence. I was offered and accepted a permanent second-grade teaching position at nearby Groves elementary. Early childhood education was exactly where I knew I'd shine best and make the most difference. Because it was our local district school, Charlie and I would be starting the next adventure together.

In September, he started for-real school. Because our school had full-day kindergarten, I'd be able to avoid any transportation and childcare woes. It felt like the pieces had fallen together so easily, perhaps too easily. We embraced the new experience in the same way we exuberantly embraced a visit to the zoo or ride on a plane. Charlie was more than ready; his natural curiosity and self-confidence made him the perfect little five-year-old kindergarten candidate. He quickly and eagerly adjusted to the new routine, and knowing I was just a hallway away helped us avoid the separation anxiety so many new students experienced.

The slowly cooling breezes of October brought the most surprising and difficult change of all, though. When Narek dropped by for one of his rare visits with Charlie, he asked to speak to me alone. I felt a heavy sense of foreboding because Narek and I never spoke alone, not ever. We'd maintained a very civil relationship, but Charlie was always present to witness it. He served as chaperone, buffer, and reminder all at once. Wearily, I sent Charlie to his room and offered Narek a seat at my table, our old table. He wouldn't look me in the eyes, and I had the sudden worry he was going to tell me he was getting married.

I eyed him cautiously. He was still a very attractive man; objectively, I could admit he might be even more attractive with age. I knew he wasn't the sort of man who slept alone. He hadn't mentioned anyone in particular, but maybe one of his conquests had dug in deeply enough she'd convinced him to make the ultimate commitment. That thought filled me with anger, and the idea that Narek's personal life could still make me angry twisted my gut. I pushed the anger aside. Surely if he couldn't marry the American who gave birth to his son, no other American would have that privilege. It just wouldn't make sense.

"I will cut to the chase. I must return to Armenia. My father is ill, he will not be here much longer, and my mother needs me. I have thought about this for a long time. I have felt a pull to bring my art home for a long time, but so much keeps me here. Of course, Charlie, most of all. It's hard to say goodbye, but this feels like the right time. Maybe my father and I can at least have our peace finally," he explained.

I was dumbfounded. That had been the last thing I would have imagined. Narek was barely around, but I at least knew in an emergency he could be found. And Charlie! Charlie had me completely, but he needed a father too. That father might be a completely flawed, unreliable human being, but it was better than not having one at all.

"But your son! How can you just leave him?" I asked in horror, irritated to discover he still could upset me so much.

"Nell, I'm not leaving him, just moving. I will still send money. He can come to visit me in Armenia. My mother would even like that; you don't know how much she's softened in past few years."

I felt chilled by that idea. I wasn't sure what would happen if Narek actually pushed the point. He surely had some kind of legal standing for visitation but would the courts ever actually allow that kind of arrangement? Just a moment before, my biggest concern had been how Charlie would adapt to being fatherless, but now I realized I needed to be very careful.

"We can talk about that when he's older, right now, he is too young to fly unaccompanied overseas. In the meantime, he will miss you though, will you come back to see him?"

Narek nodded enthusiastically and said, "Yes, of course, will be like I never really left even."

I ignored the lie in his eyes and bit back the desire to tell him exactly what I thought about a man who would leave his little son. I didn't want to make an enemy of this man; I didn't want to create a dynamic where he'd feel motivated to challenge me legally.

We told Charlie together. His big brown eyes staring trustingly as we explained Papa would go away for a while, but he'd be back to visit soon. I fought the nausea that accompanied the lie. His sweet little mouth scrunched up into a delicious-looking pout, but then he nodded and said, "I'll miss you, Papa." Narek at least had the decency to shuffle uncomfortably in his chair at that. "I'll miss you too, little Charlie."

8

Charlie was hit by a car when he was eight years old. It happened right in front of the school, on a crosswalk, just feet from the school crossing guard. It was the safest time and place in the world for a little boy with big brown eyes and an overflowing Spiderman backpack to cross a street. Witnesses told me later that the driver, an older woman in a green Honda, had slowed near the intersection and then suddenly hit the gas. She'd explain in court she'd meant to hit the brake but had gotten confused. The crossing guard had urgently blown her whistle as the car sped toward him, but the whistle hadn't magically stopped the vehicle.

I was in my classroom, taking my time entering marks into my grade book. Charlie's after-school scout meeting at the church across the street would last an hour, and it made no sense for me to go home, only to have to turn around and come right back again. The striking thing about that afternoon was how blissfully unaware I'd been. In the movies, the mom always knows when her child is suddenly at risk, but I'd barely even spared him a thought. There was no strange, mythical maternal premonition. No "something odd" in the back of my head that suggested my world had almost ended. No hint at all, until the classroom wall phone rang.

"Nell, it's Leslie. You need to come down here right away." The school receptionist sensed my hesitation, my lack of urgency, and added, "It's Charlie."

I remember running down the hallway, past the long, colorful counting caterpillar that spanned the distance of the entire hall. Each green ball segment of its body was emblazoned with a number, and I counted down with each segment as I ran. 17, 16, 15…. I counted methodically until finally, I reached the smiling head that marked the end of the hallway. I paused in front of the school and scanned the scene below and sprinted. Several of my coworkers were calling my name and running after me, but I didn't bother glancing back at them. I could see the crowd on the street and could hear the sirens approaching. He was maybe a football field away from the front door I'd exited, but it felt like miles as I ran. When I reached him, I thought for a moment he had died. His eyes were shut and he lay so still, but then he sighed and opened his eyes and said, "Hi, Mom," as if it were the most natural place in the world for us to meet up.

"Oh my god, Charlie, are you okay?" I cried out.

"My leg hurts." He was trying to be brave, but I saw the tears in his brown eyes. I looked at his leg, it lay at an unnatural angle and I knew it must be broken. I choked back a sob and grabbed his hand.

"Does anything else hurt?"

The paramedics were rushing toward us then, and he nodded and admitted, "My tummy."

As the medics swooped in to assess him, I tugged the sleeve of the closest man and cried out, "His tummy hurts."

He nodded in understanding, and I tried to reign in the hysteria threatening to overtake me. A broken leg we could deal with, an aching tummy could mean anything. One of his tiny vital organs could be bleeding out inside his torso even as I stood there. I'd watched enough medical shows to know that!

In the end, it was his spleen, which, as far as organs go, was probably about the best we could have hoped for. He went into surgery twice, first to have the spleen removed and then to have his leg reset. He spent four days in the hospital, where he became a minor celebrity of sorts. Between the endless parade of friends and teachers and the gaggle of nurses and medical attendants who seemed to love popping in on him, he was never alone. My parents flew in from Michigan, to my great relief. I needed someone to lean on because my own emotional wellbeing had been stretched to the absolute limits. Mom and Dad were the two best shoulders I could have asked for.

As a rule, I normally never called Narek. We'd spent our years of separation since his return to Armenia, parenting independently of one another. My role was taking care of my son physically, nurturing his emotional growth, ensuring his public school education was subsidized at home, being the disciplinarian and tear wiper and chief encourager. Narek's role was to sometimes send child support money and talking on the phone every few weeks.

He'd gifted Charlie with a basic cellular phone the year before that was pre-programmed with his phone number and a stash of international calling cards. Trembling, I'd picked up his phone and hit the contact named "Dad." Narek answered on the fourth ring, and it was clear I'd woken him up.

"Narek, it's Nell," There was silence for a moment, and then he replied, "Nell? What is it? Is Charlie okay?"

"Yes, well, sort of. He had an accident today, a car hit him, and he's in the hospital." Again, a long pause, and it finally occurred to me the pauses must be a function of speaking to him overseas and not just a loss of words on his part.

It was a difficult conversation, awkward because of our shared history and made even more awkward with the technical challenges. I explained the extent of Charlie's injuries and what the path to recovery would look like and he attempted to express paternal worry. He asked the right questions, gave the right reassurances but in the end, he didn't do the one thing that might have softened my heart a little toward him. He didn't offer to come back to help during Charlie's recovery. To me, it was clear my parents cared more than Charlie's own father.

When Charlie returned to school the following week, he was the envy of his classmates; not only did he have a huge cast on his leg, but he also got to ride in a wheelchair. The kids flocked around him, eager to sign the cast, begging for a chance to push him around. He handled it with aplomb, a tiny would-be king in his royal chariot deigning to allow the peasants to throw rose petals. I watched unobtrusively from a distance. I knew he would fully heal, this hasn't been a tragedy, and I should be thankful for that. I was still shaken, though. I wasn't sure if I could ever feel comfortable allowing him to cross that street without me again. Like that first time I'd left him alone as an infant with my parents, I was reminded that I was the only person in the world who could keep him truly safe.

9

The week after Charlie's cast was finally removed, I went on a real date. Before Narek, I'd never lacked for male attention. In those immortal days of youth, I'd taken it for granted and felt secure in my own power and beauty with each new conquest. I fed off the thrill and energy of those romances. Charlie had changed everything, though. I'd never really intended to become a spinster, it had just sort of happened naturally after Narek and I broke up. In my nearly eight years of celibacy, there hadn't been any close calls, I'd gone on a few coffee dates with near strangers, had drinks once with an attractive coworker, but hadn't had so much as a kiss on the lips. Still, the woman I saw in the mirror wasn't unattractive. My parts were all still reasonably firm, I was pretty sure I didn't have an offensive odor or anything negative like that. I think I just projected a very strong aura of "stay the hell away," and men heeded it because no one wants to court a bruised ego. Friends had been pressuring me for years to rejoin the land of the living. I chafed at the suggestion as if what Charlie and I had wasn't life. Another truth was that I wasn't entirely sure how to proceed, even if I did want to date again. It had been so long since I'd played those reindeer games, and while I didn't think I was in poor shape for a woman my age, I hadn't survived the early mommy years completely unscathed. As Charlie grew older, and busier with his own life, I recognized it might be nice to go out now and then and I felt myself growing more receptive to the offers.

A friend introduced me to Jan, an electrical engineer in town for a few months to consult on the new arena project. He was handsome in that tall, blonde, Nordic lumberjack sort of way and the fact he was Norwegian was a huge plus. I knew he wasn't sticking around long; the temporary nature of his time in the states made him a safe flirtation. The last thing I wanted was to meet a man I'd have to eventually bring home to Charlie. It wasn't just the potential of Charlie not liking him; it was the thousands of hours of research and training on the realities of child abuse that drove me to protect him from any newcomers.

Jan knew about Charlie, and I'm guessing he understood he was getting a much more reserved, watered-down version of me, but my emotional distance didn't seem to bother him much. He knew he would be returning to Norway soon, and he was decent enough of a human being he didn't want to stoke any unrealistic expectations. We went out on a few dates, and then one night, when Charlie was spending the night at a friend's house, I followed Jan back to his hotel room. It turned out sex was a lot like riding a bike, my eight-year hiatus meant I was a little wobbly at first, but then instinct and muscle memory kicked in.

We continued to see each other for the next few months, knowing full well the futility of it. I reasoned with myself that sometimes the reward of putting yourself out there was the satisfaction of the moment. Sometimes you don't ride off into the sunset entirely, and that was okay.

I had asked Jan if he thought he might ever move to the states if the right opportunity presented. I'd meant professional, but his slightly uncomfortable look made me realize he thought I was fishing for a possible future that he'd made clear wasn't an option. I laughed out loud, startling him, and then quickly clarified I was strictly talking about career goals.

"Ah, yes, well, I don't say never for anything, but I can't see that happening. I enjoy visiting this country, it's a beautiful and exciting place and I love most of the Americans I get to know, but there is still so much that as a Norwegian I cringe at. Your roads are confusing and these big vehicles everywhere make them worse. Your gun culture terrifies me, I do not like this crazy anti-smoking thing here, and I do not understand all these churches everywhere, even on the television."

I'd grinned and said, "You forgot apple pie!"

At his confused look, I laughed again and said, "Well, big trucks, guns, and God, that's America all right, but you forgot the apple pie!"

He smiled devilishly and conceded, "I really like the apple pie."

When Jan returned to Oslo a few months later, our goodbye was a fond one. It felt more like an old friend was departing, than a new lover. I was better for having known him; I felt a part of me I'd kept locked up for a lot of years relax. In the years since Narek had left, my identity had been wrapped up in one thing. Charlie's mom. Even my choice of career had been all about Charlie. For the first time in a very long time, I felt a spark of potential to be something else, something more, that just the sun in the center of my child's galaxy.

Charlie himself didn't seem to have minded my split attention. His own social schedule was pretty packed between school, scouting, his newfound joy in soccer, and his friends. Still, we spent more of our evenings together than apart, sitting side by side on the couch enjoying the same kind of comfortable silence I'd always enjoyed with his father.

As he'd grown older, he had also become more aware of how our little family looked a little different from most of his friends. Some also had single parents, but they also had siblings. He knew very few true "just the two of us" families. When he commented about that realization to me, I asked him if it bothered him.

"Nah, I mean a little brother might be cool, but the problem is you don't know what kind you'll get until they're already here. It could end up like Mikey Shmidt, his little brother is a psycho."

"Charlie, that's not nice…" I cautioned.

"No, Mom, he really is! Mikey's mom caught him eating dog food!" he insisted.

I fought a laugh and explained, "Sometimes little kids do weird things. When you were four, you once ate an entire stick of butter."

"Gross. Never tell me that story again."

"Ha! I could tell you some even worse ones from your babyhood, but I'll save those for later. Anyway, the important thing is I hope you're okay with it just being the two of us," I said.

"It's not really, I mean there's Dad too," he reminded me, and I bit back my comment. "Also, Grandma and Grandpa and Aunt Sarah. They don't live with us, but we do usually live with them in the summer."

Ah yes, there was Dad. The mysterious Narek of far away Armenia, he may as well have been off fighting intergalactic criminals as far as his son was concerned. Having grown up in a very traditional home, with a very traditional father, I felt conflicted and confused when Charlie referred to his father. There didn't seem to be any of the resentment and anger in him that I'd steeled myself to deal with for years. Usually, I decided that was a good thing, but sometimes I wondered if I'd maybe done too good of a job at building Narek up in an effort to shelter Charlie.

Charlie was right about my family. We lived with them for a good six weeks every summer and it was always a magical time for Charlie. I reveled in seeing him surrounded by all that love and attention, even if it did occasionally nip a bit at my maternal guilt complex. I looked forward to the journey all year, and we were about to embark again.

When Charlie and I did return to Michigan for our annual summer pilgrimage shortly afterwards, I felt the weight of my responsibilities lift from my shoulders. My mother eagerly stepped in to be caretaker to both of us. Large, home-cooked meals once again filled our bellies. Family game nights were loud, raucous affairs. The best part, though, were the long summer days on Lake Michigan. I'd deemed Charlie old enough the previous summer to introduce him to my childhood love, a sun-faded old 13' Sunfish sailboat I'd stubbornly named George as a child.

We spent hours each day teetering between George and the rocky beach at the end of the jetty. I snapped hundreds of photos of our progression from pale white to a soft caramel color. Sarah worked in the summer but pulled occasional days off to come join us, and for a little while we were just 14 and 18 again, sipping a stolen beer and giggling about the Vargas brothers.

My parents came in handy in another way. Dating Jan had effectively broken my dating seal. Taking advantage of live-in child care providers and the temporary nature of our visit, I enjoyed a few very short-lived flirtations with some of the old "local boys." None of it was ever meant to be serious, it was a beautiful summer reminder I wasn't an old maid at all. Men still found me desirable, and I could still let go and just have a little breathless fun.

As the magic of summer dwindled down, I toyed with a crazy idea. What if we packed up and moved here for good? I could get my MI teaching license. Charlie would do fine with the transition, I was sure. It would be nice to have the support of family nearby.

My sister brought me back to earth, commenting, "You're so lucky, you get to escape before the annual snow-hell commences."

I remembered then what had drawn me to Virginia. The history was appealing, the arts and culture scene was far superior to our little corner of northern Michigan, the diversity was better, but most important of all, the winters were mild. In the end, the temporary madness faded, and we returned to Virginia as we always did. So bitter is the taste in my mouth, when I remember making that choice.

10

When Charlie was ten years old, he graduated from children's art classes at the Virginia Museum of Fine Art to private lessons with accomplished artist Ben Hamilton. One of the fresh-faced eager teachers at VMFA had approached me after class one day to suggest the tutorship. She felt like the simple arts and crafts offered in her class were doing Charlie a disservice, and she had a personal connection to Ben through his private curator. She explained Hamilton would mentor one or two young artists a year, and she thought Charlie was the perfect fit.

"He's special, Nell. Raw talent needs to be cultivated, so it isn't wasted. Ben won't be cheap, but he can identify and really pull that potential out."

I knew who Ben Hamilton was. He wasn't just a local celebrity, he was a national treasure. I'd seen his exhibit numerous times at the VMFA and reproductions of his works decorated the walls of many local businesses. He was something of a mystery figure, though, the kind of man who granted a print interview with a publication like The New York Times or Salon every few years and otherwise seemed to disappear. I turned to internet sleuthing to learn more.

Hamilton was 70 years old and lived on a large farm just outside of Richmond. He fell on the radar of the local art scene after his first juried art show at 15. A well-known New York art critic with Richmond ties took an interest in him and with his assistance, Hamilton found himself eventually attending the esteemed École nationale supérieure des Beaux-Arts in Paris. His meteoric rise following was somewhat unusual and legendary in the art community. Ben Hamilton would not have to wait until he was dead to collect his earnings. Very little was mentioned about his personal life in the articles I found, but I did deduce he was single and had two living sons. There was also a vague reference to losing a third son in an old Art Scene Now article.

For Hamilton, the palette of grief is blue, not black. When you study the catalogue of his paintings, it is difficult to find consistent works that rely heavily on blue tones except for that brief period following the death of his adult son. I ask him about this anomaly, and he smiles and then reminds me he isn't here to discuss his personal life.

I was intrigued and excited about the possibility of Charlie studying with such an acknowledged genius. When I told him about the possibility and asked if he'd be interested, his excitement mirrored my own.

"Heck yeah, Mom!" he'd said, beaming.

"I don't think it's guaranteed." I warned him, "And Ashley did warn me he won't be cheap, but let's see if we can make this happen."

But "not cheap" was an understatement. I was a public school teacher who depended on increasingly unreliable child support from overseas to keep us in the small house I'd so proudly purchased four years before. Our idea of a vacation was driving to Michigan every summer to spend a month at Grandma and Grandpa's house. We splurged and ate out once a week, every single Wednesday at Joe's Pizza Shack and that was pretty much the full extent of our restaurant budget. I was also seriously saving for Charlie's college; I knew the value of higher education, but I also knew the cost. Every spare penny was being socked away in a 529 plan for his future. The price Ben quoted us was completely out of our range.

After spending a few hours with a spreadsheet, trying to make the numbers work, I finally threw my hands up in surrender. There was just no way to make it work. I reasoned that Narek had had no special art lessons as a child, he'd still pursued his passion and succeeded at it. Charlie, too, could always focus on art when he got to college. I'd made one critical mistake though; I'd told Charlie about the opportunity and now I had to let him down.

I felt a lump in my throat as I told him, "Buddy, I am so sorry, I know I said we would make this happen, but I screwed up. We just can't afford what Mr. Hamilton charges."

Charlie smiled at me, and I tried to resist the urge to poke the dimple in his cheek because the older he got, the louder his protests were when I did that.

"It's okay, Mom. You know all those art lessons are on YouTube, anyway. I can just teach myself, like Dad, right?"

"Yes, your father learned all on his own at your age. Later though, he had proper training at art school. Someday you can have that kind of training too. I'm just really disappointed I couldn't make this work, because I know how excited you were."

"I'm disappointed too; we should probably get ice cream!" he suggested with an impish smile.

The disappointment was short-lived, though. Charlie's teacher at VMFA contacted Ben directly and sent him a few more samples of his artwork. When he learned that Charlie was only ten years old, he called me back with an offer I couldn't refuse. The samples he'd seen excited him and he was willing to negotiate down the price to something that felt reasonable to me. I thanked him profusely and then rushed to tell Charlie the good news.

"Really? That's so cool! I can't wait to tell Dad!"

I'd long since mastered the art of a fake smile whenever he mentioned "Dad." Whatever I might have gotten not completely right during his early childhood, I'd protected him from my own feelings about Narek. In the past seven years, Narek had visited exactly twice. He was fairly dependable with his text messages to Charlie, but far less dependable with his child support payments. Too often, I was forced to send emails that made me feel like I was begging for coins. Several times I'd had to escalate to actual phone calls, something I absolutely hated.

My feelings had recently become even more complicated, as Narek had finally married the year before, and he now had a two-month-old son in Armenia. A son he would raise legitimately, I thought bitterly. I wasn't jealous of his wife or even the fact he'd found happiness. I fought an angry jealousy, though, when I thought about his new son, Davit, and what that might mean for Charlie. It was impossible to envision Narek playing house, being the dutiful husband and father, a half a world away and yet apparently, he was doing just that. With Herculean effort, I kept my bitterness hidden from Charlie.

"Hm, yes, I'm sure your father will know exactly who Ben Hamilton is and why this is such an exciting thing. I'm sure he'll be proud of you," I said in the cheeriest voice I could muster.

Narek was proud. He had eschewed personal social media, but maintained a professional presence on all the major platforms. Occasionally, I liked to torture myself by skimming his Facebook and Instagram pages to see his latest work. He had been a decent artist when we first met, but I had to grudgingly admit he was much better now. There was an emotional depth that his earlier work had lacked, that was present in his more mature paintings. I'd hesitantly opened his page after Charlie told him the news and was surprised to see an actual personal post, translated from Armenian to English by Facebook.

"My son Charlie is being mentored by the great Ben Hamilton. Someday he will be a far better artist than me."

I felt a tiny twinge of something between melancholy and shared pride. So many years had passed, I rarely even remembered what it felt like to love Narek. It was unsettling that for just a moment, I indulged in a memory, a sweet one. Laying naked under our champagne-colored sheets, I was on my side, my belly large with Charlie. Narek lay behind me, spooning my figure perfectly, his arms wrapped around me, hands resting warmly on my belly. His rough chin nuzzled against the delicate back of my neck, and I felt him become hard at the same moment Charlie began kicking. Narek jumped a little, and then we both laughed. At that moment, everything was possible.

Shaking the memory away to the secret place inside me that kept such memories locked away to keep them safe, I shut down the computer. Whatever other feelings I might have had, I did feel validated by Narek's post. Ben Hamilton was exactly as big a deal as I'd surmised in my brief online reading. Charlie would be studying under a true master!

His first lesson was on a rainy Monday afternoon. If he felt nervous at all, it didn't show. I felt plenty of nerves for both of us as we made the drive to the outskirts of Powhatan. Ben's studio was a large converted barn on his spacious rural property. His work might hang in some of the greatest museums in the world, but his personal preference was to stay out of the limelight, cocooned in a place where privacy and nature inspired his oil work. Driving down the mile-long dirt road that connected his art barn to the main road, I could see what drew him here. The scenery was beautiful, but more than that, the sheer serenity of a world without people mucking it up was enticing.

He was waiting for us at the entrance to the barn. He was shorter than I'd imagined, based on the headshots I'd found online. At 5'5', I could stand eye to eye with him. His wild white beard needed a trim, but his blue eyes sparkled with intellect. The callouses on the firm hand I shook surprised me; he wasn't a stranger to physical labor. He looked at Charlie and for a moment, seemed to study him as if he were the subject of his next masterpiece.

Charlie stared back confidently, and I realized with a start he was mirroring Ben's studious look. "Hi, I'm Charlie," he said simply, as if that was all the introduction he ever needed in the world.

Ben smiled, and I liked the way his eyes crinkled. It gave him a kind face that put me at ease immediately. "I'm Ben, and I'm very pleased to meet you. You understand why you're here?"

Charlie nodded solemnly, we'd discussed needing to take this very seriously and I could see he was working hard to do just that.

"You're an art master, even better than my father, and you're going to teach me how to paint right," he explained.

Ben laughed at that. "First lesson is, art is subjective. People can have favorite artists, but there isn't really a magical scale that determines which artist is best. I looked at your father's work after your mother contacted me, and he's quite good. There's a lot of debate over whether talent is actually hereditary, but having seen work by both of you, I think we can settle that debate once and for all."

He turned to me and said, "I know I live pretty far out here. You're welcome to relax in the gazebo or your car, but I can also recommend a great little cafe downtown if you'd rather."

I understood; I wasn't invited into their session. I glanced at Charlie, who seemed completely at ease with this stranger and back at Ben. I'd never been comfortable leaving Charlie with someone I didn't know very well, as in years long well. Perhaps I was a little overprotective, but it kept him safe from harm for over ten years so I called the method successful. Still, this was only for a few hours and I knew exactly where he was. Charlie gave a tiny nudge of his head towards my car, and I smiled. It was time to let him fly.

Following the directions Ben had given me, I made my way to Mabel's where I hid in a corner with my book and a huge milkshake adorned with an actual donut. The rush of carbs and calories helped curb whatever worry I was trying not to indulge in. As I glanced around the dining room, a small painting caught my eye. I got up to investigate and was excited to see it was one of Ben's. A tiny kingfisher sat on a branch overlooking a pond, its reflection in the water obscuring the faintest hint of a tiny fish below the surface. A placard identified the painting as a gift from Ben Hamilton. I couldn't help but be impressed, this was an artist whose work was displayed in the Smithsonian, yet he was humble enough to donate work to a small local business.

When I finally returned to the barn, a thrilled looking Charlie ran out to greet me. They hadn't painted at all today, he explained. Instead, they'd talked a lot about color and had studied color wheels. I couldn't help but smile at his excitement even as part of me wondered how I'd feel if I'd paid full cost for a few hours of chatting. As if reading my mind, Ben laughed and said, "Don't worry, mama, he will be painting soon enough!"

He had been telling the truth. Soon Charlie was painting. His earliest efforts were beautiful but also obviously juvenile. Then they began to evolve, and even my amateur eye could see something was happening with the work Charlie brought home. It was as if I was watching my child grow up on a canvas, well before the little boy himself would be grown. On his

12th birthday, Ben gifted him with a new set of what I could only assume were very expensive brushes, and the card said, "To my protege." and I teared up at how Charlie beamed at the word protege.

That birthday was "the best ever," he proclaimed, and Ben's gift was just part of what made it so great. His other favorite gift was from his father. Narek had been pushing me to allow him to send a "smartphone" to Charlie for some time. I saw no reason a child that young needed to walk around with a pocket-sized computer all day. He argued if Charlie had an iPhone, then he could Facetime him all the way from Armenia, and Charlie could get to know his brother more that way. I hated to admit it, but his point had merit and finally, I relented. The phone had been a massive hit with Charlie and his friends. As reluctant as I'd been about it, my heart swelled a little at his joy.

The day after his birthday, after his friends had left, he made his first Facetime call to Narek. I popped into view for a minute to wave hello after Charlie insisted and felt a pang of something close to grief when I saw Narek's smiling face and the small boy on his lap. I'd seen his picture before, but that felt different from seeing Narek physically engaging with the child. He was slightly darker than Charlie, and the dimple in his chin must have come from his mother's side, but the resemblance was uncanny. If I'd put Charlie's 18-month picture next to Davit's, anyone would have known they were brothers. Brothers who would be almost strangers. Soon Davit would have a brother or sister to play with in real time. Narek's wife was pregnant with their second child, something I tried not to think about too much. Charlie would always be my only. I was certain of that. I couldn't help but envy that Narek knew what a real family felt like.

Later, so much later, I could look back on Charlie's 12th year and be thankful for how special it was. His hours with Ben, his growing talent in the studio, his boyhood friendships, his tenuous connection with his father from half a world away, his excitement over getting to know his brother and eventually his baby sister. Later, my hurt feelings and resentment didn't matter anymore. The last year of Charlie's life was also the happiest year of his life. I'm certain of that.

Part 2

11

I've always disliked April. Other than Charlie's birth, nothing good has ever happened in April for me. If I wasn't miserably trying to avoid pollen and the requisite sinus infection, I was running to escape the relentless rain. I resented the fake summer-glimpse April offered, that naïve way I'd step outside and say, "Oh, it's so nice! I'm so ready for summer!" only to discover temperatures back in the 40s the next day. Charlie's 13th birthday was on one of those glorious fake-summer days, and I let myself indulge in it. I let myself forget to be weary.

You spend so much of your life imagining the worst, fearing the worst, watching for the worst, but the worst rarely happens when you're looking for it. The worst is what happens when you're blithely going about the dogged routine of your life, those moments when you've forgotten to have a guard up at all. The jogger obsessively checking his watch for calorie burn as he dreams of an indulgent lunch, runs right into a bus. The file clerk who argues with her husband about whose mother gets to see them for Christmas, over a Bluetooth earpiece as she carries a few large boxes of records down the hall, steps into an empty elevator shaft. A couple returns home from Disney World, eager to finally get their child to sleep in her own bed, and Dad has an embolism on the plane. As humans, our sense of doom is grossly overstated in literature and movies.

Our morning that day was like every other school year morning, Charlie scarfing down a bowl of cereal as I finished my hair and makeup. Returning to the kitchen, I eyeballed the overflowing garbage can and stripped out the bag. Tying it, I sat it by the door and called out, "Take the trash out when you're done eating." and was rewarded with a grunt I hoped was an affirmation. A short while later, there was the familiar moment of me asking, "Do you have all your homework?" and his sheepish smile as he ran back into his room. There was really only one remarkable thing on that day to note, it was Charlie's birthday.

"Let's go to Gino's tonight to celebrate," I suggested. Gino's was his favorite, and it was how we usually celebrated things if it would be just the two of us. This year, Charlie had insisted he didn't want a real party. Instead, he wanted to go to Washington DC with me for a weekend when school let out for the summer. I was totally on board for that experience, but we needed to celebrate today nonetheless.

I dropped him off at the middle school, only two blocks from the elementary school I still taught at. He jumped out of the car and then turned around to me and waved. Thirteen years old, he was a teenager now. He'd started to sprout up, and as his friends approached him, I noticed he was one of the tallest in the group. He walked away with them, backpack slung over one shoulder, with a hint of a swagger. Manhood was lurking somewhere in that lithe body, threatening to emerge at any moment. Shaking my head to chase the thought away, I headed to my own school.

I'd only just parked when I heard my message alert ding.

Mom can I stay late with Bryce, we're gonna work on his robotics project...

I guess, what time should I pick you up?

He invited me to his house afterward, his mom's making tacos.

My throat tightened a little at this. I felt unreasonably disappointed. Of course, he wanted to spend his birthday with a friend, but I felt a little left behind. Was it happening? Was Charlie hitting that age where I'd no longer be the most important person in his life? I knew this was the natural progression of things, I couldn't pinpoint exactly when it'd happened in my own childhood, but I could distinctly recall at some point my friends became more important than my own family. Still, it was just dinner, I reasoned, we could do cake and ice cream tonight at home. I'd find some new movie on Amazon he'd been wanting to see and we'd make the evening special with that. I bit back the disappointment and replied.

Sure, just be home by 7! School night!

K...

Love you...

You too...

My second graders didn't allow me to think about the cancelled plans for long. The unseasonably warm weather had them in rare form. I spent the first hour of the class day trying to harness and corral way too much sun-fed seven-year-old energy. If we were having a battle of the wills, I had to admit they were winning. I decided this was drastic enough behavior; we needed drastic action, and I turned the classroom light off. Silence temporarily descended as I spoke as quietly as possible without going into a full whisper.

Everything isn't just a hazy memory. It's like any other day in my life; I can recall bits, pieces, but not everything. I remember one child interrupted me and earned my sternest yes-ma'am face, and I remember when the alarm sounded. I don't remember just what bit of wisdom I'd been about to impart on them, though. That wisdom has been lost forever.

When the alarm first sounded, I had been confused. I assumed I must have missed an updated drill date. This was rote by now, we'd practiced it so many times. I held up a hand to quiet the already stimulated kids who seemed far more excited about having their lesson time interrupted, than worried about what the alarm might actually mean. I called out, "Go to the back of the room," as I marched up the door to lock it. Then the vice principal's voice came over the intercom, and everything changed.

"Lock down! Lock down! This is NOT a drill, teachers ensure you are following full lockdown procedures, repeat LOCK DOWN this is NOT a drill."

I glanced back at my students. They were quieter and I saw a few decidedly worried-looking faces. Summoning my inner mom, I smiled and said cheerfully in my quiet voice, "All right, you guys know how this drill goes. We're going to sit very quietly in the back of the room and wait. This is probably just like last time," I promised.

Last time had been the day First Union was robbed just three blocks away. They'd put us in a precautionary lockdown as police chased down suspects who were never actually anywhere near the school. Better safe than sorry, our school superintendent would say.

I did a quick headcount to confirm what I had already known; everyone was here. Thankfully, it was so early in the day no one had pressed for a restroom pass yet. The whole time I was listening intently, and I heard nothing concerning. Certainly, no gunshots, but also no yelling or heavy footsteps or any other sign I imagined that might indicate this was a serious situation. The last announcement had momentarily quieted my students, but they were beginning to whisper and even giggle again. It was a fine line to straddle; I was supposed to keep them quiet, but I also didn't want to terrify 16 seven-year-olds when it wasn't necessary. I settled for periodic "Shhh, voices down" reminders, as I listened intently for an announcement that would tell us this had all been a drill, or some silly mistake.

One of my students, a very serious little girl named Becca, crawled across the floor and whispered nervously, "I think I have to go to the bathroom."

She was a shy girl, the type who blended into the background and worked so hard to escape attention and notice. Her mother had confided at our last parent-teacher conference she suffered from social anxiety night terrors. Of all my students, the look on her face made it clear she was having the hardest time with this lockdown. I groaned inwardly but keeping my voice calm explained, "Not now, sweetie, you have to hold it in for a little while. I'm sure they'll open the doors soon."

Her chin quivered a little, but she nodded and sat back next to me silently. I had just relaxed again when the phones started their show. My students knew they couldn't have a phone on their person during class, but most had one stuffed away in their book bag or jacket. A lone vibrating sound was quickly joined by a chorus of various alert sounds. From somewhere in the cacophony, I heard one that sounded distinctly like my own.

The last time we went on lockdown, phones had sounded off, but it hadn't been with this same sense of urgency. What the hell was going on? I looked at my students, who were now decidedly quieter, and could see the dawning realization on their faces this was something different. Becca grabbed my arm, and then as tears fell down her face, pointed at her lap. I could see the darkening fabric of her crotch as her bladder let loose. I grabbed her hand and squeezed and whispered, "It's okay, we'll get you cleaned up soon, no one will know."

Summoning every bit of reserves I had, I faked a big smile and said in a low but cheerful voice, "Well, I guess our phones are all working! I'm going to go get mine and see if maybe there's a phone company test sending messages. Everyone stay here, and I have a funny game we're going to play while we wait. Before I go to my desk, I'm going to whisper something into Becca's ear and then she's going to whisper it into Thomas's ear, and so on. By the time we get to Jamal, I'm betting he's going to report back to me with something quite different. Let's give it a try!"

Their faces looked relieved, eager for a distraction. I leaned toward Becca and whispered, "The white cat jumped a fence, and went for a swim," then got up to creep my way toward the front of the classroom.

Halfway to my desk, I paused. I was about to pass the door and there was a window in it. I was torn between wanting to duck past it and wanting to peek out to see what might be happening. My phone alert sounded again, and I glanced back at the kids who were now fully enthralled in their whisper game. I was already taking a chance; I couldn't take a bigger one. I concentrated on my breathing, remembering the technique I'd learned when I'd trained for a 10K, eerily similar to what they taught us in Lamaze classes. In through the nose and out through the mouth. Repeat. Ducking low enough I thought I wouldn't be visible from the hallway, I swept past the door and ran to my desk. The phone was in the top drawer where I'd left it, and I grabbed it desperately. I hadn't really believed I was in harm's way before the journey across the classroom, but the sprint past the door left me feeling vulnerable.

I looked toward the back of the dimly lit room at the hunched figures of my students and gingerly repeated the trip in reverse. I reached the children just as they completed their whisper game. Trying not to sound out of breath, I asked, "Well, Jamal, what did you hear?"

"Dwight's cat shuts the fence and winter storm," he replied proudly to the giggles of his classmates. Feigning enjoyment, I didn't actually feel, I started a second round and then finally turned my attention to the phone. Multiple messages were waiting to be read. I started at the top, the first was from my mother.

We just saw the news! Call us as soon as you can.

My sister had sent multiple messages.

Are you guys okay?

OMG call me!!

Goosebumps erupted on my arms. That my family, all the way in Michigan, knew something was happening terrified me. But if I'd felt chilled at that moment, the next message left me frozen. It was from a friend who taught kindergarten down the hall.

What's going on? Any idea?

OMG Nancy just texted she heard it's actually at Cooper.

This is crazy, look at the CNN page!

Cooper? That was the name of Charlie's middle school. For a moment, I was confused. Whatever was happening, it wasn't happening at Cooper; we were the ones on lockdown. Then in a rush, it hit me. Cooper was only two blocks away; if something happened there we would go on a precautionary lockdown. In the background, the rings and alert sounds continued, and I glanced at my students. Then I looked back at my phone and with a trembling finger opened the internet browser and typed in CNN.

ACTIVE SHOOTER AT COOPER MIDDLE SCHOOL IN RICHMOND, VA. Police confirm there is an active shooter situation in progress. They report there are victims, but are not releasing further details at the time. Parents and media are being asked to stay away from the school; students are still locked down. Nearby Groves Elementary School was also placed on a precautionary lockdown. School officials say once the situation is resolved, they will coordinate a student release.

When people say, "my heart stopped," you understand unless they literally had a heart attack, it's empty hyperbole. Usually, when someone uses that phrase, it feels dramatic and empty. Except my heart stopped. I frantically opened my messenger and clicked Charlie's name.

Hey, are you okay?

Charlie if you can, pls answer me...

I love you.

I watched desperately for the tell-tale ellipsis that would indicate he was typing a response. With each passing second, I felt my panic grow. I looked blankly at my students as if they might somehow have a solution. One of the little boys closest asked, "What's wrong, Miss Sanger?"

It snapped me out of my paralysis, and I took a deep breath. "Nothing Christian, I'm just letting people know we are okay and it seems this is all just a drill after all."

The alerts from the coat hook wall kept coming, and I realized the parents of my students were as frantic about their children as I was about Charlie. If I gave them their phones, it was possible they'd see the news and feel more scared than they were already, but the truth was the constant ringtones and message alert sounds had us all on edge already. If their parents knew they were okay, the assault of sound might slow down. I glanced at my phone again, still nothing from Charlie. Maybe his phone was also in his backpack, stuffed in a locker or under a desk and he just couldn't reach it. When this was all over, he'd complain about how stupid and boring it was, how someone had played a prank and dropped some firecrackers in the boys' room or something, and all the adults had overreacted.

I looked at the coat wall and told the students to remain where they were, then made my way to it. I grabbed every jacket and backpack that hung along its length, and feeling like a Sherpa leading a group onto Everest, and walked back to the kids with it all.

"Okay, if you have a phone, you may use text only on it. You may contact your parents. We're not going to make phone calls, only text. We're not going to play on the internet. Only text. You can share your phone with a classmate who doesn't have one if they know a phone number to send a text to. Only text. Do you understand?"

They all nodded and eagerly held out their hands for their items. Soon the dimly lit classroom was filled with bright screens. I could see their little faces relax as they received comforting words from home, and I felt a stab of envy. Come on, Charlie, talk to me. *Hello???*

I hit refresh on the CNN page and found there hadn't been many more details released. There was a photo now, though, of the front of the school. There were several dozen police vehicles, ambulances, and a few media trucks with big satellite dishes extended on the roof. I couldn't see any students or teachers, the few people in the shot were obviously law enforcement or media. Then, as I studied the photo closely, the page refreshed with a new headline.

AT LEAST SIX STUDENTS INJURED AT COOPER MIDDLE SCHOOL SHOOTING (updated, 10:29 am) At least six students have been shot at Cooper Middle School, in Richmond, VA. Their condition is unknown at this time. An anonymous source reports the alleged shooter is no longer considered a threat. It is unknown at this time if they are among the casualties or if they are in police custody. Students are now being evacuated from the school and will be reunited with their parents at a soon to be disclosed location. Nearby Groves elementary school remains on lockdown, that condition is expected to be lifted shortly.

I sat back against the cold, plaster wall and closed my eyes. I couldn't hold it together any longer. I feared I wouldn't be able to stop the scream of terror that was welled up in my throat. I pictured Charlie as he had been that morning, faded Levi's, red and black checkered shirt unbuttoned, over a Gryffindor t-shirt, blue LL Bean backpack slung cooly over one shoulder. Charlie, smiling at me as he waved, looking at me with Narek's brown eyes. There were so many students at Cooper, six wasn't such a big number. Six was still reason to believe he was okay. I felt a tug at my sleeve and looked down to see Becca staring up at me.

I forced a pained smile and felt my lip shaking. "It's okay, Becca. Soon, I promise." A second after my reassurance, the vice principal's clearly shaken voice came over the intercom. "Lockdown is lifted, at this time classes will resume, teachers we anticipate an early release to some parents. Please check your faculty email for more details."

I jumped up and ran for the light switch. "Okay, everyone, head to your desks. I'm going to speak to Miss Giesinger for a moment, indoor voices, please." and ran from the room before they had a chance to comply.

I pounded on the door of the room across the hall and when a very frazzled-looking coworker opened it, she mouthed the words "holy shit!" to me. I grabbed her arm and said, "I need to speak to you now," as I pulled her to the hallway.

As soon as we were out of earshot of the students, she explained, "This is absolutely insane. I can't believe the headlines."

I cut her off. "My son goes to Cooper."

She put her hand up to her mouth and asked if I'd heard from him. I hadn't. He wasn't answering his texts. I had to go. She nodded and said, "Go! I'll take care of your kids until we can get a sub in."

I ran back into my classroom and told the children they'd be looked in on soon, and someone would take my place. I was proud of how well they behaved during the lockdown, but I had to go help someone, and then grabbing my purse, I ran back into the hallway. Up ahead, I saw someone else running. I realized as he opened the main doors it was Robert Edwards, one of the sixth-grade teachers, and I remembered he had a wife who taught at Cooper. I yelled, "Robert!"

He turned and the look on his face mirrored everything I felt, a veritable stew of emotions that in the end boiled down to one thing, terror. He nodded and said, "Let's go."

We knew cars wouldn't be able to get anywhere near the school, so we ran the two blocks. We ran past the gawkers who stood with cell phones recording the scene, past the reporters who milled about the pavement speaking solemnly into microphones, past the first layer of first responders who seemed to be packing up, and straight into the inner circle of authorities who formed an iron wall against any further forward movement. "My son." I tried to explain to the officer who had blocked me.

"I'm sorry, ma'am, but the building is off-limits right now, students are going to be bussed and released at the high school stadium."

"No, you don't understand. I'm a teacher. My son, he's here. He isn't answering his texts."

His face wasn't unsympathetic, but it showed no hint of acquiescence. "This is a crime scene. We can't allow anyone in."

I was about to argue further when I heard a piercing sound from somewhere to my left. I turned to see two ambulances pulling out as authorities shouted at the media to get out of the way. I glanced at Robert and saw he wasn't having any more luck than me at crossing this line. He shook his head in frustration and walked over to me. "They won't budge. I understand why, but this is chaos. Do you want to head to the high school?"

I nodded. The adrenaline from my run and encounter with police was wearing off and a wave of exhaustion washed over me. We walked back to our school and got into his car. The high school was only 3 miles away, but it felt like an eternity to get there.

"Your wife... you haven't heard anything from her?" I asked.

His jaw clenched and then he replied, "No. She teaches science, and I know she had a first-period class today, but she hasn't answered any calls or texts. I'm hoping maybe she just forgot to charge it or something. And your son?"

Tears rolled down my cheeks as I shook my head. "Nothing. I know he had his phone; he'd texted earlier before all of this. I don't know why he's not answering."

We pulled into the overflowing parking lot and grabbed a haphazard spot. As we faced the mass of parents searching incoming busloads of kids, he reached over and put his hand on mine and squeezed.

12

Charlie never stepped off of one of the busses. If I'm being honest with myself, I knew he wouldn't. I'd somehow known from the moment I first read the damning headline back in my classroom. When the last bus left, those of us who remained were corralled by a woman with a clipboard who started collecting names. Feeling dazed, I shared Charlie's name, his description, my contact information, and then was advised to head to VCU Medical Center for further updates. I stood still, staring at her uncomprehendingly. As the small crowd disbursed, I finally shook myself out of my paralysis and turned to leave. It was then I remembered I didn't have my car. I was having trouble thinking; I knew there was a solution to this, but nothing came to me.

I heard a throat clear and turned around to see Robert, standing with his arm around a woman I knew must have been his wife. They were both looking at me with a look I could only identify as pity, and those looks only added to my dread.

"Can we give you a ride to the hospital?" he asked. I nodded, unable to speak.

On the ride there, Robert introduced his wife, Sandy. I instinctively said, "Nice to meet you." and then felt a hysterical laugh bubble out. I had no more control over that laugh than I did the sob that punctuated it.

Sandy turned around and reached her hand back to me. I stared at it for a second and then clutched it, hard. "Did you... were you near it?" I asked her.

She nodded. "Other end of the hallway." Her face was expressionless, she seemed to gaze off at something a thousand miles away. "We heard the shots, and I ran and locked the door. I went to call 911 and realized I'd left my phone in the faculty lounge. I never forget my phone; I just couldn't believe it." She shook her head, as if freeing it of cobwebs.

When we arrived at the hospital, I followed Robert into the building. Sandy was planted firmly at my side. I was confused, where was I supposed to go? The emergency room? Was he in intensive care? Robert turned to us and said, "The information desk is over there."

When we reached the clerk, I struggled with the words I needed to say and Sandy explained softly, "Her son, he was at Cooper Middle School."

The attendant pulled out a folder discreetly placed under his keyboard and compared my driver's license to whatever document was placed inside it. He avoided eye contact with any of us and then directed me to a private lounge on the second floor.

I turned to the Edwards. Robert was looking down at the floor. Sandy was so pale; I'd never met her before, but I knew instinctively it was an unnatural pallor. She didn't speak but instead nodded subtly at me, and Robert finally said, "I think the elevators are around the corner, we'll go up with you."

I shook my head. I wanted to do this alone. I managed to thank them and tell them to please go, then turned and slowly made my way to the second floor. With each step up the stairway, my stomach clenched harder. They don't send you to the second floor for an emergency. They send you to the western side of the building for that. They don't send you to the second floor for ICU. They send you to the fourth floor for that. I wasn't sure what was even on the second floor. As I reached the landing, I suddenly recalled an odd memory. Narek, describing the horror of the Baku pogrom and how he got over it.

"It was just a week."

If Charlie was okay, even if he was hurt, then someday I would be able to say, "It was just a day."

The doors along the long, empty hallway were numbered, and I knew when I'd reached the designated place, but I didn't stop walking. Instead, I walked past the door I'd been directed to and headed straight into the restroom. My stomach was cramping so badly, I was afraid I was about to soil my pants. After leaving the stall, I washed my hands and splashed cold water on my face and stared into the mirror. My own face was barely recognizable. It was splotchy and swollen; a stranger's eyes were looking back at me. There were dark circles under my eyes, the product of mascara that had run and smudged. Had I really just put that mascara on this morning?

I stared down at my sensible grey sketchers and willed them to move across the dingy white tiled floor, back down the hallway, toward the designated room. I paused outside the door. I could just leave, just turn around and call an Uber and head home to wait for Charlie. Surely, if I reached the safe haven of our home, the world would right itself again. He would come charging through the front door and I'd admonish him to slow down. I'd nag him for not texting me and letting me know he was okay. He would tell me how he'd left his phone behind and a friend's mother had scooped him up and taken him home for safekeeping. We'd have a somber talk about how dangerous the world could be, but I'd remind him most people were still good. I'd tell him the chances of ever being in that situation again were so statistically low, he had nothing to fear. Probably, he would drag his feet about returning to school whenever it finally reopened, and I'd wrestle with my own fears, but common sense would prevail and I'd scootch him out the door with his backpack on that morning.

Then I thought about calling my parents, giving them an update, letting them know I was okay and that I wasn't with Charlie yet but soon would be.

Thinking of my own worried parents, I suddenly wondered if anyone had thought to call Becca's parents, to bring her a change of clothes. I'd forgotten to pass that message along. As I tried to think of something, anything, that would require me to leave that hospital and avoid that room, a woman appeared in the doorway.

She looked a little startled to see me standing there, so close to her, and asked, "Mrs. Buyukian?"

"Miss Sanger, I'm not married to Charlie's father," I corrected automatically. This address was an oft-repeated mistake I'd experienced many times over the previous thirteen years by people who knew Charlie before they met me. But she didn't know Charlie, I reminded myself. She was a stranger in our world.

She nodded, and with a gentle voice, said, "Miss Sanger, I'm Diana, one of the social workers here; why don't you come inside and sit down so we can talk about what's happened."

She motioned into the room, and I looked around wildly, desperate not to go in there. I shook my head feebly and said, "I don't think I can."

"I understand, but we need to talk about what's happened to Charlie, and it's best not to do this in the hall. Miss Sanger, just take my arm and we can go in together." We stared at each other for a moment.

My phone made a sound, and I broke eye contact to pull it out of my purse. It was Mom again.

Where are you and Charlie? Neither of you are answering your phones.

I looked at my call record and saw four missed calls from her. Did that mean Charlie also had four missing calls?

Glancing back at the social worker, I held up my phone and said stupidly, "My mother tried calling me."

She nodded again and put an arm around me and began to physically steer us into the room. I felt my strength depart me; I wasn't sure if my legs could even get me to a chair; I gave up resisting and leaned on her as she led me toward a chair.

"Miss Sanger…"

"Nell," I said dully.

"Nell, I'm so very sorry to have to tell you this, Charlie didn't make it."

I wondered vaguely if perhaps I was having a stroke. The room had tilted, and I couldn't focus my eyes on anything. A strange siren wailed in my ears; maybe it wasn't a stroke, maybe it was an aneurysm. The siren wailed louder; I threw my hands over my ears to protect them and that's when I realized the sound was coming from my own mouth.

13

A half dozen fish were suspended in the cerulean, pebbled world, oblivious to the drama beyond their glass prison. I envied their singular purpose, simply surviving until they didn't anymore. Nobody asks a fish if it's okay. Nobody tells a fish anything at all.

I thought I'd called Ben, but as I sat watching the tank, I suddenly wasn't sure. I couldn't remember actually speaking to him. Maybe I hadn't really called. Maybe I'd sit here and just wait out the end with the fish. I did remember shrugging off the legion of nurses, doctors, and social workers upstairs, ignoring their pleas for me to rest in a private room for a while. I'd swallowed the Xanax that was offered to me and then told them to leave me the fuck alone and made my way down to the lobby to wait.

I'm not sure why I chose Ben, I had plenty of friends I could have called to come get me after all, but maybe it was just an innate need to be with someone who loved Charlie too or maybe I'd chosen him because he too was solitary. Maybe I wanted to be around someone as utterly alone in this world as myself, someone who valued silence.

Outside, a huge crowd of media had assembled. Every time the massive, tinted sliding doors automatically opened, I could see their reflection in the fish tank across from me. The hysterical thought occurred to me, they were not just disturbing me; they were disturbing the fish. I imagined they were supposed to stay beyond the main walkway because that's where most remained, but periodically one or two would walk boldly into the facility and try to get past the security personnel at the information desk. It never worked, staff spotted them and turned them around and out the door they'd go again. I watched it all, dispassionately. The meds had kicked in and I felt like I existed within a liquid world where words were muffled and everyone moved in slow motion. I was a fish too.

At one point, I heard a woman in the lobby say to her companion, "It looks like number four won't make it." then she glanced over at me, grabbed his arm and moved along quickly.

Number Four. I wondered what number Charlie was. Somewhere in this hospital, Number Four's mother was about to join me in hell.

He'd snuck in through a side door. I didn't see him coming, but suddenly he was right in front of me. His wise old eyes brimmed with tears, but his face looked otherwise calm. I looked up at him, unable to speak. He reached down for my arms and pulled me up, and I allowed myself to rise and then fall into his arms.

"This way, Nelly girl," he said calmly, as he led me away from the fray. We didn't speak at all as we wove our way through the hospital and out of the side exit, he'd chosen. He led me to his truck and helped me climb in, still silent. I glanced at him as he began to drive toward my house, and realized his hands were covered in paint. I'd interrupted his work, and I wondered if I should apologize for that. Then I remembered again that Charlie died. Numbly, I turned back toward the road, staring straight ahead until we reached our house.

Our house was now my house. My house needed tidying. Breakfast dishes cluttered the sink, and the full garbage bag sat tied by the door. Charlie hadn't taken it out when I'd asked. A basket of clothes that needed to be folded erupted from the sofa. I glanced at Ben to apologize but could only manage the smallest shrug. He led me to the living room and moved the clothes to some unseen corner so I could sit on the couch. I cleared my throat and croaked out, "They didn't let me see him. They said I couldn't yet."

Ben nodded. "They have to clean him up properly. It's hard to wait, though. Part of you just can't believe it's real until you see it firsthand."

I remembered he had lost a son. Not that he had lost a son *too*, the too part wasn't real yet. I shook away the thought, I was too immersed in my own horror story, to think about his. He nodded and said, "It's okay, Nell," then sat next to me, seemingly losing himself in his own memories, whether they were of his son or my own, I don't know.

We sat in silence for a while and then I confessed, "I don't know what to do."

He wrapped his arm around me and pulled my head onto his chest and then said, "You don't have to do anything right now. Nell, is there someone you want me to call? Your parents maybe?"

His offer made me think of someone else who would have to be called and I shuddered.

"Oh god. Narek."

I'd forgotten Narek had even existed. Of course, someone had to call him, but who? I wanted to ask Ben to do it, I knew he would, but Narek shouldn't hear this from a stranger. I'd taken another pill, I wasn't sure I could even speak without slurring my words, but I had to get to him before he somehow heard about it online.

As if reading my mind, Ben said, "Nell, I can call him. It's fine. We don't have to do it right away either. There are no rules here."

I looked across the room and fixated on Charlie's latest completed painting. It was one of Ben's horses, the red one, munching on an apple in the field next to the gazebo. It wouldn't have passed in a gallery as the product of a professional artist, but it also wouldn't have been something people would attribute to a twelve-year-old boy. Thirteen. Thirteen-year-old for one day of his life, boy.

"He told me you offered to let him ride her. He told you he wasn't feeling well, but really he was scared," I said, my voice sounding strained.

"I knew. They're big animals, a lot of people are scared of them. I told him when he was feeling better if he wanted to give it a try to let me know."

I couldn't look at Ben, I choked out, "He loved you." and Ben replied quietly, "I know. I loved him too."

Finally, I said, "Okay, I can do this," and I picked up my phone. Narek answered on the fourth ring, and I realized it was still early morning there.

"Nell?"

"Narek. I had to call to tell you..." except that I couldn't tell him. I couldn't say the words out loud. I looked at Ben pleadingly and he gently took my phone from me.

"This is Ben Hamilton, Charlie's art tutor." There was a pause where Narek must have expressed his surprise and then Ben said the awful words. "I hate to have to say this, but there's been a situation. Charlie is, well he passed away." Another pause. "Yes, it was an act of violence at his school. No, no, she isn't."

I couldn't listen to another word. I got up and walked into my hallway, toward my bedroom. Charlie's door. It was wide open; he wasn't a shut-the-door kind of kid. I stopped in his doorway and peered in. He hadn't made his bed; he pretty much never made his bed. As I stared at the tangle of blue sheets and blue and white comforter, I felt an overwhelming desire to drown in them. I crawled into the bed and wrapped the linens around myself. I imagined some essence of him was still in the sheets and I could absorb it if I breathed deeply enough. I curled into a ball, almost suffocating on the comforter that now enveloped my face and sobbed. Once I started, I knew I would never stop.

After talking to Narek, Ben called my parents and broke the news to them. Meanwhile, I lay helpless in Charlie's bed and tried to imagine a world where I'd actually stand up, walk out, and keep living.

I closed my eyes and remembered our last dinner together, a quickie chicken stir-fry I'd thrown together from a frozen bag mix and slices of fresh chicken. Charlie was super animated, as he explained two of his classmates had a father who used to be in the NBA. The father would visit school soon and share how he had made academics a priority even when he was being scouted for college ball programs. I didn't recognize the name he gave, but I wasn't exactly a basketball fan. I'd just smiled and nodded, enjoying his excitement over almost knowing a hometown celebrity.

I'd finally had to tell him, "Hey, make sure you take some bites before it gets cold," and he'd given me this gesture I'd seen a hundred times before, long before he was ever born. A casual, little wave of the hand, that he must have picked up from Narek during their regular video chats. Sometime around the time I pictured the wave, I drifted off into blissful oblivion.

My parents and sister Sarah arrived the next afternoon. My father was a shell of his former self, I recognized his near-paralysis; it mirrored my own. He sat in the big armchair Charlie usually sprawled out on and stared mutely at the painting on the wall. My mother greeted me with tears and hugs and a whole lot of prayer talk I didn't want to hear. I knew she wanted me to fall apart on her. Her unsevered maternal strings needed to carry my burden, but her drive to be functional and helpful threatened to suffocate me.

When my stiff shoulders and one-word answers rejected her efforts, she turned to Ben, sharing his productive energy. Sarah was uncomfortable being there at all. I knew she loved her nephew, but she had never been gifted with EQ. Sarah lived in a world where emotions were stifled, and a stiff upper lip won the day. I spent a short time in the living room with them, nodding but not really talking, hoping the pill I'd taken from the old Percocet bottle I'd found would kick in quickly. As the numbness washed over me, I excused myself, retreating once again to Charlie's room.

When I awoke, Sarah was standing in the
doorway, holding a mug and a plate. "I brought you
some tea and a sandwich. Ben says you haven't eaten in
over 24 hours."

I sat upright, and I felt a wave of nausea hit. For
a moment, I feared my otherwise empty stomach would
expel whatever remnants of the pills remained. Finally,
after a few deep breaths, the room stopped spinning.
Sarah sat on the edge of the bed and said, "I'm so sorry,
Nell. I really can't believe it. I'm so angry this could
happen."

I tentatively took a small bite of the sandwich
and fought the urge to vomit it right back up. I wasn't
sure what Sarah wanted from me, but we'd never been
very close and I wasn't going to start pouring my heart
out to her now.

"I saw on the news Misty Framingham's aunt
and uncle are already organizing a march for next
Monday."

"What?" I asked, confused. "Who's that?"

She stared at me and seemed surprised. "Misty
Framingham, she was one of the other lost children."

Oh. I hadn't asked their names. I didn't like the
way Sarah used her name so casually, as if she
personally knew her. I also didn't like the way she said,
"lost children." No one had been lost. They'd been
exactly where they were supposed to be.

"Anyway, I was thinking, maybe you could
reach out to them and participate too. Maybe that would
be good for you. You know, to have something to focus
on?" she continued.

I put down the sandwich. "Participate in what?"

Again, that strange look. "The march. It's
against gun violence. It's past time our elected officials
do something to stop this madness."

I tried to understand what she was saying; it was as if the words were hanging there in the air, out of order, waiting for me to decode them. Something was buzzing in my head, though, and I couldn't quite figure out the word puzzle through that distraction.

"Why would I do that?"

"Nell! So that they can prevent this kind of tragedy in the future."

The future? What future? Why would I care about the future, my own or anyone else's? She was suggesting the earth would continue its journey around the sun without Charlie. Was that even possible?

"But Charlie's already dead," I finally said.

She was about to speak again, and I cut her off., "Sarah get out." and I lay back down and turned my back to her.

She waited a moment then said quietly, "I'm sorry for upsetting you Nell, I just thought maybe having a purpose would make this easier somehow. I'm sorry."

I lay silent as she left the room, desperate for the darkness and fragile peace of sleep to take me again.

14

I dreamt of Stoagie, my childhood dog. He was running down a trail, unleashed, and when he turned around a bend, I lost sight of him. I called his name and peered through the thick maple foliage for the telltale hint of his brown coat without success. Then I realized I'd somehow walked off the trail myself. For a moment, the forest was completely silent, and I stood still, trying to reorient myself. A crackling sound came from ahead, footsteps on dead leaves. I ran toward it, calling his name again when I saw him step out from behind a large tree. Except it wasn't Stoagie, it was Charlie.

The sound of Narek's voice stole the dream from me. He was yelling at someone, although I couldn't understand the specifics of what he was saying. My door opened and my mother walked in. "Hi, honey," she said softly. I tried to respond, but my throat was so tight and dry, I couldn't get the words out. Seeing my distress, she handed me the water glass from the nightstand and explained, "You've been out for fourteen hours."

Fourteen hours. My son had been dead for fourteen more hours. I wondered dully if parents of dead children counted deathdays, in the way we once counted birthdays. When you bring the baby home, you always start with days, then weeks, then months, and finally, at age two, years were the units of measurement but maybe with death you start with hours. Charlie was now 13 years old and 49 hours dead.

"Did I hear Narek?" I asked, struggling to push the thought of hours from my head.

She nodded, "Yes, he arrived this morning. A reporter just showed up at your front door and he was chasing him away."

I rubbed my eyes and tried to focus in the darkness of Charlie's room. I didn't really want to go out. I didn't want to have to interact with other humans at all. And then there was Narek. We hadn't seen him in almost four years, not in person anyway. He'd all but left our lives completely, and yet here he was pretending to be the doting father. I felt none of the nerves or conflicting feelings that usually plagued me when I knew we'd have to interact. Our last tie had just been completely and irrevocably severed and I wished he hadn't come at all. If I didn't go out, though, he would come in here into this sacred space. I couldn't stand the thought of him breathing Charlie's air, so I forced myself out of bed.

When I walked into the living room, everyone turned to stare. I had been in bed for almost an entire day and night, the looks on their faces made it clear they would have preferred the lie of smoothly brushed hair and a washed face, but I didn't really care if I made them feel uncomfortable in all my squalor. I saw Narek but barely registered his presence because something else had caught my eye. The television was on and a photo of a balding middle-aged man was displayed with the text "Hero of Cooper Middle School." My father reached for the television remote, but I held up my hand and said, "Wait."

Mr. Goldsby taught earth sciences at Cooper; he'd been in the classroom across the hall from the room where it had started. Upon hearing the first gunshot, he'd told his students to lock the door and ran out to confront the scene. He'd rushed in and tackled the gunman, easily wrestling the gun away from him. Gunman. The gunman wasn't a man at all; he was a tall, skinny, 13-year-old boy with red hair and acne. A video clip showed him arriving at a courthouse for arraignment. As detectives and lawyers rushed him past the throngs of reporters, he kept his head low, refusing to meet their eyes.

I stared at the boy, willing his face to memory. I knew I should feel something now; rage, grief, compassion, something that normal human beings felt, but at that moment, I felt nothing. It was as if the living me had become one of Narek's painted versions of myself. I looked like a version of a real person, but ultimately, I was just a two-dimensional facsimile of a human being.

Narek spoke finally, "John, the television, please?" and then he approached me. He looked older; a few silver hairs now flecked his tightly shorn beard. The lines at the corners of his eyes were deeper, and I could tell from the bags under them he hadn't been sleeping much.

For a moment, we just stood there, staring at each other, two solitary sailors on passing boats adrift. Then he walked toward me, as if to embrace me. I recoiled before there was contact. I didn't want to touch him and not feel anything, and worse yet was the possibility I might feel something after all. I wanted to remain alone and detached from all of them.

"Hello, Narek." My voice sounded cold.

"Nell... I am so brokenheart."

"Heartbroken," I corrected automatically.

"Heartbroken. I cannot believe our Charlie is gone."

I turned to the others, still seated awkwardly on the sofa and chairs. I heard my mother attempt to muffle a sob as she wiped at her eyes. My father's face was bright red with the exertion of holding his own tears back. Sarah was the only one with the grace to look uncomfortable instead of just sad. Locking eyes with her, I said, "Can you take Mom and Dad somewhere, please. Go get lunch maybe."

She corrected, "Dinner, but yes that's a good idea. We'll text before heading back."

When we were finally alone, I sank into one of the dining chairs and refused to look at him. He paced behind me. It was as if he'd absorbed every bit of energy that had drained from my pores and now, he didn't know what to do with it.

"Nell..." he began, and I put my hand up to stop him.

He finally stopped moving and said, "You need to eat."

I shrugged but didn't protest as I heard him opening cupboard doors. Something hit the countertop, and then there was the sound of pots and pans clanging as he dug through their cabinet. I turned finally, to see him opening a can of soup.

We didn't speak as he prepared and served a simple meal of soup and slices of days old crusty bread. Through the blessed silence, I felt my stomach unclench enough to swallow a few bites. If we had failed at so much else, Narek and I had at least always been very good at silence.

When I was sure the soup would stay down, I drew a breath and finally spoke. "My parents, I'm not sure how much longer I can handle them being here. They mean well but their grief... it's exhausting me."

He nodded. "I can see that in just the shorter time I was here. I think it is ideal if you can help each other but maybe now is not the good time for that."

"Where are you staying?" I asked, making an obvious point with the question.

"Marriott on Broad Street," he replied, not seeming to take offense.

"And you are... alone?" I asked hesitantly. I didn't think I could handle it if he'd brought his family, Charlie had never met his half-siblings when he was alive, it would have been ridiculous to bring them here now.

"Yes, of course." His eyebrows furrowed, and a small part of me felt a spark of satisfaction at his obvious disapproval of the question. I could still feel something after all. "Look I know he was your only son, you were the best mother too. I have other children and I was not a good father, not good enough anyway for Charlie, I know this too. But I am truly brokenheart over this. I would not hurt you by bringing the other children here; you should know this about me."

I sighed, my head was pounding again, and I remembered the Percocet, it was time for another pill.

After taking it, I returned to him and said, "I don't know what's happened since..."

He nodded at my unfinished words, he understood. "John and Nancy talked a little of it. They said Ben Hamilton has introduced them to the person who arranges the ceremony, but they need our input."

He looked away and when he turned back, I was surprised to see the tears rolling down his cheeks. "I would do this all for you, anything to make this easier, but I do not know how to bury my son."

His raw emotion bothered me. I resented that he felt entitled to it. I hadn't cried since the previous afternoon; the pain had been replaced by the numb reality that some part of me had also died yet here he sat crying. Narek had not earned the right to grieve. It was a relief when I heard the text alert interrupt, from the phone on the counter. I replied with a brief acknowledgement to my sister's warning they were returning soon and then scrolled through a seemingly endless list of unread messages from friends and coworkers. Glancing up at Narek and seeing his still stricken face, I turned back to my phone screen, hoping to lose myself in it. "I have to answer some messages," I explained without looking back up.

I couldn't find a single person I actually wanted to reply to. Any reply I sent would surely be met with one back, an expectation of conversation. I knew what society was expecting from me at the moment, and I was nowhere near ready for that kind of dialogue. I didn't want to hear about prayers I didn't even believe in or to reassure people I was okay (I wasn't okay.) I knew they meant well; they wanted to offer me some comfort, some confirmation I wasn't forgotten, but I didn't need that. What I needed was peace.

As I scrolled down, I suddenly happened upon the last text from Charlie. My hand froze for a moment, and then I opened it.

Love you.

You too...

I sheltered the screen with my hand and glanced around. Narek was at the sink, tidying the dishes. Looking back at the phone, I typed.

I feel as if someone reached into my chest and tore my literal heart out. Undo this.

I can't go on without you.

Everyone misses you, but they will be whole again. I won't ever be.

Your father is here, you know how crazy that makes me. His grief makes me feel so unreasonably angry.

Grandpa and Grandma are trying to help, Aunt Sarah's here too.

They're all making me a little crazy.

Missing you makes me the craziest of all, though. Please undo this. Just hit refresh. Make it all go back to the way it's supposed to be.

I heard the front door open and quickly closed the screen. My mother spoke too cheerfully, too brightly. "Well, that was such a nice meal!"

I looked at her and said truthfully, "I'm really tired. I need to go lay down for a while." I ignored the look on her face, the one that made her worry and disappointment quite obvious. I'd had exactly as much human interaction as I could handle for the day and I craved the encompassing forgetful comfort of sleep.

15

Try as I might, I couldn't get that old rhyme out of my head. April showers bring May flowers. The flowers were early; there were still 13 days left in April. The funeral hall overflowed with sickly-sweet smelling displays and bouquets. There seemed every imaginable floral combination arrangement of cross and wreath lining the entrance, the hallway, and the actual viewing room. When we arrived, the two men in suits with somber faces had shaken my hand and then led me to see him, although "seeing him" wasn't really a fair way to describe what I was actually offered.

Struggling to walk through the veritable…
jungle… I approached the awaiting casket on shaking
legs. It was closed, although I couldn't bear to
remember why we had to leave it that way. His likeness
was there, though, captured perfectly on canvas that
rested on an easel. It was fresh enough; I could still
smell the paint and the slightest hint of turpentine. Ben
had worked tirelessly on it, and I could not bear looking
at it after my first glimpse.

My parents and sister had stopped at the back of
the room, giving Narek and I a private moment. I
glanced at him, his eyes so disturbingly mirrored
Charlie's eyes in the painting. He reached over and
took one of my hands and we each placed our free
hands on the stained oak surface of the box that now
held our boy. I tried to imagine him sleeping inside, his
eyes shut peacefully, his mouth making that tiny smile
he always had when he slept. I knew that wasn't what
he looked like anymore; the carnage had been absolute.
The damage so severe even makeup couldn't make him
presentable enough for an open casket. The irony was
the nature of his injury meant that he hadn't known. He
hadn't felt it. We'd learned he was indeed Victim
Number One. When the first shot was fired, it had gone
directly into the back of his head. He hadn't had time to
be afraid. That was the single fact I clung to in my
darkest hours. He hadn't been afraid.

I found a seat in the front row of chairs and soon
the public doors opened. We were not prepared for the
crowds that lined up and wove their way through the
facility. Some faces were familiar, coworkers and
friends, a few of Charlie's closest friends and their
parents, some of his former teachers, a few old college
friends of both Narek and I. Many of the visitors were
complete strangers though, they'd stop to offer me a

personal condolence and I felt awkward giving a perfunctory nod. The children were the hardest of all. Hundreds of children, mostly of middle and high school ages. They'd been casual friends of Charlies through various organizations and events, classmates at some time, and sometimes seemed to have no connection at all.

At one point, a woman and her little girl paused in front of me and I stared up at the crying woman through uncomprehending eyes. It didn't click until I glanced again at the child. It was Becca, the child I'd had glued to me during the lockdown.

"I just wanted to say I am so sorry this happened to your son and also to say… thank you. Becca told me how you kept her safe that day," she said in a rush of tears.

I looked back at Becca and opened my arms, inviting her in for a hug she eagerly accepted. Her hair smelled like strawberry suave shampoo, and for just a moment I allowed myself to inhale her essence, the freshness of it so much better than the cloying scent of a thousand dying flowers. Grasping her tiny frame to me, I closed my eyes and allowed myself to pretend for a moment, it was Charlie at that age. He'd been all knobby knees and chubby cheeks, obsessed with trains and hot air balloons. For months, every drawing he did featured one or the other. Then I felt the child jerk back. I'd held on too tightly and she was suddenly scared. I let go and watched her grasp her mother's hand. They said an uncomfortable goodbye and then disappeared into the crowd.

The service and burial were the following day. I'd toyed with attending unmedicated, allowing myself to drown in the pain of the living, but in the end, I'd taken a pill and chased it with vodka. My mother said nothing, but I saw the look on her face. She was worried, and she didn't approve, but she didn't dare say so out loud. I sat through the service, once again numb. I had only one inappropriate moment, when the 70-year-old minister said, "To everything there is a season, and a time to every purpose under the sun."

I couldn't stop the loud "ha!" from escaping my lips. I heard a few soft gasps and my mother grabbed my hand, but I wasn't sorry. What did that old man know of my Charlie? What purpose would God have had for allowing his brilliant little mind to explode all over a cheap, shitty tile floor? I remembered then that I still had to pretend, so I sat mute for the rest of the service.

At the cemetery, the medication seemed to be wearing off. I could feel the pain in my feet from the new pumps my mother had foisted upon me, and soon I could feel the pain in my soul as I watched the box containing my only child being lowered into the ground. In a panic, I grabbed at the figure next to me. I somehow thought it was my father, but it was Narek. I looked at him, desperate for help. We had to stop them from doing this; we couldn't let him be buried. Once he was buried, that was it. It couldn't be undone. He put his arm around me and pulled me tightly against him and rested his chin on top of my head. With the solid wall of Narek supporting me, I stayed upright, and I stifled the screams building in my chest.

Afterwards, at my house, I made my way into the bathroom and locked the door. I turned on the shower and the overhead fan, and then I finally did scream. When they banged on the door, asking if I was all right, I shouted back through the wood I was fine, and then I screamed again.

My family finally left four days after the funeral. They'd been in town for nine days already, and it was time. My mother had suggested she stay behind, she thought my father could get my sister back to Michigan so they could both return to work and she could take care of me, but I told her with as much self-serving kindness as I could muster that wasn't a good idea. I needed to be alone for a while. As they were leaving, I allowed myself to be hugged for far too long by both of my parents and promised to visit soon and then I turned to my sister. I had been pretty chilly toward her for the entire visit and now I regretted it. I might never see her again and I didn't want her carrying those feelings. "I'm glad you came Sarah... I haven't been myself I know."

She shook her head and pulled me into a hug, whispering in my ear, "Call me anytime, day or night."

Narek visited that evening, bringing Chinese food from our old favorite take out place. I was eating a little more, but it was still difficult to actually taste whatever was going down. He broke our comfortable silence, sharing the burden that was uniquely his. "I am so angry at myself. I always want to visit, but I always put it off. In a few months, I have enough money to travel, in a few months, I take time off work, in a few months, Nazani and the children don't need me so much. Always an excuse! I would take it back now, any way possible. I would like even just one more day with him."

I could see the pain and guilt in his tear-filled eyes, and despite the previously impenetrable ice wall I'd erected around myself, it touched me in some small way. I felt a momentary urge to reach a hand out and pat his, but it was far too weak an urge to be acted on. For his entire life, Charlie had idolized his mysterious father, a man he'd met a handful of times after the age of three. He too would have done anything for just one day with him. If Charlie were still here, he'd keep growing and maturing and I am certain the day would have come that he would have resented this man and how absent he had truly been. At that moment, I felt resentful on Charlie's behalf and that resentment warred with the unwelcome whispers of sympathy.

Narek's eyes dropped in shame, as if he were reading my mind. "I wish I could stay and take care of you, the way I didn't when I was young and foolish. If I did not have children waiting for me, I would insist on that, actually. I cannot do this thing again, though; I cannot leave more children like I did Charlie."

"Oh, good god, Narek," I burst out. "I don't want you to leave your family! I want MY family back. I want my son here. You being here doesn't fix that."

I glanced at the clock and reached for the ever-present pill bottle on the table. Narek's hand shot out and covered mine. "I think you are taking too much; I think is not good for you at all."

I withdrew my hand quickly, as if a snake had touched it. I didn't want to justify myself and my choices, and the easiest way to avoid that was to not take a pill. I looked up at him and shrugged my shoulders angrily. "Fine, I'm having a drink, though."

As I had always been able to do, I handed Narek a glass and convinced him to drink with me. I refused to be the slob who was falling apart while he got to play cool, restrained, rescuer. He was every bit as fucked up inside as me and we both knew it. When the vodka bottle was empty, I walked crookedly into the kitchen and rummaged through the cabinets. I was drunk, but not drunk enough. I found an old bottle of cheap champagne I'd received in a Christmas gift swap a few years back and popped that. Narek groaned when he heard the cork hit the ceiling, but he didn't say no when I shoved a glassful of bubbles at him.

"You're leaving tomorrow still?" I asked, unable to decide if the prospect made me feel relieved or distressed.

"No, in two days, I have an early flight so tomorrow will be my official goodbye. I must visit the grave before I leave seven days after burial. I must return to my job and family, but I am not through with mourning even then. I must mourn for forty days, and even without Charlie's body, my family will mourn with me."

"Forty days?" I asked, confused. The alcohol was clouding my thinking. Was he saying after forty days he would be over it?

"Is tradition. I will not shave until the time is over, and my family will join me in dark clothes. At fourteen days, we will host memorial at my home since we cannot all go to the grave."

The Narek I'd known had been almost hell-bent on shedding the auspices of Armenian culture. Part of what had drawn me to him was my perception of him as being exotic and different, but the truth was he strived in every way to be a "normal American college student" in those days. The rites he described now conflicted with the young man I'd known and they made me both uncomfortable and angry.

"Charlie wasn't Armenian you know, not in any way that mattered," I said bitterly.

He nodded and sipped his champagne again. "I am aware. And I take blame for that. I have told you I have changed, though. I am going to church again. I am raising my children to be true Armenians. I could not do that for Charlie in life, but I will in death."

I slammed my glass onto the table and stood angrily. I didn't want to hear this, not any of it. I was so angry with him, many years of pent-up anger that I'd swallowed for Charlie's sake, threatened to explode out of me. He stood too, refusing to be cowered by my glare.

"Nell... let's not do this now."

"Don't do what? Tell the truth? Expose your fraud to the whole world?"

His hands were on my shoulders and I was yelling, horrible, terrible, yet true things.

"You left him! You left *us*! You broke every promise. You let me bring that beautiful boy into this terrible world, and you left me to raise him alone. You replaced us! We were all alone and he died. He died because you weren't here to protect him!"

He didn't argue with me. He didn't look away, even as his face twisted in anguish and tears rolled down his cheeks.

And then I was crying too, and my tears weren't angry tears; they were tears of loss. Loss of Charlie, loss of my youthful naivete about love, loss of dreams for the future, and perhaps most astonishing of all, loss of Narek.

"I'll never see you again after you leave tomorrow."

He shook his head in protest, but he was too drunk now to say the lie out loud.

"Never again," I repeated. He pulled me to him and when the kiss happened, it was desperate and hard enough to cause pain in my lip. Afterwards, after the kiss and the sex and the sobbing into each other's arms, I watched him fall asleep and was thankful. Thankful he'd reminded me how to feel angry, and sad, and loved, and connected. I knew I'd go back to being someone in a painting and not a flesh and blood human being again after he left the next morning, but for a brief period I'd been a real woman again. One last chance to feel.

With morning came a stabbing headache and a much more restrained goodbye. Narek stood awkwardly in the doorway and said, "If you need anything…"

I nodded. "I know where to find you."

Still, he hesitated before walking away and finally, I had to say, "Go on, it's time," and then I watched him walk away for good.

16

My heart was locked away in a steel box, and my body was locked away in my small ranch style home. I'd become a hermit. I had spent the three weeks after everyone left holed up in my house, the only faces I saw were my grocery delivery person and the mailman. I avoided phone calls as well, deferring to voicemail and quick "I'm okay" responses via text to my family and Ben to ensure they wouldn't rush in to check on me. The only person I really spoke to was Charlie. I'd taken to texting him regularly, throughout the day.

> I keep telling everyone I'm okay, but it's a lie and we all know it. They accept the lie because it's easier for them to go on with their lives that way.

Your father texted today, I ignored it. I
can't absolve him of his guilt any more
than I can absolve myself for not being
there when you needed me...

I found your baby book today, there's a
lock of hair in it... it was so silky and
black, I smelled it, but it didn't smell
like you.

I don't think I believe in heaven, but I
want to. I want to believe you are
someplace happy. Mostly, I want to
believe that if I die, I'll see you again....

I may have checked out from society, but
society kept trying to find me. The stack of unopened
cards, letters and bills on my kitchen table grew. I could
afford to pay the bills; I was currently on paid sick
status, although summer break was about to begin.
Somehow though, the act of sitting down at my
computer sounded like a task too taxing to bear. As for
the cards and letters, I knew they'd be filled with empty
words of sympathy that couldn't have come close to
touching the part of me that was locked in that steel
box. They, like everything else, felt pointless.

More disturbing, were a few voicemail
messages I'd received from a stranger. My number was
unpublished, so someone, some mutual contact, must
have passed it along. When I heard the messages, I'd
immediately deleted them from my phone, wanting to
forget the determined, strong voice I heard but not
succeeding at that goal. I thought of it, of her, too
much. I told Charlie about it.

I'm glad I don't answer calls, just got a voicemail from the mother of Number Three. She's reaching out for mutual support she says. As if I am capable of offering anyone support…

Why does that call bother me so much? Is it the fact she is so incredibly arrogant to think she is able to offer some magic salve or the fact she is so delusional to imagine I, myself, have that power?

Phone rang with unknown number, tensed up, was it her? Finally braved the voicemail and no, it was the police department. They want me to pick up your belongings.

Number Three's mother left another message. She said Number Four is arranging a visit to the capital to discuss gun reform and hoped all of the affected families would go.

Where is Number Two in all of this, I wonder.

She called again. Am thinking of having my number changed to avoid that woman, but am afraid that might somehow delete all of our texts.

The police call had prompted a whole new set of problems. I desperately wanted to get his belongings, but I also desperately wanted to not leave my house. If I didn't pick them up immediately, would they destroy them somehow? Grudgingly, I dialed the phone number they had left. My hoarse, neglected voice, sounded like a stranger's voice and it felt surreal to be discussing my dead child's belongings over the phone, but in the end, I was reassured they would be held until I could pick them up. I wasn't sure when that would be.

With each passing day, I felt myself withdrawing more from the world outside my walls. I'd pulled the curtains tight and turned off the porch light. That life could so casually go on for everything and everyone on the outside was far too painful to consider. I preferred to pretend it had all stopped. That at this very moment, as I lay curled under Charlie's old Star Wars blanket on the couch, with only my book to keep me company, so too had everyone else ceased to exist. Surely, they too were all holed up, dormant, in the darkness awaiting the moment I signaled, "Okay, we can all get up and go on now."

I made the mistake of turning on the local news. They were saying he attempted suicide in lockup. No one knows where he got the belt from...

Ben dropped off your unfinished work. I refused to open the door and asked him to leave it on the porch. I was afraid to bring it inside, but more scared someone might come steal it so I finally grabbed it. The little fox in the unfinished field, it will always be unfinished...

I was almost out of pills, but then I remembered the stash I'd put under the

sink after your surgery. I now have 8
Vicodin in addition to my remaining 2
Xanax. I didn't take one, I don't want to
waste it.

I made it 31 days. On the 32nd day, I accepted
that nothing would change. I knew I could get up and
leave my house and go to work, and the empty pit
inside me would persist. I could win the lottery, fall in
love, go to Paris, whatever, and nothing would change.
I would live with this feeling until the day I died, and I
would indeed die one day. Every waking moment
between this moment and that day, however many years
away it was, would be meaningless and pointless pain. I
was delaying that eventual end and, in the meantime, I
was suffering needlessly.

I burned my hand today on the stovetop.
It was on purpose, I wanted to see if I
could still feel. I did feel the sear, but I
didn't care.

When I try to picture a future, I see only
bleakness. There is no happy ending I
can imagine that would make living
through this hell worth it.

I am going to take the pills.

I poured a glass of cheap cabernet and sat down
at our kitchen table with my pills and my notepad. I
wrote a letter and explained where my accounts were,
specified my parents should have the balances, thanked
Ben for his help, and requested to be buried next to my
son. Then I rest my hands, palms down, on the smooth

wooden surface. We'd eaten so many meals on the cheap Ikea table, but I couldn't remember what any of them tasted like. How strange that I'd stressed over clipping coupons and chasing sales while somehow ensuring whatever landed in the kitchen was deemed healthy enough to feed a growing boy. Why had I bothered with any of that? The money I'd saved had gone into his 529 plan and that was irrelevant now. Whatever nutrients I'd offered him had only gotten him to age thirteen; they too were irrelevant now. It was disconcerting, it occurred to me not only was the entire future moot but so was the past.

I poured another glass and opened the bottle that housed the pills I'd saved. Lining the caplets up side by side, I studied them. They were so small and innocuous looking; tiny, white bullets. I remembered a line from a song, "just prayin' to a God that I don't believe in." and wondered if I should pray. If there was still a God watching over this world of pain and misery, he hadn't made his presence known to me in a very long time. If there was something more, though, some afterlife I couldn't really envision, then I wanted to be there with Charlie.

Finally, I said aloud, "I don't believe in you and I don't forgive you, but if you're there, then let me be with my boy. You owe me that much."

One by one, I swallowed the pills, needing to refill my glass of wine when I was halfway through with the task. When they were all gone, I went into Charlie's room and lay down on his bed, awaiting what happened next, but first, I sent Charlie one last message.

I'll be with you soon.

I almost ignored the text alert from the nightstand, I was already feeling very sleepy and the room had begun to tilt. I glanced over at the lit screen though, the glow drew me in and without thinking, I reached for it.

Mom call 911 now. It's not time yet. Please...

I blinked and tried to focus on the screen again, but it was blurry now. A whir of grey walls spun mercilessly around me as my stomach spasmed within me; whether it was a product of the pills or the text I'd just read, I wasn't sure. The alert sounded again. I couldn't read the text! My eyelids were so very heavy, I couldn't keep them open. I grappled weakly in the darkness, pressing on the phone screen and then everything faded.

17

Everything fucking hurt. My head was pounding, my throat felt raw, my chest hurt, my stomach was cramping spasmodically even as waves of nausea crested over me. My hand felt bruised and raw under the taped gauze bandage that covered the IV port entry, and my muscles from my neck to the bottom of my back were screaming in protest. I could hear the beeps and whirs of various monitoring machines, but it hurt too badly to turn and look at them. At first, I only knew the pain, but then I suddenly remembered Charlie in a panic. Where was he? And then, a moment later, the delicate thread of amnesia floated away, and I remembered what had happened to Charlie.

It was as if I'd lifted a large log from a dam where there'd been a faint trickle. There was now a rush of memory that couldn't be stalled. Charlie, dead. The burial. My parents leaving. Narek walking away. The darkness of my house. The pills. The phone. *The phone!* I struggled to sit up because I needed to see the phone, needed to see if the text had been a drug-induced mirage, a Vicodin fueled hallucination. As I struggled to sit, a small clamp on my finger fell and the machine beside me gave a warning beep and suddenly, a nurse was there.

"Ms. Sanger, it's okay, you need to stay lying down," she said kindly.

"I need my phone," I explained hoarsely. My throat was on fire. Why did it hurt so much to talk?

"If the paramedics got it, it will be with your personal belongings, and I'll check for you in a minute." She fiddled with the machine beside me for a moment and then explained, "I'm getting the doctor and he can explain what's happening now. I'll also check to see if your phone is here."

I struggled to remember how I'd ended up in this bed, but anything I could recall ended with reading that text. *Mom call 911 now. It's not time yet. Please...* I needed to see it again. I knew that it was crazy to imagine it had been real. I knew some subconscious part of myself that still willed my body to live must have manifested itself on what was actually a blank screen. Knowing that didn't make me any less desperate to confirm the truth with my own now-sober eyes.

My thoughts were interrupted as the nurse returned with a short, middle-aged man.

"Hello, I'm Doctor Patel. You're at VCU Medical Center. Do you remember coming in last night?"

I shook my head and rasped out, "I don't remember anything but falling asleep."

"This is not surprising. The hydrocodone in the Vicodin you took is an opioid, you were unconscious through most of the event. The paramedics who brought you in used Narcan to counter it, and we were able to pump your stomach and administer IV acetadote for the acetaminophen poisoning. Medics were able to recover the empty Vicodin bottle, so we knew what we were working with and that helped. Vicodin presents a dual problem, though, while the hydrocodone portion presents the immediate threat, the acetaminophen presents a more long-term concern even with the acetadote. At this time, we are still running liver panels and you'll need another blood gas test before we can move you from ICU. The good news is you are awake and alert, and that signals we got it out in time."

I felt tears well up in my eyes; what he described sounded so invasive and embarrassing. I imagined the medics into my messy house, going into Charlie's room, tearing my clothes from my body to tend to it. They probably thought I was a junkie, someone who hadn't once been a normal human being. Someone who hadn't been a mother, a teacher. And now, this doctor was privy to all my body's secrets. Then another thought occurred to me.

"How did they find me?" I asked in as steady a voice as possible.

"I understand you activated the emergency call option on your phone. You are very lucky you did. This could easily have ended another way."

Lucky. Was that really the right word? Every part of me hurt at the moment and I knew when the physical pain finally passed, I would still be left with the gaping wound that couldn't be touched. I glanced at the nurse and asked, "Did you find my phone?"

She shook her head. "Sorry, no, it must have been left behind at your home."

Home. "When can I leave?" I asked.

They glanced at each other as the doctor closed his clipboard and he stepped even closer to my bedside. "Not yet. As I said, we do need to run some more tests here. Once we confirm you are out of danger, you'll be moved to a recovery room so you can rest a bit and then we can talk about what happens next."

What happened next was a three-day visit to the hospital's psychiatric ward, where I experienced repeat lab work, counseling sessions, and a new antidepressant prescription. I'd been given access to a telephone and dutifully called my mother to let her know I was okay but would be off the grid for a short while. In the version I told her, I was just tired and needed a little self-care. I think she suspected there was more to my short stay than what I'd shared, but she didn't press. When she mentioned coming to visit me soon, I demurred as politely as possible, telling her I needed to focus on me for a while.

As I was about to depart the psychiatric floor, a nurse stopped me and said my assigned psychiatrist, Dr. Huber, wanted to speak to me briefly. I dutifully followed her into the office, willing to do anything so I could finally leave and check the phone message that had plagued me for days now. Dr. Huber, a heavyset woman who looked like she accomplished the brutal chop of her hair all on her own, without a mirror, smiled and invited me to have a seat.

"So being honest, I'm not so sure you're really ready to go home, but since you claim you don't have a desire to self-harm and it's been 72 hours, we don't really have a means to force you to stay. What I can do is try to ensure you have as many tools as possible to get through this grief and transition period."

She handed me a business card and explained the address and phone number on it were for a grief support group. Apparently, if you put multiple grieving mothers in a room, it would somehow be better than if I were to just sit in a room alone. I had no interest. I doubted it was any better for a pair of lobster to boil in a pot together than separately. Shared misery sounded like misery squared. I nodded, though, and pretended the concept interested me, then shook her hand and made my way toward the exit. Outside, I walked to the nearest trashcan and dropped the card into it before entering my waiting taxi.

I knew I hadn't completely hoodwinked her. I wasn't feeling resilient and hopeful at all when I was finally released, but it was also true that I wasn't an immediate threat to myself or anyone else. Whatever resolution I'd felt the night I sat down with that bottle of pills, had faded momentarily in my need to understand what had happened with my phone. If I delayed taking any further action for a while, it would be okay, I reasoned. I had the rest of my life to die after all.

18

My home was a museum of The Life That Wasn't Anymore. As I hesitantly entered the familiar back door we'd always favored over the front, I felt like a trespasser. If part of the old me had died with Charlie, the rest of whatever had once been Nell had departed on the night of the overdose. Ignoring the fossils of days' old dirty dishes stacked on the counter, a pair of discarded blue medical gloves I stepped over in the living room, and the unkempt child's bed I'd almost died in, my focus was singular. As I shook the linens and crouched beside the bed to peer underneath, I fought the rising anxiety. It had to be there somewhere. Finally, as I kicked through the pile of clothes on the floor, my toe met the solid, reassuring form of my phone.

Unsurprisingly, the battery was dead. I plugged it into a charger and then waited for the screen to turn on and refresh. My heart pounded, but it was as close to exhilaration as I'd felt in the previous month. Finally, the old familiar Apple icon flashed and it was ready. I tapped the message app and then, without any grand countdown, tapped on Charlie's name.

> *Mom call 911 now. It's not time yet.*
> *Please...*

I stared at it, as a symphony of cicadas buzzed in my ears. I hadn't imagined it. Sitting down on the bed, I tried to process what was happening and how to react. It would have taken a tremendous leap of faith to believe Charlie had actually sent me that message, and I was completely out of faith. That isn't to say I didn't try, though.

As I'd done so many times in my adult past, I found myself lost in a momentary childhood memory. I was seven years old and my family had taken a vacation to Disneyland. After a long day of exploring the park, we'd retreated to the orange and goldenrod hued decor of our cheap Howard Johnson's motel room. Dad had turned a baseball game on and I'd absent-mindedly started to fiddle with my loose front tooth. Suddenly, I'd felt a pop sensation and the tooth was ejected into my fingers. I'd wondered out loud how the tooth fairy would find me. Mom happily explained the tooth fairy was magic so she could find me anywhere. That night as I tried to fall asleep, I obsessed over the tiny, toilet paper wrapped piece of me that was under my pillow. The truth was I kind of didn't believe in the tooth fairy. I kind of thought if I could stay awake long enough, I'd see my mom tiptoe over and swap the tooth out for a shiny quarter. I wasn't certain, though. I wanted to believe in that kind of magic so badly. I willed myself into falling asleep quickly so I wouldn't have to know the truth.

I mostly didn't believe Charlie had sent the message. I guessed that someone had found his phone or perhaps this was some kind of hacking game. It could have been someone who knew me, who wanted to reach me and thought that using Charlie's identity would be the easiest way to do that. It was also possible this was a complete stranger. I mostly didn't believe the magic was true. Mostly.

Still, I was unable to resist doing what I did next.

Are you there Charlie?

When your heart stops beating, you have three to four minutes before your body tissues start to die. I remembered that nifty fact from my college biology class. Ten minutes? That's a lifetime. An eternity. You don't understand how long it is when you're flipping television channels or waiting on a prescription. You don't really know how long ten minutes really are until your heart stops beating, or you're waiting for a return text from your dead child's phone. After ten agonizing minutes without a response, anxiety gave way to anger.

How dare someone intrude in my life this way? How dare they use my dead child in whatever sick game they were playing? If this was a scam of some kind, I wasn't sure what they hoped to accomplish. Usually, such things involved monetary rewards. I certainly didn't have a lot of that to steal. Maybe this was an identity theft thing though, Charlie had his own social security number and it occurred to me scammers might target the identities of people who died. I realized

I really needed a second pair of eyes and an unbiased mind to bounce this off. I needed Ben.

Grabbing my phone, I headed back into the living room where I paced as Ben's phone rang again and again. Finally, on the fifth ring, he answered. He sounded both apprehensive and surprised, "Hello Nell, everything okay?"

"Yes, well no, well as okay as it can be. I need your help on something, actually," I confessed.

"Anything. What can I do for you?"

"Let's talk in person, it's hard to explain over the phone."

"Sure, do you want me to come by this afternoon?"

I thought about it, as my eyes scanned the mess I was standing in. "No, let's meet for coffee, I can head down to Mabel's if that works for you? Three o'clock?"

I made it to Mabel's before Ben, and was seated by a familiar waitress. She smiled at me and said, "Haven't seen you for a while! Welcome back!"

Here I was, a regular face, but no one knew my name or story. I relished the feeling of being an anonymous near-stranger. "Thanks, been busy. I'll just have my usual latte."

As I sat at my favorite corner table with my drink, I allowed myself to savor the normalcy of it all for just a moment. How often had I sat in this exact chair, drinking from this exact mug, as Charlie toiled safely just down the road at Ben's farm? When I heard the bells over the door jingle, I looked up to see Ben walking toward me. He had that familiar, comfortable smile on his face, but his eyes were searching mine and I recognized the concern and sadness in them. I stood and hugged him and let him stand back and examine me. I knew what I looked like, I was showering again, and I'd brushed my hair, but my face had aged unnaturally.

"Nell, I'm so glad you called," he said as he sat down.

"Me too, I've missed you. It's been difficult, but I needed some time alone."

He chuckled at that and reminded me, "I'm a man who understands the value of alone time."

Of course, he did, he purposely chose to live in a rural area, on a large, very private property. He skipped most of the "society" event invitations he received. He was even known for not being present at his own exhibition debuts. He wasn't antisocial; he took in a handful of students like Charlie and had a small circle of friends he'd visit, but at heart, Ben was most comfortable alone.

"I'm really glad you called, but you said there was something specific you needed help with?"

"Straight to the chase, as usual, I've always liked that about you. All right, I have a strange story to tell you and I need your opinion. First, though, I have to ask that you not fixate on how this came to happen. I can assure you I'm not thinking about doing anything like this in the future," I lied before continuing truthfully, "but I'm sort of overwhelmed here by something that's happened and I don't trust my own instincts on this."

He raised an eyebrow, and nodded. Taking a deep breath, I recounted what had happened the night of the overdose. He didn't interrupt but did reach across the table and take my hand when I described laying down in Charlie's bed, and my expectation I wouldn't wake again. When I finally finished the entire story, he asked simply, "The phone, can I see it?"

I opened the message and handed it over. He glanced up as he scrolled through and I felt a moment of embarrassment. Then he looked back down again before passing it back. As he thoughtfully stroked his beard, he said, "I can see why you're unsettled. Are you asking for my opinion on the authenticity of the text or do you want to hear how I'd handle it?"

"Both, I guess. I'm having trouble wrapping my mind around it all, I do know I can't just ignore it," I said.

"Well, as to the authenticity, no, I don't really think Charlie sent this. I'm sorry, Nell. I think somehow someone has gotten ahold of his phone or phone number and I doubt they intended to play a cruel trick or anything, but they saw your messages and felt genuine concern. I don't think that replying back anymore is a great idea because you're just opening yourself up to possible heartache and maybe even fraud of some kind. I'd suggest having the number disconnected."

I felt my stomach lurch at the suggestion. This tie, tenuous as it was, was really all that remained of Charlie. I could still hear his voice on his voicemail message. I could still reread all of our old texts, following the actual flow of the conversations. I could still send him messages.

"Thank you, Ben," I said a little too stiffly, "I really do appreciate you taking the time to meet me."

He shook his head gently and said, "Nell, I know you're not happy with my opinion on this. Ultimately you can do whatever you want or need to do with this; I don't know it all. I've also experienced loss first hand and I know how much a person wants to cling to some hope. I also know how desperate a person can feel when the grief is all-consuming. How a person can be pushed to the brink, where just surviving one more day sounds like too much to bear. I want you to know there's another side, though. You do eventually pass through this part of it to that other side. You're changed, but you find new things to live for. You eventually appreciate the gift of waking up in the morning again, I promise."

I felt tears threaten at his words. Part of me yearned for that thing he described, but that part warred with the part of me that knew it could never apply to me. I didn't want to hold out false hopes that would only be dashed in another Vicodin haze when it finally hit. I could not imagine a future where I was any form of normal again, and certainly not one where I was actually happy.

"I'm hearing you, truly. That's the best I can promise right now, though, that I'll keep trying to hear you," I confessed before a thought occurred. "Your son, you hadn't mentioned him before all of this. Do you want to tell me about him?"

Ben smiled, and it was striking because of how genuine the smile was. He wasn't masking pain; he was actually happy to talk about his son.

"Ben, that was his name too. I actually fought against that. I wanted him to have his own identity, but his mother insisted and any man with an ounce of intelligence knows when it's time to stop arguing with a pregnant woman."

I chuckled at that and realized with a start it was the first time I'd felt anything close to a laugh since Charlie's death. Feeling guilty about it, I forced the momentary slip back down, but Ben had noticed. He smiled again and then continued his story.

Ben Jr. was his oldest son. He'd come into the world screaming defiantly, and the defiance never really left. As a young boy, his daredevil streak was further antagonized by his naturally rebellious nature.

"If there's a bone to break, he broke it," Ben explained. "We were constantly trying to get him down out of trees, out of rough surf, away from the road's edge. It seemed like no matter what sort of natural consequences he had, he'd be back out there doing whatever the fool thing was again as soon as he healed."

Thinking about Charlie's inheritance of Narek's artistic ability, I was curious about Ben's experience with his own son. When I asked, he threw his head back and laughed.

"The boy couldn't draw a straight line. Seriously, he was a horrible artist. He had his own gifts, though; he was a talented musician. We'd gotten him into guitar lessons in the hopes he'd maybe turn to safer, indoor hobbies, but he soon graduated himself to the electric guitar and throughout high school played in a punk band. The clubs they played at were rowdy, tough places. He might have been safer outside."

Somehow, they'd managed to get him through his high school years and he eventually went off to UCLA. He scraped by his first semester with a 1.5 GPA and when Ben found out, he'd been furious. "It wasn't cheap, not even back then. But the bigger issue was I felt like he was Peter Panning it; he was the boy who refused to grow up. I couldn't understand his party lifestyle, I knew he was using drugs, he was drinking too much, I doubted he was making it to class most days and it made me so angry. We had a huge fight over the phone one night, and I told him if he didn't straighten up, the bank of Mom and Dad was officially closing. The worst thing you could ever do with Ben Jr., of course, was try to control him. His response was to use one of my own credit cards, without my knowledge, to buy a motorcycle."

Ben had understandably been furious and after another loud argument over the phone, had told his son he was on his own financially. Two weeks of silence passed when Ben and his former wife got the dreaded late-night call about his son's accident. Ben Jr. had been riding along a canyon road when the driver of an oncoming truck fell asleep at the wheel. Ben swerved to miss the oncoming vehicle and crashed over the guardrail. He'd been killed instantly.

"Oh my god, I'm so sorry, Ben. Losing a child... well, it's the worst pain imaginable," I said, fighting the tears that threatened to overflow.

He closed his eyes for a moment and nodded, and then said, "It is. And in my case, it was compounded by the guilt over how rocky our relationship had become. I would have given anything to take back that last fight. In the end, though, I learned to accept this wasn't something I could change or influence. Ben was who he was, and along with that rebellious streak, he was brave and visionary, and he lived every moment of his life to the fullest. Two weeks of silence may be two weeks we can never have back, but it was a blip on the wild, colorful radar that was Ben's life."

After a few minutes of silence, I said, "I don't know how you got there Ben, I'll admit I hope to someday view my memories of Charlie through that kind of lens, but right now, I feel pretty positive I will never be anywhere near as healed as you."

He nodded and grabbed my hand again. "I know it feels that way now, Nelly. I've had 32 years to come to terms with this, and there are still days when it's harder than others. It does get better, though, and right now, when you have your lowest moments, I want you to focus on that promise. It does get better."

Before we parted, I promised to carefully consider his advice and take his words of comfort to heart. We both understood I was lying, but he said goodbye gracefully.

19

Are you there? It's me.

I called it my beautiful lie, and I lived for it every day. Each morning when I awakened, I felt momentarily content. For about fifteen seconds of the day, every day, I lived in a world that had not changed on April 12th. For that brief period of time, everything was exactly as it should be. Not that I was consciously thinking about Charlie, not usually anyway. This was fair; when he was alive, I didn't wake up instantly thinking about him either after all. What happened was more subtle. I simply awoke feeling safe and whole. Then the cruel mistress of reality cracked her whip and everything would come back at once. The beautiful lie dissipated as the bedroom ceiling came into focus. It made me both crave and resent dawn's first light.

After I remembered again that my life was shattered, I reached for my phone to see if the text I'd sent in the middle of the night had garnered any reaction. Once again, though, it had gone unanswered, just as I had expected it might. Coward, I thought bitterly. Of course, he won't answer me anymore; he knows he did something really disgusting. Stealing a dead boy's phone or hacking into his account was an ethical line I imagined they realized now that they should never have crossed. That was when it struck me then that I could find out for certain whether anyone physically had Charlie's phone. I simply needed to pick up his belongings from the police department.

I'd avoided going to the station. Other than my time in the hospital, I'd managed until that point to avoid places where I might be identified as one of the Cooper tragedy moms and I was nervous about revealing myself to the police. I didn't want attention; I especially didn't want to see sad, sympathetic eyes that somehow made me feel obligated to lie and say I was doing okay. I just wanted my son's belongings.

As soon as I nervously checked in with the desk clerk, I realized I'd wasted a lot of worry because I'd grossly overestimated her interest in doing her job at all. I'd stood there clearing my throat to get her attention, as she'd stared down at her phone while chewing her sickly grape scented gum and was finally rewarded with a bored glance and a dry, "What do you need?"

When I explained I needed my son's personal property, she asked his name and didn't bother asking any more details. Twenty minutes later, I was walking out the door, my trembling hands holding a large clear plastic bag that held his backpack and a separate large brown bag. I tried to focus on the road as I drove home, but my eyes kept glancing to the backpack on the passenger seat. I'd been so paranoid about airbag safety, I'd only just started letting Charlie ride in that seat about six months before his death. Now his backpack sat there alone, a dog awaiting a master who would never return.

At home, I moved into the living room with the bags and took a deep breath for fortitude, then explored the contents. The heavy math and Spanish textbooks took up the bulk of space. Charlie had hated both math and Spanish, they were his least favorite classes and the fact that they just happened to fall on the same day had always felt like a cruel joke to him. He'd been a good student in general, but his last report card had reflected his dislike of these subjects. Despite earning A's in every other class, math and science had been twin Cs. We'd had one of our rare arguments over that. As a teacher, I took it personally when I learned he wasn't doing his homework or completing assignments fully. I felt like it was somehow a reflection on me as a mother, but also on me as a teacher. There'd been a slammed bedroom door, really a first hint of the adolescent pushing to emerge in him. Afterward, we'd calmed down over bowls of ice cream and a Marvel movie.

Reaching in, I next withdrew the battered-looking blue binder stuffed to the gills with handouts and notes. Opening it, I caught my breath. There it was, his infinitely neater than my own handwriting. The page I turned to was from his science class. He'd carefully drawn an example of a plant experiencing photosynthesis under a glass dome. The subject wasn't extraordinary, it was basic middle school earth science. The drawing was breath-taking, though. Detailed, with shading and exact labels, it could have been published in a textbook or naturalist guide.

As I flipped through page after page of notes, I saw that most were adorned with doodles and pictures around the edges. Sometimes they were silly, a cartoonish rat with his own tail in his mouth. At other times they were just abstract shapes, those I could picture him absent-mindedly doodling without even looking down at the paper. Still others were detailed illustrations that offered a glimpse into Charlieworld in a way words never quite could. I could picture him sitting at his desk, trying meticulously to keep up with the lesson, but unable to resist creating a small galaxy in the margins with a pencil in his slender left hand.

After I finished perusing the binder, I dug deeper into the bag and felt plastic. A smooshed Twinkie still in its wrapper, thankfully. We hadn't had twinkies in the house for months; there was no telling how old it was. A single glove, a wadded-up piece of paper that turned out to be a field trip form he'd never given me, and a small stash of pens and pencils completed the bounty. No phone. I opened the paper bag next and inside it was the black and red checkered shirt he'd been wearing *that day* over his t-shirt. I couldn't resist lifting it up to my face, inhaling the scent deeply. I flashbacked to a similar visceral reaction to his clothing when he'd been an infant. I'd carefully laundered those first outfits in Dreft; then, when they were still warm from the dryer, I'd hold the tiny garments to my face. I'd never been able to resist giving those early, tiny, wash loads a good sniff as I folded them.

The shirt was still clean, unblemished by the horrors of that day. That confused me at first, but then I realized he must have been warm and removed it at school. I could picture him hanging it crookedly over the back of his chair. On a sunny April day, this shirt hadn't been needed for warmth, its entire purpose had changed to simply bearing witness. I felt the front pocket, and it was empty. Digging back into the brown bag, I realized it, too, was empty.

Someone else had the phone. The thought made me feel uneasy. I pictured some grey, shadowy figure pouring through my child's personal photographs and text messages, learning his most intimate secrets. How had he even accessed it? I'd ensured it was all password protected. I knew hackers could accomplish some scary things, though, and clearly, there had been some method that worked. The more I thought about the invasion of privacy, the angrier I got. I needed answers, and only one person could give me any. I picked up my own phone and opened the text chain again.

Who is this and how do you have Charlie's phone?

FYI I am going to the police.

Do you know how fucking cruel this is?

My child DIED. You stole a dead child's phone.

Why are you such a coward? Answer me!

I'm sorry, I'm upset. Please talk to me, it's important.

A moment passed, and then I felt the phone vibrate in my hand. I stared down at it.

I'm sorry.

I'd known someone was in possession of the phone, but even as I'd lashed out my demands, I hadn't actually expected a response. Now that I had one, I suddenly felt unsure of what to do next. Did I continue to encourage this bizarre back and forth or did I just do the sensible thing and report the phone stolen? It felt like nothing good could come of further communications, yet I was drawn into the fantasy of a conversation with the shadow person on the other end.

> Why are you doing this? I want his phone back.

> *I just want to say u should stop being sad.*

Someone had my child's phone, a phone they must have stolen from the scene of his death, and now they were taunting me and pretending to care about my emotional state. The entire situation left me feeling a fury that, on the one hand, felt a little excessive but, on the other hand, was a vast improvement over just feeling crushing sorrow. I felt driven to solve this mystery. I had no idea who they were, where they were... and that's when I realized I actually might know where they are.

I flipped quickly to my "find friends" app and waited for the map and updates to load. Finally, the familiar blue dot that had once represented my child's location in this world revealed the phone's location. Cooper Middle School. It was almost 8 pm on a summer break day and the school should be locked up tight. How could anyone be messaging me from it? I wondered if perhaps there was a night janitor, maybe he had been cleaning and had come across the phone. Maybe he hadn't even intended to steal it, he just thought he'd lucked out, and now he just hoped I'd go away. Well, that was not happening.

For the third time that day, I got into my car. For over a month, I'd been unable to leave my house at all, but my anger motivated me to break free of the safe bubble. When I reached the school, I drove down the familiar drop-off byway, trying not to remember the last time I'd traveled that path. I spied no cars in the adjacent visitor's lot and headed toward the back. It was empty. I didn't trust the emptiness, maybe he lived nearby and walked there or maybe his wife dropped him off. The sun had set, and twilight was rapidly disappearing as I marched toward the back service door. I thought I heard something behind me and whirled around, but it was only a feral cat.

When I reached the door, I pushed and pulled on the knob. It was locked, and when I peered into the glass window, I could see no evidence of movement inside. Not satisfied, I worked my way around the building, peering into each set of windows I passed, trying each door handle along the way. When I reached the last one, I conceded no one was there; they'd either been spooked off by me or had left before I'd arrived. Defeated, I walked back to my car when I heard the short siren blast. Blue lights flashed, and I heard, "Richmond police department, stop and put your hands up."

It felt like a surreal dream, but I complied with the request and turned to face the officers. The female shined her flashlight on my face, and I winced, closing my eyes. "What are you doing on school property?" she asked sternly.

"Someone stole my son's phone. I traced it back here and was trying to catch them," I explained, but I could see by the looks on their faces they didn't believe me.

"Is your son a student here?" the male officer asked.

"He was a student but isn't anymore," I explained, "Someone else has it, and they were here tonight."

"Ma'am, you can put your hands down now, just keep them at your side. Do you have ID on you?"

I nodded and explained it was in my purse, then retrieved it for them. The female officer went back to the cruiser with it, while I sat waiting on the curb. I looked up at the male officer and commented, "I have the find friends app on my phone, I can show you the location if you want, although obviously, he's not here anymore."

He shook his head. "Let's wait for Officer Baker to come back and then discuss it."

When she finally returned, I knew. The bright light of the streetlight shone fully on her and she wore the same expression I'd seen on hundreds of other faces at the services after the shooting. It was a look that combined pity, horror, nervousness and a tinge of survivor guilt. I knew that she knew.

"Lieutenant Morris, can you please come here for a second? Ms. Sanger, we'll be right with you, I promise we'll get you out of here soon," she said, gesturing to the male officer. I saw his look of surprise at the soft tone of voice she was suddenly employing and he looked at me again curiously before following her.

When they returned, the female officer said, "Ms. Sanger, is there someone we can call for you?"

I stared incredulously. "No. What you can do is find the person who stole my son's phone. Here, I'll show you the GPS!"

I ignored the uncomfortable look they shared as I scrolled to the find friend app and pulled it up again. "Here. Look! They're still inside the school."

The male officer took my phone and looked, then said, "Ma'am, perhaps the school office has it stored for safekeeping. I'd suggest you call them tomorrow and ask. In the meantime, you can't stay here on school grounds."

"You're not listening; someone has it. They were texting me earlier tonight. I'm not crazy, if that's what you think. It's not like I want to be here either."

"I understand, but there's nothing we can do tonight here. Call the school tomorrow, if you don't feel satisfied by what you learn then here's my card, you can call me personally. I'm the sector chief, I'm not usually out on patrol, but we do annual appraisals. I can promise you I'm in a position to ensure this is followed up on if you need it. You need to go home now, though. Are you okay to drive?"

His voice wasn't unkind, but I heard the firm "no" in it. I pulled the card from his hand, perhaps a little too violently, but he didn't react. I reminded myself I'd only been released from the hospital's psych ward the previous morning. I needed to chill in front of these officers or I might end up back there quickly. Biting back my frustration, I said, "Thank you. I know this all sounds crazy. I'm fine and am headed home now."

I returned home, slamming my front door behind me. Tingling with angry adrenaline, I looked at the scene around me. Shit was everywhere. It was barely inhabitable. I bent down and picked up clothes and trash. Charlie's backpack went into his room, with that old familiar drop I'd employed a hundred times before when he'd left it in the middle of the living room floor. I spent almost an hour washing dishes, scrubbing counters, and mopping the kitchen floor. Finally, exhausted, I walked down my now-clear hallway and paused at Charlie's door, then turned and walked into my own bedroom. As I lay in my own bed, plotting my next move with the phone situation, sleep came quickly.

20

We need to talk.

I started my morning with a text, and then moved on to making actual calls. These were difficult calls I'd put off long enough. My mother was obviously relieved to hear from me, and even more relieved when I mentioned I'd gotten out of the house and had coffee with Ben the day before. I felt some guilt at that I, of all people, understood how badly a mother wants to see her child thrive. Mom not only had to grieve the loss of her grandson but also feared for the future of her daughter. I wanted to give her reassurances I was healing, I was okay, I would come out of this stronger in the end, but those lies were too heavy for my tongue to bear.

I avoided mentioning the mystery of Charlie's phone. I was certain she wouldn't approve of my efforts; she'd tell me to let it go and move forward after canceling his line. I redirected the conversation away from me quickly and for the first time since he died, it occurred to me to ask her how she was doing. She, too, was struggling, she revealed. They all were. She had her faith, though, and her church family was giving her a lot of support. For her, her faith offered comfort, shoulders to lean on and a promise of eventual reunion with Charlie. My father, she confided, had a much harder time handling this loss. He was angry at God and felt abandoned. He didn't understand how God could have let this happen.

Religion had always been a sticky wicket between us; my parents were regular churchgoers, pillars within their church really and I was of the less convinced tribe. I had some vague, shadowy idea of who or what God was, but most days I was pretty sure I didn't actually believe in him. Usually, when religion came up in discussion, I quickly steered us toward some safer topic. This time though, I listened. I could hear the pain in her voice, as she described my father's conflict. Despite her concern for him, she was optimistic he would find peace with God sooner rather than later. I found myself wishing I could experience that kind of peace too; I knew that such a wish was folly. This was my own personal onus, one that could not simply be shed.

"All right, Mom, I have to go now," I said, after our conversation drifted into more casual territory.

"Oh… I hate to be pushy but are you sure it wouldn't be a good idea to come home for a while? I think it might be nice for all of us."

Not that Michigan didn't sound appealing. Maybe leaving Richmond was exactly what I needed. I'd always loved Michigan in the summer, I had many happy memories on that lake from both before Charlie came into our lives and after he finally existed. I couldn't wrap my mind around leaving him, though, the trace of him anyway, that still existed somewhere here in Richmond.

I rejected her idea in as soft a way possible and then promised to call again soon. Taking a deep breath, I moved right into my next call. My sister Sarah had borne the brunt of my immediate pain during the darkest weeks and I felt nervous dialing her number. She answered on the first ring, "Nell?"

"Hey, sis."

"Oh my god, how are you doing, are you okay?" she asked in a rush.

I assured her I was, as okay as someone in my position could be anyway. We chatted a little about my parents, and she reassured me they were managing as well as possible. Finally, I said, "Look, I still feel bad for the way I treated you. It's been on my mind."

"I wish it wasn't. Just let that shit go, girlfriend. I certainly have. I understood then and I understand now," she reassured me.

"So, how are you doing?" I asked her.

I meant how was she handling the loss of her nephew, but she lowered her voice and replied, "Not so bad actually, you're not going to believe this, but I met a guy on tinder of all places and I seriously think he may be the one."

I closed my eyes and reminded myself that I, too, had once been young. I thought about meeting Narek in those days. I'd been so self-confident back then, so aware of my own feminine power and so utterly unaware of what everyone around me was actually dealing with. I remembered a few months after we'd met, a waitress I worked with lost her husband to a sudden heart attack. We'd taken a collection up at work, and I'd dutifully donated because I knew everyone else expected me to. I felt sorry for the woman, someone I didn't know very well but spoke to regularly, yet I'd resented handing over that measly $20. It had taken the birth of Charlie to disrupt the trajectory of the earth's orbit in my head.

I finally interrupted her story and explained I hated to go, but I had an appointment I couldn't miss. She sounded so relieved and happy to hear from me, I forgave her silently for not being perfect. We reassured each other we would talk again and then said goodbye.

My next call was more intimidating. With trembling hands, I pulled up the familiar contact and hit the call button for Charlie's phone. I didn't actually expect the thief to answer, but some tiny part of me held out hope they'd surprise me. After five rings, it went to voicemail, and I once again heard my boy's voice. "Hey, it's Charlie, you can leave a message but remember no post on Sundays."

After hanging up, I began to text again.

You can answer me. Are you there?

I'm not just going to give up. You owe me an explanation.

I want his phone back, if you come forward now, I won't press charges.

Hello????

Do you even care how much this is tormenting me?

Finally, an ellipsis signaled across the screen... he was typing again. I held my breath as I awaited whatever might come next.

Im not trying 2 but I wish U'd stop texting. I don't know what 2 say.

Tell me your name.

I cant...

Are you a student from Cooper?

I don't like 2 talk about myself. U should talk to real people tho, not me.

I was around real people yesterday. Where are you right now?

I'm laying on a roof, looking at the clouds.

What roof? Are you at Cooper?

No.

Where?

Heaven. Thats what I pretend up here anyway

If I could just keep him talking, eventually he'd drop enough clues I'd be able to track him down. I was now convinced this had to be a kid, and kids might think they're smarter than their teacher, but that was pure fantasy. I needed to push for more details.

What's heaven like?

Real heaven? Beautiful. There r angels and flowers everywhere.

No one yells and fights and u don't have to hide from anything bad. In heaven you dont have to ask for protection because they dont let any bad people in.

Like, what kind of bad things would you have to hide from here in the real world?

All the dark stuff...

Such as the shooting?

I guess, and all the other ways people hurt u.

I felt a chill. I'd grown convinced the thief was definitely a student, one who had been in the science room when the shooting happened. This exchange was taking an odd turn though, I reread the exchange and kept focusing on *Yeah and all the other ways people hurt u."*

I'm not going to pretend you're Charlie, but I'd like to call you something. What name do you want me to use?

IDK i guess u can just call me C.

Is the C for Charlie or is it for your real name?

IDK, I just want u to use it

C I'm not mad, I was at first but I promise I'm not now. I need to know something, has someone hurt you?

No I have to go now.

C you can tell me the truth.

U don't really care.

Yes, I do. I'm a teacher. If someone is hurting you it can stop.

No one really cares. No one even sees me.

But someday I will make it stop myself.

How?

I have a gun 2

Do you really? Okay this has gone too far, tell me your name.

C… are you there?

I began to pace, trying to decide what to do next, when I remembered the police officer from the night before. Digging into my purse, I found his card. Lieutenant Dan Morris. I'd gotten the distinct impression he thought I was half off my rocker when we'd met, and I wasn't feeling very optimistic as I dialed his number.

"Lieutenant Morris, can I help you?"

"Yes, well, hello. This is Nell Sanger, we uh, met last night at Cooper Middle."

There was a pause and then in a cautious tone, he replied, "Yes, hello Ms. Sanger. Were you able to reach anyone at the school?"

"Not exactly, to be honest, I haven't tried yet. But there's been a situation I think you should be aware of. I'm not quite sure how to handle it," I explained.

"Situation? Ma'am, like we told you last night, your best bet is to reach someone—"

I cut him off. "I know what you told me, things have changed, and I need your help. The police still help people, correct?"

He sighed, then said, "All right, tell me what's happened."

"It's easier to show you, can I come down to the station and meet you?" I asked

"All right, I won't be in until after 1:00, though. When you come in, let the guy at the desk know you're there to see me and I'm expecting you."

I heard the doubt in his voice, but I knew that if I could just show him the texts, he would better understand. I wasn't thrilled about going back into that station, but that teacher part of my brain indelibly interwoven with that mother part, recognized the faint buzz of alarm that my mystery texter had sounded.

21

There is the sanity you feel, and there is the sanity you display. Most people don't really care about the first one; they just wanted permission to avoid your crisis. For the first time in months, I sat at my vanity and opened my make-up bag. The woman who stared back at me wasn't exactly a stranger, she was someone I spied from a moving bus window who I thought I might recognize but couldn't quite place. My cheekbones were more pronounced, the hollows beneath them were new. Dark circles hung from my heavily lidded eyes. Where before, a few grey strands had appeared, now wiry silver tendrils had completely overtaken the new growth at my temples. I needed work.

My face eagerly drank the moisturizer it had been deprived of for too long, then with the dab of a foundation laced sponge, the light brush of blusher, a few strokes of mascara and a smudge of neutral lipstick, I watched my face emerge from the ghost in the mirror. I needed a haircut I noted dispassionately, but it was easy enough to pull the mane back into a simple, elegant clip, trying to ignore the shock of grey. Finally, I slipped into my normal parent-teacher conference uniform, dress pants and a casual blouse. There, totally sane looking.

At the station, I was led to a private room where Lieutenant Morris soon joined me. Sometimes large men were intimidating, simply by nature of their stature and girth. Lt. Morris wasn't one of those men. He was about six feet tall and looked like a man who worked out regularly yet still had an extra ten stubborn pounds around his waist. His face made him seem approachable. I guessed him to be in his mid-40s, but there was something boyish about the soft curves of his cheeks and jawline. His blue eyes were kind and intelligent. He wasn't exactly handsome; he was the sort of man who would easily blend into a crowd. I wouldn't have really noticed him at a bar, nor would I have crossed the street to avoid him in the city.

"Good afternoon, Ms. Sanger. What can I do for you?" he asked in a steadying voice.

"Hello. Well, I have a situation…" I broke down what had happened, starting with the first message from "Charlie" after his death. I felt awkward opening myself up to this stranger about my darkest moment, but I knew he'd want to see the message chain and there was no point in trying to avoid that uncomfortable subject. After I explained my own desperate attempts to reach out and the initial response, I looked up to gauge his reaction. He was nodding and listening intently. If he felt any judgment, it didn't show on his face.

I opened my message app and scrolled down to show him the latest messages. He took it from me and read it thoughtfully, but I couldn't guess what he was thinking. Finally, he looked up and asked, "and the GPS location is always the school?"

I nodded. "Yes, I was just assuming that meant this kid was only texting from school grounds, even after hours, but it occurred to me last night that there could be another factor, so I googled and discovered phones can have fake locations listed, spoofing, and apparently this is well-known stuff in kid circles because they don't want their parents tracking them. Now I think maybe that's what's been done here. Its location is just always set to Cooper."

"It's definitely a possibility," he said. "We do deal with stolen phones pretty often, and this is one of the tricks they sometimes undertake. Usually not children this young though, I'm not saying they aren't capable, it's just not been the norm in my experience."

He rested his chin on his hand and studied the messages again. "Have you reached out to your service provider?"

"No, not yet. To be honest, I feel like this all came to a head yesterday, and I went from being curious and irritated, to feeling like this might be something really serious."

"Okay, I don't want to keep you here too long, but would you mind waiting while I confer with someone else about this?"

I nodded and then waited for his return. When he finally reentered the room twenty minutes later, he was accompanied by a younger man in civilian clothes who shook my hand and introduced himself as a detective. Morris had explained the situation to him and he wanted to see the messages himself. Unlike Morris; he seemed impatient. When he began at the top, he paused and glanced at me and I had the distinct impression he was a little put out by the crazy lady taking up his valuable time. Still, he went back to reading, and then by the end, he had a different expression. Concern.

"I'm going to need your phone. We need a record of the messages and we may need to reach out to the child." He turned to Morris and said, "School being out for summer both helps and hurts here, we don't have to worry about lockdowns or other students being at risk, but it would be a lot easier to ask questions and get answers if we had every kid in one place."

I interrupted. "Wait, no! I need my phone." I felt a growing sense of panic; there were hundreds of photos on there of Charlie, hundreds of texts, emails, voicemails, snapchats. Stupidly, I hadn't backed it up in years. I'd never paid to upgrade our Cloud space; whatever was on that phone would be lost forever if it was taken from me.

The detective began, "Ms. Sanger, we need—" but was cut off by Morris.

"Jim, I have an idea. Let's get copies of the messages, and it seems to me the best way to reach out again is to let Ms. Sanger do it. She is well trained to communicate with children, this is her area of expertise, and her voice is authentic. Sticking someone on there to pretend to be her could backfire."

My eyes widened at his defense and then relief flooded me when the detective grudgingly agreed. It was decided I would contact the child only when in the presence of Morris or one of the other authorities, and if the child reached out to me first, then I would contact them immediately. My role would begin right there, in the interview room.

Under Detective Fish's direction, I sent my first text.

Hello C....

Are you there?

Three minutes passed and then the telltale ellipses showed on my screen.

Yeah

Good, what are you doing?

Just sitting in my room. He's coming home again.

Your father?

C....

Its okay, I don't know who you are so you can tell me the truth.

Dill was my friend.

I went cold. For a moment, I forgot to breathe. I stared at the screen and felt a hand on my shoulder. I looked up to see Morris standing beside me. He nodded and asked softly, "Do you need a break?"

I'd tried not to ever think of his name, his face, his life. It was more than not wanting to give him the power of living in my head, I'd worked hard to accept

Charlie's death was real, but I hadn't been able to accept the violent nature of it. Better to imagine he'd been in a car accident or had cancer or suffered an anaphylactic reaction than to accept someone had deliberately taken his life. I'd heard the name before, as much as I tried to avoid the news, I sometimes came across it accidentally. But whenever that happened, I quickly pushed it away, rejected it in whole, lest it crawl into my brain and burrow into a spot where it would hang tight and never let go.

Shaking my head at Morris, I typed again. As I did so, Detective Fish announced that he had to make a quick call and exited the room. I understood. Friends with Dill. A breadcrumb had been tossed, and he wanted to follow up on it.

Oh? Do you know him well?

Just a little. I didn't know he would do that. But he was nice 2 me and not many kids are.

Do they bully you?

Maybe sometimes but mostly ignore. Dill would sometimes talk 2 me. They didn't just ignore him u know, they called him names all the time.

Thy used to call him pickle cuz of his name but this year they were mostly calling him loser and fag.

But he was nice to you?

Yeah. He said hi sometimes and once he gave me half his sandwich. I don't always have lunch and he felt sorry for me I think.

Charlie… was he ever nice to you?

…

Does that mean no?

I mean he was ok. He smiled at me a few times but he didnt really talk to me tbh. He wasn't mean to Dill either, I dont think.

The really mean boys wasn't even in that class cuz I know what science class they were in.

Why do you think he did it in there then?

I don't know. Maybe he didn't mean to but he just broke b4 the bell rang. People can only take so much b4 they break.

Were you scared?

Yeah. Everyone in school was.

Now I think it was stupid to be afraid. If I died the angels would take me to heaven, and no one would ever hurt me again.

What about your dad? You seem afraid of him.

Have 2 go.

No wait, C you said you had a gun?

C?

I looked up at Morris and he nodded. "That's okay, you did great. We're going to be working with your provider to trace this if possible, and we're contacting the school to get more information on the students who were present that day. This'll be resolved soon. I'm sure."

"All right, so I guess I'll just wait for you to call and if he sends any more texts, I'll get in touch sooner," I said.

"Yep, and Ms. Sanger, thank you for coming to us. I know this has to be very difficult for you."

Difficult. It was such a sanitized, proper word for what I was feeling. Calmly discussing Dill Hobert, the boy who had taken my son's life, was like pinching the flame of a candle and refusing to flinch in public. I'd had entirely enough of other people observing me, worrying about me, making assumptions about me, though, so the facade of calm would remain firmly in place.

"Thanks, I'm fine. I'll be in touch," I said, perhaps a little too curtly, before I saw myself out of the building.

22

Sanitized, cleaned, my house was a mausoleum and the ghost it housed was me. Outside was real life; open the door and enter the place of memories. This was the place I'd turned to as a refuge when life stopped on April 12th, 2019. I'd spent that first month so heavily medicated, or if I wanted to be honest with myself, drugged, this home had felt like the entire world. The only surroundings I'd even known during that time had been in the cave of masochism that was once Charlie's room. Now, with the opioid haze lifted, I viewed it all through more realistic eyes. For as long as I remained under this roof, I would never be able to truly move forward.

I made my way to Charlie's room and gave it a frank visual inventory. It was messier now than it had been when he lived in it. My dirty clothes on the floor, glasses and various bits of trash cluttering the nightstands and desk. What was striking was how empty it felt despite that clutter. Whatever life force that was left of Charlie, and surely it existed somewhere, it wasn't in this room.

My quiet moment was interrupted by the chime of my phone. Unthinkingly, I removed it from my pocket and answered.

"Hi, is this Nell Sanger?" a woman cautiously asked.

Shit. I knew better than to just answer the phone, I'd let my current mission distract me. Assuming this was a telemarketer, or worse, a reporter, I replied "Yes" in a tone that made it clear I wasn't buying or selling.

"Hello, this is Ronda Jenkins," she replied. There was a pause, and I realized she must have assumed I knew who she was. She had to be a reporter.

"Okay, and?" I said as coldly as possible.

"My son is DeShaun Jenkins," she said simply, and then it clicked. Number Three. I cursed silently for having answered the call. I still wasn't ready for this.

"I'm sorry, yes, of course. I got your voicemails… I just haven't had a chance to respond."

"I understand," she said, in a tone that sounded suspiciously like she really didn't. "As I mentioned before, I've been working with Calvin and Sherry Framingham as well as the parents of the injured children. We've already met with our district and state representatives, but we feel like our voices would be more powerful if you and Charlie's father joined us. We're still trying to reach the Carters as well. It's a lot to explain, it would be easier if we could meet in person."

"I.... I'm not sure," I confessed. The thought of uniting in grief with a bunch of strangers sounded horrible. I preferred to handle things privately, although I had to admit that hadn't worked out so well for me. The other issue was the fact I had no idea exactly what kind of reforms they were pushing. I had followed none of their efforts in the news, and while on an intellectual level, I could appreciate the value of directing anger toward a cause, my overwhelming emotion wasn't anger. I was sad. The whole gun issue was a quagmire I tended not to think too much about even before this happened. Of course, we needed fewer guns on the streets, but realistically it was too late. Too many of the "bad guys" already had guns, so wasn't it only logical that the "good guys" would want them too?

"Ms. Sanger, can I call you Nell?" At my affirmation, she continued. "Nell, just come meet us and hear us out. If you're not interested after that, we will understand, but at least come listen."

Against my better judgment, I heard myself saying, "Okay, when and where?" as I wrote down an address. She wanted to meet up tomorrow and that meant it would be three days in a row I had to pull myself together. I felt exhausted at the prospect.

After the call, I sat down and considered the day's events. Between the text conversation and the intrusion of Ronda Jenkins, I felt like I was being forced to think about that day, the day I tried to never deliberately think about. Given the details the texting child had shared, and the fact I would be walking into a discussion about those events tomorrow, I felt dread at what I knew needed to be done. I needed to do a little research; I needed to know more about that morning, and the boy who had shattered my world.

His name was Dill Hobert. He was a tall, skinny boy with a shock of red hair and vacant blue eyes. He wasn't a boy I'd seen before, and with that red hair, if he'd passed through my school, I would have recognized him. He must have fed into Cooper from one of the other elementary schools, or perhaps was a recent transfer into the district. I studied his picture, searching for some hint of the malady that had poisoned him. He didn't look like a monster, but there was something troubling about him. I was clearly a biased witness, but I didn't think I was imagining it. He stared straight ahead in the released police photo. He didn't seem to be hiding from the camera; he displayed no shame or fear, his face seemed to hold no expression at all.

I poured through articles, learning he'd always been labeled a troubled kid. He had been diagnosed with learning disabilities; former teachers had commented he'd been a challenging student. I remembered the texting child's comments; Dill had been a target for bullies and after reading about his learning and behavioral challenges, I wasn't surprised. As a teacher, I tried to protect the vulnerable ones, but my protective wings could only spread so wide. Some children could be very cruel to those who were different.

The gun had been his father's. His parents were divorced, and he apparently spent time between both households. His father's criminal record included several domestic abuse charges later dropped, multiple DUI arrests, and a misdemeanor assault conviction. His mother was a stage 4 breast cancer patient, with a terminal prognosis. Not a lot was known about her, other than the fact she'd apparently been married to an abusive man and that as some speculated, she likely wouldn't live to see the conclusion of Dill's trial.

On the morning of April 12, 2019, Dill Hobert had packed the 9 mm handgun he'd picked up off of the kitchen table the night before into his backpack and carried it into Cooper Middle School. The gun was loaded with a magazine carrying 15 bullets. At school, he would go to his first-period class and about ten minutes into class, as students were standing to find their lab partners, he would remove the gun and turn to the boy nearest him. That boy's back was turned, Dill would aim at the black curls on the back of the boy's head and without saying anything, fire the gun.

Charlie, of course, died immediately. Dill would immediately aim again and hit 12-year-old Misty Framingham in her torso. She would die before paramedics could load her into the ambulance. He would fire next at 13-year-old Sam Keller, hitting him in the shoulder. Sam would survive. He'd fire one shot into the wall behind Sam, and the next 2 shots would hit DeShaun Jenkins, killing him, as he hovered over his twin sister Aliya. She was miraculously spared any injury. Number Four, Jessica Carter was struck in the head but initially survived. She would die later at the hospital. As Mr. Goldsby rushed into the room to tackle him, the gun would go off one final time and would graze Louisa Gonzales's thigh, leaving her with a very minor injury and permanent scar. He fired eight shots, and seven of them hit human flesh. Four of his six victims were fatally injured. Dill Hobert, for all of his shortcomings, was an amazing shot.

I had grown up with guns. Every kid I knew back in Michigan learned how to shoot a gun before they learned how to drive a car. Like Dill Hobert, I spent many days with my father firing at targets. His had been sheets of paper with human form on them, at an indoor shooting range. Mine had been tin cans and water filled milk jugs on saw horses, set up across the field on the back end of our property. Our family used guns to hunt, our freezer was always full of wild game. We also kept them for protection, people often think of the city as being where you need extra protection, but when you live in a semi-rural area, you're vulnerable in a different way. Home robberies were not unheard of, and the police aren't just a whistle away. No, guns had never scared me. People sometimes did.

Dill hadn't spoken publicly since the shooting. His attorney, a frazzled looking middle-aged man with wiry white hair and a permanent frown in every photograph and video clip, just repeated often that his client "will eventually tell his story."

I had my doubts about that, I'd seen kids like Dill before, kids with dazed lifeless eyes and mild cognitive challenges and they were not the tell your story kind of kids. Whatever secrets were locked up inside Dill's head, would probably remain there. He was, in essence, a walking corpse. He'd never be fixed, because he hadn't been whole before the shooting. He'd likely never leave prison. He'd stay locked up inside that head, with the monsters that inhabited it, and eventually fade away from public remembrance entirely.

I was curious about his mother, but found little information to fill the gaps. There were a few photos, one was from Dill's early childhood. She was standing behind him on a porch, staring straight ahead. She was fuller then, but not by much, her long thin arms dangled at her side with a three or four-year-old Dill mimicking her pose directly in front of her. Neither of them were smiling. Even then, in her presumably healthier days, they looked sickly. In a recent photo, she stood outside the police station, tall and skeletal, wearing a scarf and a dazed look. She, too, had made no statements, but what was there for her to say?

The only photo released of the father was a police mugshot from an old arrest. He was the source of Dill's red hair, but he didn't share his son's thin build or his vacant eyes. The senior Mr. Hobert's eyes burned with anger and hatred toward the unseen cameraman. He was the image of a man I'd have avoided sitting next to on a crowded bus. Unsettled by his picture, I slammed my laptop shut and stepped away from my table.

Between my uneasy stomach following my research on Dill, and my anxiety over what was happening with C, I couldn't rest. I felt the heavy burden of impotency fill me as each minute ticked by. Pacing, I clung to my phone as if it were a talisman and willed it to do something. As it remained inanimate, I was reminded yet again that the universe didn't particularly care what demands I made of it.

I needed to distract myself from the anxiety threatening to seize control of me, and for the first time since Charlie's death I dug into the hall closet that housed my treasure trove of photo albums. Randomly, I chose a fat, unlabeled, green album from the middle of the pile and brought it back to the living room.

The cover stuck lightly to the first page, and there was a distinct stale smell that promised this wasn't one of my recent albums. Good, my recent life hadn't worked out so well. I smiled when I saw the first page of snapshots. Tucson 1995. It was an out-of-place vacation for us. We took a trip each summer, but typically they were much closer to home. We stuck to places like the Wisconsin Dells, Cleveland, Chicago. I'd flown just twice as a child, once to Disneyland and once to Tucson. I learned later that Tucson wasn't a random destination, my father had actually scored a free plane ticket and a free hotel room as local union rep to a national convention. At the time, though, the trip had seemed so exotic, so different, I imagined it to be my parent's dream vacation.

In the first photo, six-year-old Sarah smiled wildly, her nose scrunched up, her eyes squinting, as a ten-year-old me pointed at a saguaro cactus next to her that was easily three times her size. It really hadn't been that long ago, all things considered, yet the two innocent girls who had their entire lives before them were strangers. As I thumbed through the pages, I was struck by how happy we all seemed. Mom in her sundress, her hair still a deep, dark, auburn, holding up a dreamcatcher she'd purchased. Dad, in the hotel swimming pool, waving with his sunglasses on. A candid shot of me in a botanical garden at night, staring intently at a rare cactus flower that only bloomed at night.

I'd been lucky, I knew it. I'd grown up in a home where there was laughter and love. I yearned to feel as safe and confident as the young girl in the photos again. How had these years of promise ended so badly? I'd had everything a child needs to develop into adulthood unscathed and unscarred. Even that hadn't been enough to protect me from the pain always watching and waiting. Dill's photos were of a family that knew only anger, pain, suffering and I didn't envy that, but I realized perhaps had I suffered just a little back then, it would be more bearable now. Maybe I'd been too blessed.

23

Ronda Jenkins was a force of nature, a microburst that carved a path in the solid terrain of the status quo. I'd approached the huge, brick, colonial home and knocked softly on the bright red door only to have it swing open with force. Although of similar, average height as myself, the four-inch-tall heels she wore gave her a towering impression. She wore a royal blue dress that looked both chic and expensive. Her hair was short and expertly styled, her face was made up with precise eyeliner, mascara and a deep ruby lipstick. She commanded attention. I instantly felt shabby in my faded blue jeans and Old Navy t-shirt and fought the urge to reach back and pull the ponytail out of my hair. With barely a word, she'd grabbed my arm and swooped me up in the house announcing loudly, "She's here!"

We walked quickly through the entryway, down a long hallway. More accurately, Ronda clipped along at a rapid pace in her heels while I tried not to run to keep up. I barely had time to take in the details, but the large bowl of fresh flowers, the oil paintings lining the walls, the marble-topped table displaying a white sculpture, made it clear Ronda and I were in completely different socioeconomic classes. I'd felt awkward enough about this meetup before arriving. By the time we stepped into her kitchen, my anxiety was almost out of control.

The kitchen was a chef's dream kitchen. I felt as if I was walking into a showroom bathed in a heavenly sunray as I walked toward the huge marble-topped island that four other people already sat around. I eyed them nervously and realized with some relief they looked decidedly normal, almost as schleppy as me.

"Welcome, Nell, that's Calvin and Sherry Framingham, Lulu Deters, and that's my husband, Jeremiah."

They all waved. Sometimes when people were married a long time, I'd noticed they looked more like siblings than spouses. The Framinghams had that look, with matching grey-streaked light brown hair and gold wire-framed glasses. Both had deep bags under their eyes and I sensed that they, like me, had slept little in the previous six weeks. Lulu was a large, casual looking woman who wore her long black hair in a braid down her back. I didn't recognize her name and wasn't quite sure who she actually was. My face must have given my confusion away because she explained her son Sam was one of the injured students who had recovered. Mr. Jenkins stood to shake my hand and I could only gawk at his height. I guessed he was almost seven feet tall, and I suddenly understood Ronda Jenkin's apparent affinity for high-heeled shoes.

Jeremiah Jenkins, the name sounded familiar. I coaxed the memory forward, and then I knew who he was.

"You're the basketball player," I said.

He nodded. "I was, although these days I'm the marketing man. You're a basketball fan?"

I shook my head. "No, it's just that Charlie mentioned you just before that day..." It felt strange to say his name out loud to these strangers and I immediately regretted it.

As if sensing my discomfort, Ronda said, "Have a seat, Nell, what would you like to drink? Coffee? Iced tea? A glass of chardonnay? We don't judge."

Eyeing the wineglass in front of Lulu Deters, I pointed and said, "I'll have one of those." This day would need a little liquid ambition.

I sipped on my wine slowly as Ronda filled me in on what the group had planned and achieved so far. They had initially met to discuss school security measures and gun reform, but in truth, things had morphed into something else. They were pushing for a short list of specific gun reform items, focusing mostly on accused domestic abusers. The current state laws, they explained, prohibited anyone under a domestic abuse-related protective order from owning a gun. What it didn't do was prevent anyone with a previous conviction (or future one) from owning a weapon if they were not under an active restraining or protective order. It didn't stop anyone who was under any other type of protective order from owning a gun. There also wasn't a strict impetus in place for officers to remove weapons from a household where they were responding to a domestic abuse accusation. With Dill Hobert, such a law might have kept his father's guns out of the house.

I listened intently, still grappling with the question of inevitability. "So, here's my question, if Dill was bent on doing this thing, and his father didn't have a gun, could he have gotten it someplace else anyway?"

"Possibly," Ronda conceded, but then clarified, "But we're talking about a thirteen-year-old kid here. We know that his brain was still developing; every year, he's developing more, his frontal lobe is going to be fully developed around the time he's 25. For every day that his exposure to a gun is delayed, the better the chance is he doesn't do this thing."

For the first time, I saw the dignified strength in her show a crack, as her chin trembled a bit and her voice became slightly shaky. "If this boy doesn't find a gun at home, he has to go look for one and that's not that easy at thirteen. This boy isn't running with a gang, he doesn't even have friends, it seems, like most of these school shooters, he gets his gun at home. It's almost always the parent who introduces them to it."

Everything she said made sense, but something else had occurred to me. Feeling timid, I finally said what was on my mind. "The boy, it's true he didn't have friends. I hear he was, in fact, bullied. I appreciate your efforts and everything you just said makes sense. I think, though, it's falling short."

Lulu Deters laughed suddenly, and I glanced at her. "Sorry! I just love when someone tells Miss Ronda she's wrong about something."

Ronda gave her a pointed look and said, "You shush. Go on, Nell."

"Sorry, I just think if a kid is intent on causing harm, he or she will. And maybe it won't be something as catastrophic as this, but they hurt themselves and other kids in other ways. I think it's really important as a teacher that I help identify these kids very early on and I feel there must be a better way we can handle them when we do. Any child who reaches eighth grade and doesn't have a single friend has been failed along the way by a lot of people."

I saw the Framinghams look at each other and then Sherry Framingham interrupted, "I don't feel sorry for him and I don't know how you can. I don't care what his background was; he had free choice. Plenty of kids come from bad homes and don't act out like this. My daughter is dead, while he will live for years and years off taxpayer dollars."

I rubbed my forehead; I knew this meeting had been a mistake. "No, I don't feel sorry for him. I've tried in recent days to be honest, because intellectually, I know I should, but that hasn't gone well. I'm thinking of the future Dills out there who can still be saved, though, and how important that is; because that means saving future Charlies and Mistys and DeShauns."

Ronda walked over to me and put a hand on my arm, and as I looked into her deep brown eyes, I realized all of that strength, all of that dignity, I'd seen her display, was a powerful shield against the raw grief she was still fighting. I was a person who'd needed to hide, cocooned in my son's bed, from the agony I thought might literally break my heart. Ronda Jenkins put on heels and lipstick and stared defiantly at the pain that threatened to encompass her. It was window dressing though, inside her soul, she was as much a broken human being as me.

I smiled sadly at her, now that I could finally recognize her as a kindred soul, and she smiled back. We understood each other. She broke the silence and said, "I like that actually. If we are talking about gun laws and metal detectors as preventative measures, it makes sense we would also talk about identifying at-risk kids and trying to meet their needs better. That, too, is preventative. Okay, so last time, we discussed forming an actual NFP organization and I think we should get the paperwork rolling on that. I'll have my paralegal write up a mission statement and send it to everyone. We'll have chairs for various parts of the program, and obviously, you'll be head of the at-risk youth identification part, Nell."

My jaw dropped; force of nature Ronda was back. Lulu laughed again, this time even louder. "Gotcha sucker!" she said.

"Next order of business is getting the Carters involved. I'm passing that one off to the Framinghams. I think I scared them last time I called; Sherry might be able to reach them better."

The mention of the currently missing Carters made me suddenly realize there was another family not represented here.

"There was another injured child, wasn't there?"

Ronda nodded, and clenched her jaw before replying. "Mmhmm, Louisa Gonzales. The family has left the state, maybe the country, I'm not sure. They weren't documented and with all the publicity, they were afraid ICE would show up at their door. It didn't help that every time her name was mentioned in an article, some local yahoo would comment and ask about her ethnicity and nationality. I spoke to her father shortly before they disappeared and he said they just couldn't afford to get involved."

For Louisa's family, Dill hadn't just hurt their child; he had disrupted their entire lives. They'd lost jobs, friends, and their very home. A child who had been through trauma and probably needed the security of familiarity more than anyone was thrust away to who knows where to deal with healing alone.

We spent the next hour sharing our own progress or lack of, in the healing process. The group, I learned, had taken to informally calling themselves The Tribe. It was a tribe no one actually wanted to belong to, a tribe of broken hearts and lost dreams, but it was also true this was a tribe of warriors. They shared pictures and stories of their children with me. Broken free of my self-absorbed world where I was the only one hurting, I listened to the stories and better understood just how much beauty and potential had been lost.

Ronda was clearly the anchor here; she was the strong one, the organized one. Her firm tone belied the struggle in her own home, though, I learned. When her son was killed, he had been protecting his twin sister, her daughter Aliya. Aliya wasn't recovering well; she barely spoke anymore unless it was part of an angry outburst. Aliya had already been through one round of in-patient treatment in the same VCU mental health ward I had been in, and was in intensive therapy now that she was home. Ronda confessed they weren't sure if the therapy was making a difference; the child they'd known and loved was forever changed and in her place was an angry, isolated stranger.

Dill Hobert's victim list was longer than the newspaper indicated, I thought. We, the survivors, were also mortally wounded. We were walking ghosts, phantom apparitions of the humans we used to be.

We shared more than our trauma and the physical absence of our loved ones. Each of us was plagued by the burden of "what could have been." The loss of potential stung, a question that was never to be answered. Yet what surprised me most weren't the more poignant stories, or the moments when tears threatened, the strangest moments were the occasional hints of laughter. Even as broken human beings we somehow pulled those dormant trills from each other.

When I returned home that afternoon, I felt a little less alone than I had before. I still felt completely unsure about actually becoming active in any political outreach the group might undertake, but I thought I might at least benefit from the communal moments. I knew I couldn't stay hidden in my house forever. It was scary to imagine letting anyone else in, but I had to decide before the new school year began. I couldn't carry my uncertainty about my own fate into a classroom full of second graders. I would need to decide if I could bear living for another potential 40-50 years without Charlie in this world.

24

Charlie ran ahead of me, the green hood on the back of his hoodie swaying rhythmically for a few beats, until Stoagie got the better of him and surged. Charlie clutched the leash tightly and then almost tripped over a rock. He glanced back, checking to see if I'd witnessed the near mishap and then laughed when our eyes met.

"You have to pull back when he does that, show him who's boss!" I yelled, although I knew it was pointless. The truth was Stoagie had always been boss and none of the discipline classes we'd tried throughout my childhood had ever taught him a thing.

As they broke through the treeline, there was a moment where they seemingly disappeared completely and I felt an unreasonable stab of panic. I called his name and ran faster, trying to keep up. As soon as I breached the perimeter of the canopy, I stopped and stared ahead. Lake Michigan loomed, somehow the forest of my youth now intersected the waters of my youth, although they'd never converged before.

Charlie had reached my old sailboat, and before I realized what was happening, he and Stoagie were sailing George out onto my old familiar waters. I called his name again, and he turned to look back at me and with a brilliant smile, he waved.

"No!" I yelled, willing him to come back, and then the persistent ding sounds from the phone on my nightstand jarred me awake.

> *I once read a book about a girl who fell out of a tree and died.*
>
> *I climbed up the tree in our backyard and tried falling from it but I didnt die, I just hurt my shoulder bad.*
>
> *My father wouldn't take me to the doctor bcuz it costs too much money*
>
> *Sometimes I think maybe I didn't climb high enough and I should try again...*

My eyes had finally cleared enough to read the messages, but I squeezed them shut again. I was angry to have my beautiful dream snatched away. I'd dreamt of Charlie before, but this had been the clearest, he felt so close, nearly tangible, and then it was gone. The words on my screen reverberated, though, and my concern over C overrode the anger.

Did something happen?

Nothing ever happens. Every day it is the same. He comes home and I try not to be seen.

Your father?

Yeah

He hurts you?

C? Still there?

Yeah... I just dont know how 2 answer. He doesnt beat me if thats what u mean.

What does he do?

Mostly nothing. Mostly just yells at me to go to my room. Maybe grabs my arm but never touches my face.

What about your mother?

Sometimes he hurts her but sometimes she screams at me too and thats when they seem to get along best.

Sometimes women feel hopeless, and they just don't know how to leave. There are people who are trained to help them do that though, they can get both of you help C. I just need to know your name.

U don't understand tho. He would kill us all if police came here. I know it.

Has he threatened to do that?

Yeah. And he would really do it. I know it.

I can help. Tell me your name.

No one can help....

Give me a chance C, I promise I can.

C... are you still there.

I'd been sitting upright and banged my head backward against the headboard in frustration. I wasn't qualified for this; I had no idea if this was an emergency situation right this minute or if I should report it the next day. Reluctantly, I got out of bed and went into the living room to get Morris's card. After dialing, it rang several times and then a groggy sounding Morris answered. My number must have shown on his caller ID because he knew who I was immediately,

"What's happening, Ms. Sanger?"

"He texted again. He sounded really bad," I explained. The truth was the moment Morris answered, I'd regretted the call. Morris could do nothing at this hour and it was possible this kid was just playing games. My gut told me this was a sincere child in need, but I wasn't exactly confident about my own intuitions anymore.

"I'll head over, give me about 30 minutes," he replied.

"Head over? Here you mean? Now?" I asked. When he affirmed, I tried not to panic. After hanging up, I raced to dress and tidy up a little. No one had been inside my house since Narek left after the funeral. Then it struck me he hadn't asked my address; how would he even find my house? Oh yeah, he could find out anything about me he wanted, I remembered. As unreasonable as I knew it was, it felt as if my sanctuary was under threat of being violated. I scrolled through the messages again. Had I misinterpreted? Was I making a bigger deal out of this than I needed to?

Whatever doubts I felt were moot because I soon heard the knock at the door, and I forced myself to walk across the living room to let him in. I opened the door, and my heart pounded as I motioned behind me and stepped across the threshold. He looked different, I realized, and then it hit me he was wearing khaki pants and a golf shirt, not his usual uniform.

At my raised eyebrow, he said, "Perks of being a sector chief. I can be in uniform or civvies, on the clock. I figured you might not want your neighbors to see a police officer entering your house at two a.m."

"You thought it'd be better if they just saw a strange man coming here at this hour?" I asked incredulously.

He had the grace to look a little embarrassed by that and confessed he really hadn't thought much about it at all. After apologizing for the late-night intrusion, he asked to see the phone.

"Well?" I asked after he finished reading and then scrolling and rereading the conversation. "Is it as bad as I think it is or am I being dramatic?"

"I'm concerned," he admitted. "I think it feels authentic, and at best, we have an abused child situation. At worst, it's an abused child with a gun."

"I mean, are you any closer to identifying him? It seems like he had to have been in the classroom when the shooting happened if he got his hands on Charlie's phone, and the list of kids who walked out of that room is pretty short."

Implicit in my comment was that four kids hadn't walked out at all. Two others had been injured and left on EMT gurneys. Dill Hobert left in handcuffs. The remaining student list would have been relatively short. How difficult was it to identify who on that list might have a problematic background?

"We are working it, and while the most likely scenario is the child would have been in that class, it's possible they could have come across the phone in some other way. One of the hardest things to do during an investigation is resisting the urge to jump to conclusions too fast because then we start missing the clues that point to something else," he said.

"Oh, I'm sorry. Here I was thinking maybe the most obvious explanation should be explored first. What do I know about detective work, though?" I replied, not bothering to hide the dripping sarcasm in my voice.

"Ms. Sanger, I know this probably seems slow and frustrating…"

I interrupted. "No, it doesn't seem that way. It is that way. No one could save my son in time, but this boy can be saved. You need to work faster."

Without thinking, I added, "And stop calling me that; you're not my student. My name is Nell."

One side of his mouth curled up in a half-smile and he replied, "You're right, we need to work faster.

We'll figure this out, Nell. In the meantime, just keep doing what you're doing but if it does ever feel overwhelming, let me know. This isn't your job, and it's okay to step back."

I sighed and threw my hands up in the air, so he knew I understood. He walked casually across my living room floor and studied Charlie's painting of Ben's red horse. I stood silently next to him for a moment, looking again into the wide brown eye of the mare. Charlie had added just the tiniest fleck of white there, indicating a reflection. Although I couldn't see what the reflection actually was, I knew it was Charlie himself. He'd stood there, locking eyes with her, and she had seen him. That hint of reflection was proof he had been real, he had indeed existed.

"Nice painting," Morris commented politely, and I nodded.

"It was one of my son's," I admitted.

He looked surprised and said, "Wow, that's impressive. He was thirteen, right?"

"Just. He was actually twelve when he painted this. He was studying under Ben Hamilton, not sure if you know who that is."

"Of course. We have several of his prints hanging in the station. I can see why Hamilton would choose him as a protege. Are you also an artist?" he asked with sincere interest.

I laughed at that. "Well, if you count cutting holiday shapes out of construction paper to decorate a second-grade bulletin board, I am indeed an artist! No, Charlie got all of his talent from his father." At his curious look, I explained, "Narek lives in Armenia. He's a pretty successful artist there. We were never married, it's... complicated."

He smiled and confessed, "I understand. I have a few *it's complicated* stories of my own."

I decided I liked his smile, and then I decided that was a really unwelcome line of thinking, so I cleared my throat and said brusquely, "You have everything you need here tonight?"

He nodded, and I walked him to the door and said goodnight. He walked away and then turned back and said, "Make sure you lock up. You're in a decent neighborhood, but there have been a few vehicle break-ins lately."

"Yes, officer," I said flippantly. It didn't hit me until after the door closed, just how normal the entire conversation had been. The subject was not very normal at all, but the tone of our conversation had been a natural thing. Even my anger had felt natural and normal, the type of response any person who felt frustrated with constraints might have experienced. I'd taken for granted the casual back and forth that had marked most of my life. It felt odd to notice a semblance of that sneaking back in, odd in a disturbing way. The unease that filled me was difficult to identify at first, it wasn't sadness or anger, those I was used to. It was something worse. Guilt. Every moment I allowed myself to indulge in normalcy was a moment of disloyalty. Angry with myself, I vowed not to fall into that trap again.

25

Just let me know you're okay.

I hadn't heard from him in two days. Numerous scenarios explaining his absence had occurred to me, each worse than the previous. One of the most realistic, though, chilled me. What if his father had found the phone? Had our communications possibly put him in even more danger?

Morris had called the previous afternoon to give me more bad news. Technology wasn't proving to be our friend. They'd looked into every student who had survived that classroom, and none fit the profile they were looking for. The phone company had been a bust; somehow this child had successfully spoofed his GPS location and was only accessing the device via Wi-Fi. If he turned on the cellular, they claimed they might be able to help. We'd essentially hit a dead end. I felt dejected by this, but Morris still seemed confident they'd resolve it. I tried to find solace in the fact Morris was actually qualified and experienced to know about these things, but it was little comfort in the face of the current silence from C.

Whatever overthinking I'd been about to indulge in was interrupted by a call from Ronda Jenkins. For once, I was grateful to be distracted by her pushy nature.

"We're meeting today at 1 for lunch, women of the tribe only. You'll come join us?"

I was feeling a little stir crazy, constantly staring at my cell phone screen. Maybe getting out would be a good thing. "I think I can make it…" I began hesitantly.

"Good," she interrupted. "We'll be at the Razzledazzle brewery; you know where that is?"

I ran my free hand through my hair and shook my head. "Wait, what? Lunch at a brewery?"

"Yes, there's a taco truck and trust me when I say it deserves a Michelin star," she explained.

I tried to picture the Ronda I'd met, dignified, regal, dressed to the nines, at a brewery, buying food from a truck. Did she eat her tacos with her hands, or did she use a fork? Suddenly, lunch sounded even more interesting.

"I'll be there," I replied.

When I arrived at the brewery, the others were already seated. They stood to give a greeting hug, one by one. I hadn't been sure if I'd perhaps exaggerated Ronda's presence in memory, but as soon as I saw her, I realized if anything, my memory had been a little subtle. On this day, she wore a bright fuchsia dress that clung to her curves and a pair of matching fuchsia heels. Her lipstick also matched. Lulu's hair was unbraided now and framed her pretty, round face before cascading down her shoulders. She was somewhat stuffed into a Redskins football t-shirt and a pair of sweatpants. Sherry was every "older" mother, I'd ever worked with on a PTA project. It felt uncharitable to call her oversized, khaki capris and faded floral shirt frumpy, but that was the word that came to mind. Looking around, I realized it was extremely unlikely the four of us would have ever naturally gravitated to one another.

"So, we were talking about diets before you got here," Lulu said. "I've gained twenty pounds in the last few months. Don't get me wrong, I wasn't a small woman before, but this is a lot of gain in a short period of time, even for me."

The battle of the bulge felt like such a benign topic. Had a group of women ever met for lunch and not somehow discussed diet and weight loss? I wasn't sure what I had expected, but I'd envisioned a more formal discussion about laws and organization building, not the casual girlfriend chatter of a normal world. My slight discomfort with the seeming banality of it all was shattered by the conversation that followed.

Ronda said, "Look, girlfriend, you need to stop beating yourself up. We are all coping however we can. You're not the same, you have been changed, and that's a process."

Lulu's friendly face seemed to work overtime, as multiple muscles twitched and her top lip sucked in. I wasn't sure at first if she was trying not to laugh, or trying not to cry.

"I know, but I just fucking hate laying this stuff out in front of you all. I'm the lucky one, I know it. I have my Sam at home. Compared to the rest of you, I shouldn't complain about anything ever. I'm sorry, I feel stupid for even mentioning this. I just need to eat fewer tacos."

One perfectly groomed eyebrow raised on Ronda's mahogany face and she said, "Oh no, you don't. You're in this with the rest of us. Don't forget that I also have a surviving child who was there that day. I know exactly what you're dealing with in your home and it isn't pretty. Losing DeShaun is the worst thing that's ever happened in my life, but watching Aliya try to recover is almost just as bad. No one who hasn't been here can know just what these kids have been through, how it's changed them, and what it's doing to our homes. So, don't you dare start with that survivor guilt stuff, because like I told you back on day one, I won't have it."

I could tell by the ease at which the words came out and the accepting way Lulu nodded her head, this was a familiar discussion. Lulu had apologized more than once for her son's survival, and Ronda had told her every time to knock it off. I actually had thought it a little odd Lulu was so enmeshed in the group considering her luck, but perhaps I'd been too quick with the word luck. I'd have given anything for Charlie to be in Sam or Aliyah's shoes, but at the same time, it was unrealistic to imagine if he were, we'd be okay at this moment.

Sherry, who I had figured out by now was the quiet one, commented dryly, "Well, all of this diet talk is making my stomach growl; let's go get some tacos."

After loading our table with a variety of gourmet tacos, we settled back in. I still didn't feel completely comfortable, they were just too new to me, but I wasn't exactly an outsider. I knew I belonged here. When Sherry casually asked about my classroom,

I steeled myself for questions about our lockdown that fateful day, but they kept it light and casual.

"Why second grade?" she asked.

I thought about it. The truth was I'd sort of fallen into the early years almost by accident. My daycare experience made me comfortable with younger children and my ascent into elementary school coincided with Charlie's entry into the school system. Of course, I'd thought about branching out and trying something different, but even when Charlie had moved on to middle school, I'd stuck with what was familiar.

"By second grade, most kids are reading; they're capable of sitting still most of the time. They're still young enough. They're moldable, teachable, and many of the parents are still involved. I know from peers that tends to taper down each year," I explained.

Lulu said, "That makes sense, it kind of goes back to what we were discussing at Ronda's house. That's the time to identify the at-risk kids."

"Yes! I can tell you right now which kids are going to be the loners, which kids just don't fit in at all. It's all obvious in play dynamics by this age."

Ronda asked, "If it's so obvious, why aren't there already programs in place to reach them?"

"As teachers, our hands are pretty tied in what we can do. No one wants teachers being parents, and they see any step outside of basic curriculum decisions as encroaching on a parent's role. They fight any social programs we suggest."

Lulu nodded, "Republicans, right?" and I didn't have a chance to reply before Sherry interrupted.

"Hey now! I'm a republican and I would support that!"

"Whoops, sorry, I don't mean to start a political debate. Lulu's right though, republicans do often fight us on any social issues. That said, I can't say the democrats do me any favors either. Almost every local administrative issue that's tied my hands as a teacher has been at the behest of democratic board members. The truth is the parties both say they want better schools, better teachers, safer kids, and both parties completely tie the hands of the people most qualified to make that happen in the process."

The sad truth was as teachers we didn't earn a high enough salary to be considered important enough to make those kinds of decisions. We were too far down the administrative food chain to create our own meaningful changes. Everyone in the city had a better way we should be teaching, better programs we should be working under, every parent in the city knew best how to manage a classroom, every school board member and state education officer knew best. Teachers, with their boots on the ground as it were, had to work with whatever tools and parameters we were handed.

I blushed, realizing I sounded an awful lot like what my friends and I jokingly called my old teachervangelist self. Teaching had never been my calling; I'd fallen into it as a necessity, but it had become my passion. Sitting at lunch in that brewery, I realized that was the first time I'd felt a spark of that old passion since the shooting.

Ronda pointed out the political lines made the gun safety issue so difficult to address. "We all know it's polarized now. Our challenge is getting both sides to hear us without talking over us. I don't want our goals to be hijacked, so I think we need to be really clear and specific in what it is we want to accomplish, and let's be real, that may not be exactly what any one side wants. As an attorney, I know that the true mark of a successful judgment is when both parties walk away feeling a little unsatisfied."

I felt a little embarrassed because it hit me that until that moment, I hadn't actually known what it was she did for a living. I'd been so self-absorbed, it hadn't occurred to me to even wonder. Ronda as an attorney made perfect sense. I could only imagine the groans of opposing counsel when they learned she was going to be their nemesis.

"What kind of law do you practice?" I asked.

"The ugly kind!" she quipped. "Family law, I mostly represent divorcees, I bust balls for a living."

That elicited an earnest laugh from me that was echoed by the others. It suddenly struck me how naturally our conversation flowed. I didn't feel like a newcomer, a stranger; we could have been any four women meeting for lunch and a beer, anywhere. The few patrons in the brewery didn't glance at us. There was no telltale neon sign over us. It felt almost nice to be this normal again, just four girlfriends hanging out and sort of having fun. The word fun startled me out of my reverie, though. With it came the crushing reminder that for Charlie, there would be no more fun.

Ronda was eyeing me keenly and said, "So tell us about your story; we know you're a teacher, but what about your personal life?"

"What do you mean?"

"Where's your ex in all of this?" she asked.

"Narek? He's in Armenia," I said dully. I was still numb from the chilling reminder of why I was here.

Lulu leaned in, "Is he from there?"

I didn't want to talk about Narek. I didn't want to remember Narek. Somehow just saying his name, on top of the reminder of Charlie's absence, filled me with ice water and I didn't want to say anymore. What I really wanted was to be far away from this place.

I said, "Hey, I'm sorry, I have to get out of here; I have an appointment I can't miss. It was nice seeing you all."

I saw the look of concern in their eyes, but they, too, were members of this club no one ever wanted to join. They, too, understood putting on the mask and walking away quietly. They, too, understood we were really just pretending to be four normal girlfriends.

26

It's been four days and I should stop
texting, but I continue to hope you'll
reply.

As the waters of the Chesapeake Bay warmed
in anticipation of summer's imminent return, I steeled
myself for another season without Charlie. For the first
time since I had begun teaching, I wouldn't be heading
back to Michigan. My mother wasn't happy about that.
She wanted the opportunity to serve me, to help me
heal, to witness my recovery in person. I understood
exactly why it was hard for her, but the prospect of
watching the blessed, the ignorant, the innocent, in
summer play on the shores of Lake Michigan was too
much to bear. I thought of the old hurricane rule I'd
learned when first moving to Virginia, "June too soon."

I had been healing, at least a little, I thought. I wasn't entirely trusting of my own self-analysis, though, because I recognized that when the numbness had finally worn off, when I'd finally started to feel emotions again, they often swung wildly. That small improvement in emotional health was stilted all over again with the lack of response from the child. My anxiety rose with each passing day, or passing hour if I wanted to be honest with myself, that C didn't reply.

I had just picked up the fragile pieces of what was left of my life when C disappeared. If I'd felt guilt over not being there when Charlie needed me, I'd always known intellectually that guilt was unreasonable. He was at school that day because he needed to be there. I was at my school teaching because I needed to be there. There wasn't some reasonable alternative that would have kept us together and safe. With C, it was different. He'd turned to me for help and I'd had a chance to reach him in time. I'd failed at convincing him to trust me enough to give me a name. I'd failed to protect him. With each passing hour of silence, I believed more strongly that I'd failed to save him.

I'd started ignoring calls again, first the tribe, and then my mother. I didn't want to engage in casual conversation, but neither did I want to share the burden of my guilt with anyone else. I had once again started to lock myself up in the house, afraid to leave the safe walls and the steady, dependable stream of Wi-Fi. It had been only four days since my last interaction with C, and I was already unraveling, undoing any hint of earlier progress.

The one person whose calls I did answer was Morris. Each time my phone rang and I saw his number on the screen, I'd force myself to pick up for what always turned out to be a meaningless check-in that would serve to only confirm that C was still anonymous, still missing. Morris assured me that police were not giving up, he tried lulling me with the vague suggestion that perhaps we had misread the entire situation, but it didn't help. I felt certain the child had come under some serious harm. We'd lost our opportunity. But then, on the sixth day, everything changed again.

> *I'm ok, he brought us to my grandmothers house and she doesn't have wifi*

It took me a few minutes to truly catch my breath, as the waves of relief threatened to drown me. I squeezed my eyes shut to fight the tears that rolled. My heart pounded and I reread the text several times, thinking carefully about my reply. Trying to quell my shaking hand, I replied.

> I've been so worried, but I'm glad to hear you were somewhere safe. Is grandma's house safe?

> *Yeah, he leaves me alone there bcuz hes so busy. It's nice too cuz she has a dog*

I sank back into my couch, and closed my eyes in relief for a moment.

> I used to have a dog, when I was a kid.

> *What kind?*

The fat kind! I don't think he really had a breed, he was a bit of everything, his name was Stoagie. That's what the old folks used to call cigars.

I wish we could have one but I wont even ask bcuz he wouldn't allow it

I don't really know why we don't have one. I mean, when I was living with Charlie's father I couldn't because he was allergic but I should have gotten one after that.

U still can

I guess. Actually, it's funny this comes up because I've had a bunch of weird dog-related dreams lately. Maybe the universe is telling me something.

I did have a bird 4 a while

His name was Dr Pepper

Oh that's a fun name, what kind of bird was he?

Lovebird. Mama got him from Deke.

Deke? Is that your father?

Lol no. He was an old man Mama used to clean for and when he died she took the bird.

Oh, so she cleans houses?

Idk. Anyway we didnt get to have him long. He would make these sounds, like he was sad and mama said he wanted a mate. Lovebirds wasn't meant to live alone.

:-(Did you give him away?

No. My dad hated it, he would yell at him to shut up and then one day I came home from school and he said he set it free outside

I'm sorry. You know if we get you out of there maybe you could have another bird.

Would rather a dog tbh. Nanas dog loves me more than Dr Pepper ever did. I can lie on top of him and he just lets me. He sees me.

What do you mean?

Well my dad just has angry eyes when he looks at me. And my mom doesn't look at me at all. At school no one sees me usually and if they do it's to make fun of my clothes and stuff.

Do you have any friends at school?

No.

Who do you sit with at lunch?

*Don't go to lunch. Usually dont bring
any and no one would sit with me.
Usually I just hide somewhere.*

*Once I tried to sit with some of the other
kids who don't have a lot of friends. Dill
was there. And it seemed okay at first
but then one of the girls pointed at my
dress and said she saw me wear it the
day before and even the kids no one likes
laughed at me.*

I squeezed the phone in my hand, studying my
milky white knuckles that contrasted against the light
tanned skin of my hands. I'd caught the clue. Careful,
careful, I told myself, as I struggled to respond.

I'm sorry that happened to you. You
know you won't always feel this way,
though. You will find people who
appreciate you.

*No I won't. I'm stupid and ugly.
Everyone hates me. My parents and kids
at school and u would too if u met me.*

C they're all wrong. Your life can
change, you can be happy.

I don't think so.

*I lied 2 u before. He does hit me. Not a
lot tho. But sometimes he hurts me in
other ways 2 and my mom gets mad
then. Things are very bad today. They're
fighting and I have to hide in my closet.*

C do you really have a gun?

I have to go now.

C?

C please answer me...

Of course, there wasn't an answer. I quickly
dialed Morris's number. When he answered, I blurted
out, "It's a girl."
He said, "Slow down, what?"
"C is a girl!" I explained and then shared the
latest conversation. He was quiet for a long moment
and then said he was at the station and would start
working through the student lists again. The resolute
tone of his voice was a steadying force. He believed
me, believed her, and he would find answers. Before
hanging up he asked if I would be around later in the
afternoon when his shift ended, and I told him yes, I'd
see him then.
    In the meantime, I had an idea of my own that I
wanted to pursue. I'd assumed this was all to be kept
quiet outside of official channels, but no one had
actually told me I couldn't tell anyone else. I was in it
this far, I decided it was time to go full detective on my
own. Biting my lip nervously, I dialed Ronda's number.
She didn't sound surprised to hear from me. I'd worried
after my lunch exit a few days earlier and my avoidance

of her calls she might not want to hear from me at all, but it was as if nothing had happened at all.

"I'm glad you called; I was going to actually call you tonight to see if you could make our first official board meeting on Tuesday," she said.

"I, uh, well maybe. So, I actually have a situation and I feel awkward coming to you with it, but I think I may need your help," I explained.

"Mhmm, I have a meeting with a client in fifteen minutes, but I'm free after that. Your house or mine?" she said, without hesitation.

I felt relief flood me, of course, Ronda Jenkins would be up for helping. I just hoped the actual nature of help I needed didn't turn her off.

"Mine please, someone else is coming over this afternoon and I don't want to miss him."

We said goodbye and then I tried to make my house and my person presentable for two anticipated guests. I was far more worried about impressing Hurricane Ronda than Lt. Morris. My little home was probably about the size of her garage. I knew she wouldn't judge me for it, but I felt like both my home and my person were pretty lackluster compared to Ronda. It made me feel a little embarrassed.

I wasn't concerned with Morris's opinion. I knew with the nature of his job, he surely had seen much worse, regularly, than my humble little ranch house. I wondered what sort of neighborhood he lived in. I'd noticed he didn't wear a wedding ring, so I assumed he was single. I couldn't quite picture him off duty, cozy and relaxed in his own home. It felt like Morris was just always on duty, always to be found at the police station.

When the doorbell rang, I steeled myself and swung the door open. Lime green. She wore a lime green dress that hugged every curve, and the requisite matching shoes. This time I'd armed myself a little too, though, I was wearing a summer dress and a bright red lipstick. I hoped she recognized the effort for what it was, a pledge to join her well-groomed army of one. It was imperative she see me as an ally today, that she knew my intentions were good.

I welcomed her into my home, and as I'd guessed, she didn't raise an eyebrow at its simplicity or size. She followed me into my small galley style kitchen, and we chatted casually as I set a kettle of water on the stove. After pouring two cups of tea, I sat down at my table with her and began to explain the texts I'd been receiving and what we had tried so far. Her eyes occasionally widened dramatically as I gave the full back story, but she listened intently without interrupting. When I finally got to the last conversation and C's abrupt departure as she'd avoided the gun question, she visibly winced and put a hand over her mouth.

"So, the reason I wanted to meet with you, is I had an idea. I know you're understandably very protective of Aliya. She's been through so much and doesn't need to have any more exposure to the worst elements of this world, but…"

Her chin lifted and I saw the stoicism in her raised eyebrows. She might truly feel for this child and want to help her, but Ronda had made it clear from the first time we met; Aliya was completely off-limits. I knew this wouldn't be easy.

"I'm just thinking if anyone could help identify this child, it might be another child. We know she's in middle school, she's probably low income. She mentioned not having lunch. We know she was sometimes friendly with Dill Hobert. She'd be a quiet girl, someone who has no friends. Sometimes she falls into another child's focus and they make fun of her, but mostly she's in the periphery. Invisible. She isn't a kid who has a cell phone. She lives in a house, not an apartment, it has a tree in the backyard. Mom may clean houses. She doesn't have a dog. Her parents probably aren't the type who show up for school plays and concerts. We don't know how she got Charlie's phone, but I think it's likely she was in that science wing on that morning. Maybe all of that would ring a bell with Aliya."

She took a long sip of tea; I focused on her fingers that wrapped around the delicate cup, as if they were suddenly seeking warmth. The large cut diamond that glittered from her left hand contrasted brightly with the darkness of her skin and I didn't miss when she tapped the inside of that finger purposely against the porcelain eliciting a soft "tick tick tick" sound.

Finally, she replied, "I can try, but I can't make promises she will be able to help. You have to understand, she's different now. She had to bear witness to this terrible thing, and she lost her other half, her twin. Her therapist says on top of all of that, she has severe survivor's guilt. She feels like he was killed protecting her. I told you before, she doesn't talk about that day with me, but the truth is she doesn't really talk to me at all anymore. I can't promise she will hear me if I try to ask her about this"

Ronda glanced away and I saw the tears welled up in her eyes. Her armor of stiletto heels, aggressive speaking, and chin up fortitude were weakened significantly when Aliya was mentioned. She'd accepted the loss of DeShaun on that April morning because she'd had to, but in effect, she'd also lost a second child. The prolonged slow torture of watching

Aliya struggle to find some seed of hope had worn down the strongest woman I'd ever met.

I reached over and touched her hand, "You don't always have to be the strongest one in the room. Look, if you think this is too much to ask of her, I totally understand. We will figure this out some other way. There is something, though, that you might want to consider. This... mission, it's changed my life. Trying to help this child has given me a purpose. I wonder if maybe Aliya would also get some value from that."

She smiled at me; it was a softer and more real smile than I'd ever seen her display. Taking a deep breath, she said, "I'll talk to her. No promises, it depends how the conversation goes, but I'll try."

Our conversation was interrupted by the ringing of my doorbell. "That's Lt. Morris," I explained. We agreed I wouldn't mention to him what Ronda was going to attempt. We didn't want Aliya exposed to any police questioning. With that agreement made, we walked to the door.

Morris stood on the porch and gave me a strange look. I realized this was as put together as I'd ever been in his presence. When his lips showed a hint of a smile, I felt my cheeks redden. I was all too aware of just how much leg I was showing, and just how red my lipstick was. I hadn't gone to the effort for his sake, but what if he thought that was my intention?

I hurriedly shoved Ronda in front of me and said, "This is Ronda Jenkins, Ronda, this is Morris. We had a meeting, so I'm dressed up for that. Ronda and I had a meeting, I mean. Because I mean, well, we just sometimes meet like this. It's an organization; we are forming an organization."

Ronda turned around and gave me a pointed look. I knew I was babbling, and her look confirmed it was as bad as I thought.

She stuck out her hand and in Hurricane Ronda business mode, said, "Lieutenant Morris, nice to meet you. I'm sure Richmond PD will be hearing all about our organization soon. Have a nice day."

He barely got out his own return greeting before she was sashaying down the sidewalk in her heels. When he looked back at me, I saw the confusion on his face, and I laughed, "That's Ronda! Come on in."

When he was seated in the chair Ronda had just vacated, I handed him the phone. He frowned and shook his head as he read the interaction and took notes.

"So, there are about 340 female students at the school. That's a relatively small number really to filter through, but our job is made a little tougher because of summer break. We can definitely rule out the girls who were in that room that day because we've already investigated them. That leaves about 332 more students. We are getting closer; we will identify this child."

I nodded and didn't share the details of my own little investigation. I needed to protect Aliya, but there was also the matter of not wanting to step on Morris's toes. He'd been a good ally in this. I didn't want him to think I was suggesting I wasn't confident in him or his department. I glanced back at him; he really was a good guy. He'd been so patient with me and so willing to help. I suspected a lot of this was being done off the clock. Surely, he had more junior people who could handle this role of professional hand holder.

"I know you're working hard on this and you probably have a thousand other cases that keep you busy. I really appreciate it," I said.

He smiled, "This one has become a priority for me personally. I don't want to face the wrath of the citizen-detective who hasn't given up on this child."

I smiled back and then it hit me I'd smiled more on this day than I had in months. I pictured tiny little electric zaps in my brain, new circuits forming a fragile network to the previously dead smile zone. If I could learn to smile again, at simple things, then perhaps there might be a day when I'd feel actual happiness again. Perhaps that part of me was just dormant, waiting to be teased out.

27

I want to save you. You're worth it.

She'd gone underground again. By then, I was used to the frequent breaks in communication. I wrote anyway, hopeful that C was reading even if she wasn't yet responding. It had been almost 24 hours since I'd seen Ronda and I was resisting the urge to call her for an update. I knew this was a delicate matter, and she needed time to pull it off. When she finally called, though, I could not mask my breathless anticipation.

"Were you able to ask?"

"Yes. It was so hard to get her to even look at me, let alone hear what I was saying. When I explained that she could help save a little girl, though, I saw something in her eyes I haven't seen in such a long time. It's like she just awoke. At first, she couldn't really think of who it could be, but then she remembered there's this girl, Callie, who was in Mr. Goldsby's room across the hall. She said she remembered a time she was in the hall on a bathroom pass and she'd seen the girl going through a locker. Aliya knows the girl who belongs to that locker and it wasn't this child. She saw the girl pull out a granola bar and then shut it and ran back to her class. She kind of thought maybe the girl had stolen the bar, but she didn't say anything because she doesn't know the other girl that well and maybe she'd offered it."

A wave of exhilaration hit me, a hungry child, sticky fingers, in a nearby classroom. It had to be her! I thanked her profusely and then hung up to call Morris.

"I think I know who it is. A girl named Callie, she was in Goldsby's room," I explained.

He was silent for a moment, then pressed for more details. I reluctantly explained my secret little side mission with Ronda.

"Look, I know you were following up on all of this, but I thought Aliya might know better than any of us and frankly, I don't think she's in a place yet where she could have talked to the police. I'm really sorry I wasn't more upfront but—"

He interrupted me and said, "Nell, stop explaining. My ego isn't so large that I'd sacrifice two little girls just so I can play hero. I'm going to follow up on this immediately."

I closed my eyes in relief, both at the note of determination in his voice, and his ability to accept my sleuthing on the side. We said our goodbyes and I began the painful waiting game. After hanging up, I began to pace, awaiting what I hoped would be a positive update. Surely, they would be able to roll right in and get to the child and end her nightmare.

I squeezed the phone in my hand and willed it to ring, but with each passing second, my anxiety climbed, as less welcome thoughts snuck in. What if they met resistance at the house? Could Morris actually be in danger? What if they removed her and she denied it all, would they have to return her? When it suddenly sounded a text alert, I jumped.

I'm going to real heaven now. Remember when we talked about it?

What? No wait, don't do anything!!!!!

I just wanted to tell u sorry bcuz u have been so nice.

Callie, I know who you are. Don't do it.

Doesn't matter. He told me last night we have to leave to live in west virginia. My moms not going. She left with a man last night.

He's not taking you anywhere, trust me.

He will if I let him but Im not letting him. Hes packing the car now and when he comes in to make me Im going to be just like Dill except Im gonna die too.

I dialed Morris's number and when he answered, yelled, "She's got a gun, get there now!"

then hung up without hearing his response, to get back to the text.

>Callie, the police are on their way. Your father is not taking you anywhere. You are going to be safe. You need to put the gun away right now.

>Callie, answer me.

>Callie???

I stared at my phone and thought, please, please, please, and then hit the familiar contact. Charlie. It rang straight to voicemail, his voice, but this time I didn't stop to listen to his entire message. I hung up and redialed. Again, voicemail. Redial. This time on the second ring a child answered. Her voice was quiet and shaky.

"Callie," I said, simply.

"Hi."

"Callie, are you someplace safe?"

She paused, and then in a thin voice, a voice that sounded far too tired to belong to a 12-year-old girl, she replied. "Not really."

"Do you still have the gun?"

"Yeah."

"And your father? Is he…"

"He's packing, and breaking everything he's not taking with."

"Listen, Callie, the police are on their way and they are going to help you. You think this is it; you think it can't get any better than this. I'm telling you it can. You are stronger than you ever imagined; you can survive anything. You can come back from this; you can build a life again. You can find purpose and meaning. You don't have to go down like this without a fight. You have value and worth. Callie, can you hear me?"

She was crying softly, "I don't think I can."

"Callie this is just a few minutes. This is just a day. This is just a week. This is just your first 12 years. There are so many more years for you, so many chances to experience happiness. The rest will be different. Your different will start today. Let the police help you."

She inhaled deeply enough I could hear it, a long clear breath that took in the hope that oxygen always gives. And then she replied, "I have to go now."

The disconnection was immediate and I trembled. I tried to return the call, but this time it didn't ring at all before going to voicemail. It was instant. She had turned the phone off.

My legs felt weak and I sat on the floor. I balled my hands into fists and cried out, "Oh God. Oh God. Oh God."

The seconds ticked by and I was back in my classroom, little Becca clinging to my side in the darkness. Smell of urine in the air. Phones buzzing and ringing and beeping from the coat wall. Knowing something was happening, but not knowing what. Sense of dread. Charlie and Callie. As my memories collided with my reality, panic rose up in my chest. With it came a wave of nausea. I ran for the bathroom and vomited.

As I lay on the bathroom floor under the spinning ceiling, my chest clenching in rhythmic contractions, I tried to surface from the pool of panic for air. Just one breath, I told myself, just one breath. Finally, gasping, I focused on the overhead light. The room seemed to be closing in on me as my heart threatened to pulsate right out of my chest and then things went black.

The sound of pounding brought me back. I wasn't sure where I was at first, and as the bathroom fixtures came into focus I felt confused and lost. I wasn't sure how long I'd been laying there, and everything seemed so foggy in my head. The noise continued, and for a moment, I thought that too had originated in my head. Then I realized it was coming from the front door in the adjacent living room. Without consciously meaning to, I heard myself calling out and then there was the sound of the front door slamming open, and Morris was in the bathroom doorway.

He leaned over me and was speaking, but I felt disoriented, unable to quite translate whatever was coming from his lips in the murkiness of my brain. He reached down and picked me up and carried me into the living room, laying me on the couch. Finally, through the disorder, I heard my name.

"Nell, Nell, can you hear me?"

His voice sounded different, strained, worried. Morris never sounded worried. He was a solid rock of calm. I cleared my throat and made my words work.

"Yeah, I'm here… is she dead?" I asked.

"No, I tried telling you when I first found you, we have her, she's okay. Everyone's okay. You saved her in time," he said.

I squeezed my eyes shut, but the tears rolled down my cheeks anyway. Saved.

"I'm sorry I'm such a wreck," I said as I struggled to sit up.

"Shh, you're fine," he said gently.

"She hung up and I couldn't reach her and I thought, I thought she had done it. I don't know exactly what happened, it's as if I was suddenly back there on that worst day of my life."

"That's completely understandable. You don't just get over trauma; it's not just your brain that stores it. Your body remembers it too. There are techniques to help you work through those moments. I have the name of a really great therapist who is an expert at PTSD. Many of my officers have used her with good results. I want you to give her a call," he said.

His voice was soft, calm, but there was an underlying tension in it and I glanced over at him. His forehead was slightly wrinkled and he was staring intently, and I realized that tone I'd heard had been worry. For a moment, our eyes met and there was an uncomfortable silence. He was more than just a police officer, and I was more than just a helpless citizen. I broke eye contact first, I didn't trust anything I was feeling at that moment.

"Callie, where is she now?" I asked.

"She's at the hospital right now, she's with social workers and detectives, and they're going to move her later to a protective foster home. I see that look but trust me, forget every horrible thing you've ever heard on the news. The families who sign up to work with kids like Callie do it as a labor of love and they are very carefully selected," he said.

I suddenly realized that this all meant that I wouldn't be hearing from her again. I felt so incredibly relieved that we'd found her, but the thought left me with an almost wistful feeling. Our texts had filled that lonely, empty place inside me. Talking to her, seeking her name, chasing her down with Morris had all become part of my identity. I was no longer Charlie's mom, and now I was no longer the woman who could save Callie. I couldn't explain any of that to Morris, he wouldn't have understood, so instead, I just smiled and said the right things.

When his phone rang, he said a few curt words and then hung up and said, "That was the station, I'm needed down there, but I hate leaving you like this."

I smiled, "Like what? I'm fine now. Really, go!"

I walked him to the door, and he looked at me and said, "You did good, Nell, you really helped that girl. I know it may be hard, but you can stop worrying now. We will make sure she's okay from here. And I really do hope you call that number I gave you. She's very good. I've talked to her myself before."

It hadn't hit me until that moment this closure meant I would also say goodbye to Morris. Of course, there would be no need for him to call me daily for check-ins anymore, no more late-night pop ins. Everything was resolved in a very final way. I bit the inside of my cheek to keep my emotions in check and smiled, "I think I will, thanks again, Morris, for taking all of this seriously."

There was an awkward moment on the porch. My natural inclination was to lean in and give him a hug goodbye as if we were old friends. We weren't old friends, though; he was a professional who had just been doing his job. I thrust a hand out, and he smiled that crooked smile, and then shook it before walking away.

Part 3

28

The tribe had formally organized into "Moms
Preventing Violence," or the much less tongue twisty
MPVs. I'd fought valiantly to keep any reference to
guns from the title because I didn't want us to be
portrayed as just another gun control group. We were
something more. We were looking at a larger, more
comprehensive picture and were hoping to address
everything from the systemic abuse and neglect that
provided such a breeding ground for child violence, to
the laws that allowed guns to end up in their hands.

I wanted to identify at-risk children before they
reached middle grades. Children who were lonely, the
outsiders who lacked peer support. I had developed my
own program that I'd put into action the previous
month when the new school year began. I'd created
rotating small groups in my own classroom to enjoy

private lunch buddy days. While observing my kids in the early days, I'd picked out the ones who didn't adapt easily to social constructs and matched them up with their more outgoing peers. It was my hope my classroom would serve as a model classroom and we could convince the school board to implement it district-wide the following year.

We were also pushing for better, free mental health access for children and youth. Too many families found themselves at a loss when trying to seek help for their children, stymied by prohibitive health insurance costs and a lack of available care in the region. I knew the current state of mental health care options was in crisis, and it felt like a huge mountain to climb, but with Ronda at the helm, there was no doubt we would make inroads.

Guns were also addressed. We kept our focus pointed, rather than looking at across-the-board gun regulations that would have had little to no success in passing, we would focus on gun laws as they related to those accused of domestic violence. It was crucial, we argued, that police have the legal tools to remove guns from homes where a party was accused of domestic violence. Relying on adult victims and courts to pursue and award protective orders was too risky. Allowing 24 hours even after such an order was awarded for forfeiture of guns voluntarily to friends, family members or police was also too risky. Police should have the ability to remove guns immediately from a home when responding to those calls, and any forfeiture should be to law enforcement personnel.

The governor was impressed with our efforts and his office wanted to acknowledge the organization with a formal ribbon-cutting ceremony at the capital. It wouldn't be an especially large event, but there would be some media there and we hoped we'd reach a few new potential political allies. It would also be a unique opportunity for us to honor our children. None of us had truly been in a place during their memorial services to pay tribute to them in the manner they deserved. This gave us a second chance to get that right. As part of those efforts, I was touched when Ben contacted me to tell me he would be donating the portrait he'd done for Charlie's funeral as well as portraits of the other children to display at the event.

In the lead to the event, I'd become immersed in the tribe. Sometimes, all of us would meet up with a formal agenda, but at other times we were just four friends sharing our daily lives. Grief was the awning over our patio, at times its shadow dominated, but there were other times the sun shifted enough on the horizon we forgot it was even there. We talked Sherry through her marital strains; she and Calvin were trudging through their daily lives but had completely lost connection with each other outside of survivor mode. When she shyly admitted to us they hadn't been intimate since the shooting, we forced her into a department store to lingerie shop. When she later reported the mission to be a success, we celebrated with her with toasts at a wine bar.

To the casual observer, Ronda was a superwoman. She was practicing law full-time again. She was still active in her church. She had nudged Aliya out of her shell a bit and was once again hosting girl scout meetings at her house. Only we knew about the nightmares that still woke her almost nightly. She'd sneak out of bed and tiptoe down the hall and peer in at her surviving child to reassure herself everything was okay. She had Big Jeremiah, as I fondly called him, to lean on but having made herself the steel pillar within our little community left her at times emotionally drained. We were familiar enough, and bold enough, to do what very few people were brave enough to ever do with Ronda Jenkins. We told her to knock it off and relax a little. Amazingly, she actually listened to us and we walked her down a path of self-care.

As for me, I'd become a pet project too. Although Lulu was also single, they'd pinged in on my solitary life in particular. Maybe it was because Lulu had a child living with her, or maybe it was that she'd been married until just a few years prior, but they didn't pressure her the way they did me. They were constantly tossing out names of men they'd like to set me up with. I always refused, I was doing better, but I was absolutely not in a place to start dating. I'd barely dated at all since Charlie was three years old, and it had worked out fine for me until now after all. I didn't need a man in my life to be complete.

I tried to explain this to my friends, but they were unsatisfied.

"You're still so young, Nell. I know I sure don't plan to stay single forever. Why would you want to?" Lulu asked.

I wasn't planning on anything; I was ignoring the idea of dating entirely.

Sherry looked uncomfortable and said softly, "You could have another child, you know."

Everyone got silent then. It was the one topic we never broached. None of us had ever mentioned trying to make our families larger with the loss of our children. I felt my mouth tighten in anger and said, "No, I can't, I won't. Charlie isn't replaceable."

"I didn't mean that, Nell, I just mean you don't have to be alone, and you can have a real family someday. I'd give anything to be able to have another baby. I'm 54, though. It took us 12 years to conceive Misty. My ship has completely sailed," she said sadly.

"I know you mean well, but you have to believe me, I have no desire to ever have another child. Charlie was my one and only. Not only isn't there a prospective father in the picture, but I'm also almost 34 years old. I'm doing okay now, but I still have a lot of issues that would make me an unsuitable parent."

The finality of my tone convinced them to drop the subject, and move cautiously to one less loaded, my impending return to the classroom.

In the weeks leading to the new school year, I'd been nervous but determined to get back into a classroom. I had been excited to enact some of my MPV plans in the classroom, but truthfully, I'd also wanted to prove to myself that I could still find joy in some part of my old life. My tribe had encouraged me in those preparations. I was touched when they dropped off a huge stash of class supplies in a gift basket. Their confidence in me helped me feel more confident in myself and it turned out returning to school was easier than I feared it might be.

Beyond spending time with the tribe, I'd also taken to meeting with Ben again. We didn't get to see each other as frequently as when Charlie was taking lessons, but we hit Mabel's every other week or so. I realized that as much as we'd appreciated Ben in our lives, Ben had also appreciated us in his. He may have enjoyed his solitude, but I could also tell he was lonely at times too. He opened up more about his own family. His surviving sons lived far away, but they were still trying to be a little too involved in his private life. When Ben confessed, they were always bugging him about meeting some nice older woman, I shared my own recent friendly arguments over dating.

"Your friends are right, though, Nell. You're way too young to give up on finding someone."

"Ugh, not you too! I tell you what. I'll go on a date when you do; how does that sound?" I replied crankily.

He'd laughed at that, maybe a little too hard, and I changed the subject to the upcoming portrait unveiling. I knew Ben was not a portrait artist, but I also knew he would more than do our children justice. That he had a personal connection made his participation all the more serious. A few days after that conversation, he called to not-so-casually mention, "Oh, and by the way, I'm bringing a date to the reception following the ceremony. I can't wait to meet your young man."

I couldn't believe I'd been so easily snookered by Ben Hamilton of all people. When I shared my dilemma with the tribe, they immediately threw out names and descriptions of every eligible bachelor they knew. Annoyed at myself for going along with the madness, I chose a random name just to stop the barrage. Lulu had supplied the winning name and she beamed as if she'd outwitted a worthy opponent in chess. I pursed my lips and announced, "Whatever. Just tell him to text me, I'm not texting him first," to their laughter.

We'd moved on to appetizers and wine, when Sherry's phone rang. She had a strange look on her face as she answered it and then walked away.

"What do you think that's all about?" Ronda asked.

"I don't know, hopefully, there isn't an issue with Calvin…." I replied

We'd barely had time to speculate when Sherry returned. "You guys are not going to believe who that was! Angela Carter. She said she's ready to meet with us."

It was a huge surprise. The Carters had refused all overtures until now. Jessica's funeral had been kept private, they'd avoided all press, and never answered a single one of Ronda or Sherry's voicemails. We'd speculated that maybe they just could not handle talking about their daughter or maybe they belonged to some very insular religious community, and as a rule, they avoided outsiders. We'd never forgotten Jessica, and Ben was including her in his display, but none of us had expected by this point that they'd respond to our many efforts.

"I mean, we're all kind of on our own timeline. You guys were meeting for weeks before I was able to even think about joining you," I pointed out.

"That's true, and it sort of feels like forever because of everything we've accomplished, but it's only been six months," Lulu said.

Six months. It took nine months to gestate a baby, we hadn't even had the time yet to develop a human being. Sometimes the truth was I felt like I was pushing too hard, too fast. Callie had lit something inside me, though, a need to be needed once again. When I thought back to those early weeks after Charlie's death and how desperately alone and listless I'd been, I felt certain I'd be dead right now if it hadn't been for her falling into my life.

Morris had called a few days after Callie's rescue to let me know I could come down and officially pick up Charlie's phone. At the station, he'd pulled me aside to share what he had learned about the phone itself. On the morning of the shooting, it turned out Charlie had left his phone on his homeroom desk. He must have pulled it out when he texted me about going to his friend's house and never put it away. I could picture him standing absentmindedly, joking with the kids around him, without a care in the world. He'd simply walked out of that room and left it sitting there.

Callie was also in that homeroom and she didn't have friends to talk to. There was no one who wanted to joke with her, and as she trudged toward the front of the room alone, she spotted the phone and pocketed it. The mystery of how she accessed it was also answered. Charlie, despite the rules I'd put in place, had disengaged the password. I could only guess at his motive, but the most likely one was that he didn't want to waste two seconds to enter it each time. His tweenage rebellion had saved Callie's life.

When I thought about how we saved each other, Callie and I, I felt Charlie's fingerprints all over it. If that was possible, then I couldn't help but wonder if maybe the deity I'd so consciously avoided most of my life had more than a passing interest in me. Six months had not healed my broken heart or my yearning soul, but it had given me a purpose and reason to keep living.

29

I'd refused my date's request to pick me up before the ceremony. I explained brusquely it would be best to meet after that part. I spent the day of the ceremony awash in a kaleidoscope of emotions. While our grief would be central, this was truly a day about accomplishment. We had done it; we had overcome that which might have otherwise killed us, and we were moving forward with purpose. Everyone who would be there was window dressing; this was about us. The reluctant survivors.

I wore a soft green sweater dress and chic black boots, but not to impress the stranger supposed to be taking my arm. I was dressed up for Charlie; I wanted him to be proud of me. When I walked through the underground tunnel from the capital lawn into the main building, a kindly usher took my arm and walked me toward the rotunda where the main event would take place. My Tribe was there, and we beamed at each other. Then, I saw Sherry's smile widen as she motioned across the room to a petite pale woman who seemed to drown in baggy black dress pants and a black blazer. She walked hesitantly toward us and Sherry said softly, "Angela, this is Ronda, Nell, and Lulu. Everyone, this is Angela Carter."

We rushed around her, and soon Lulu had her wide arms wrapped tightly around the frail woman. I felt the warmth of her embrace echo through the chamber, and I glanced around to see the crowd watching us. That's when I noticed the easels. I murmured that I'd be right back and made my way over. In the first, Jessica Carter smiled widely, unashamed of her slightly crooked teeth. Her long blonde hair was held back with a clip and a faint smattering of early summer freckles dotted her nose. She was sitting on a swing, looking heavenward, the picture of innocence and joy.

In the second painting, I saw the boy whose picture I had seen many times. He'd never looked this alive though in those photos. DeShawn Jenkins had a slightly impish smile, his smooth dark skin crinkled at his eyes in the same way Big Jeremiah's did. He was close up, in profile, smiling at a distant figure across a field. The figure was a small black girl in a pink dress with braids flying behind her and I knew without being told it was Aliya, DeShaun's twin.

Misty Framingham lay on a blanket in the third painting. She was smiling softly, with her lips closed, up at the sky she had been gazing at. A book lay folded open across her belly and in one hand, she held a daisy. She was the picture of serenity and peace.

Finally, my heart beating rapidly, I moved to the final painting. I'd seen it once before, but on that day, I'd barely been able to register it. Now I was in a place I could finally appreciate it. He, too, was smiling, of course. His brown eyes, the eyes I used to call Narek's eyes, but now I called Charlie's eyes, were open wide, framed with their luscious lashes. His head was slightly crooked, and his eyes were focused, studying something off canvas. He wore a blue t-shirt, and on close inspection, I could see the dab of paint on the sleeve. In his left hand, there was a paintbrush. In the background, I could see a hint of Ben's barn, and overhead the sun shone so brightly, a ray seemed to shine directly on Charlie himself. Tears pricked my eyes; it was the most beautiful painting I'd ever seen.

I moved back over to my tribe, and Ronda reached her hand to give mine a squeeze. I smiled back, and then we focused on just breathing as the governor began his introduction. When he finally finished, he gestured back at us, and as we had practiced, Ronda stepped forward.

"We thank you for this opportunity to introduce the city to our organization. Our goal, as was so eloquently stated by the governor, is simple. We want to prevent any other family from ever knowing the pain we have known. We believe that preventing gun violence in our schools begins long before a child ever feels desperate or angry enough to pick up that weapon. We believe that a comprehensive strategy is needed, starting in kindergarten to identify children at risk. While our goal is to identify and help 100% of these children, we also know someone may still slip through the cracks, so our approach is threefold, identify at-risk children, improve mental health access for youth and children, and enact sensible gun laws to keep guns out of the hands of children."

When she finally concluded her speech and thanked everyone, there was robust applause. I knew the news cycle ticked by quickly, and tomorrow, these same people might forget all of this, but at least for now, they were on our side.

We then made our way into the old senate chamber for the small reception. I spotted Ben across the room and made my way to him. "Oh my god, Ben, they're perfect, absolutely perfect. Thank you." and leaned in to kiss his cheek.

He smiled and said, "I was the greatest labor of love I've ever undertaken. I'm glad I was able to do it."

I glanced around and asked, "Where's your date?"

He shrugged and smiled. "I guess I forgot her."

"Ben! You didn't! You totally cheated."

Before he could reply, I heard Lulu exclaim excitedly from my side, "Nell, Peter's here! Peter, this is the Nell I'm always talking about."

I turned to face a nervous-looking man in his thirties, who was overdressed in a suit and tie. I shot Lulu a look and then an even darker one at Ben.

"Hi, Nell, good to meet you, finally. I feel like I know you from all our texting!" he said way too enthusiastically. The truth was we'd barely texted at all, at least, I had barely texted. I was sure this Peter was a nice guy, but I felt nothing when I looked at him except annoyance. I glanced back at Ben and saw the corner of his mouth twitch. Glancing around furtively for an escape, my eyes stopped when they met Dan Morris's eyes across the room.

I spun around to Peter and said, "Hey, so I'll be back in a minute, I see an old friend," and left him standing there next to a slightly embarrassed looking Lulu.

"I didn't expect to see you here," I confessed after I reached Morris.

He smiled, "When I read about this in the papers, I had to make it. Congratulations on setting up this initiative, from a law enforcement perspective, I really appreciate the focus on prevention."

"Yes, well, we needed to do something. Just hiding at home wasn't accomplishing much."

He nodded. "I can see it's been good for you; you look good."

As soon as the words came out, he shuffled his feet and looked away awkwardly. I knew he wasn't here in a professional capacity; he was here to see me and I knew intuitively that he liked what he saw. I wasn't sure how I felt about that, but what was striking was that I didn't feel an immediate urge to discourage him or push him away. I felt vaguely curious.

Wanting to smooth over the moment, I asked, "And Callie? Any word on how she's doing?"

"She's good, she's actually really good. She's in a terrific foster home and they have her riding horses as part of her therapy. She's really opened up and I think it's finally started to sink in, she's actually safe. Her father will spend some time behind bars. Maybe he'll even get help, although I don't have a lot of faith in that. He won't be in her life, though."

"What about her mother? I'm really confused about where she is in all of this."

"She's a victim and a perpetrator. She was a classic battered spouse in most senses, but she doesn't seem to have any interest in her own child. It's bizarre.

I haven't dug into her background, but I wouldn't be surprised to find out she, too, had been abused as a child. She's left the state with a new boyfriend, and this one has a record a mile long. I don't see social services allowing her in Callie's life unless she makes some huge changes."

I felt him before I saw him, Peter, suddenly at my side again. "Hi, Nell, just wondered if you wanted to get out of here and go get a real bite to eat."

I glanced up at Dan who was watching us without saying a word. "Hm, actually, I don't think that's going to work for me, Peter. It turns out I need to get some work done with Officer Morris here."

Peter glanced down at his feet, uncomfortably. I added sweetly, "Why don't you go talk some more with Lulu. She might want to go out for a bite with you!" I turned my back on him.

After a moment, I shrugged at Morris's sardonic look, and mouthed, "Is he gone?"

He nodded. "New friend?"

"Mm, something like that. I hope you don't mind that I used you as an excuse."

He smiled and said, "Not really, but I'm a big believer in telling the truth. We're going to have to actually leave and do some work now, you know."

I was a little confused, "What work would that be?"

"I don't know, maybe the work of getting a cup of coffee?"

"Oh, well, I don't know…" I suddenly felt a little nervous.

"Hey, I'm a police officer. It's my job to keep people honest," he explained, again with his wry smile.

I looked him over again; he was the kind of guy some women would call "nice looking." He'd never grace the cover of a magazine, but there was an appealing side to his strength and those blue eyes that seemed to miss nothing. I'd only really dated a few men in my life, and they had all been the sort who might be described as "devastatingly handsome." They'd also, coincidentally enough, all been foreign. I was drawn to people who were different, who changed the boring landscape of my daily life. I'd particularly always liked the quiet, brooding, artsy types. Narek had been my great love, but he was really an archetype for every guy I'd ever been interested in. Dan Morris was the complete opposite of my "type." But so far, my type hadn't worked out very well for me.

"Mmhm. If you say so. I suppose I don't really have a choice; I'd hate to be arrested for lying after all," I quipped back.

30

"It's the right thing to do," Morris reminded me. I leaned back, focusing on the light flurries kissing the windshield softly. It was too late to change my mind; everyone back home was eager to see me and if I cancelled at this late moment, my mother would probably buy her own ticket and show up on my doorstep. Whether I was in Michigan or Virginia, I'd be facing my first Christmas without Charlie. It wasn't as if I could completely escape that reality. Still, it would have been easier to hide from here. I knew my parents' home would be dripping with holiday decor and expectations.

I finally looked at Morris and gave a tight smile. He raised his eyebrows and nodded, "Yes, you can do this."

"Mm, if you say so," I said doubtfully.

Finally, I opened the car door and stepped onto the sidewalk. Morris walked around to the back of the car and opened the trunk to retrieve my bag and then joined me in front of the door marked departures. He pulled me into his arms, and his body helped counter the nearly freezing air temperature. I pulled my head back and locked gazes with his blue eyes and asked, "Are you sure you don't want to come?"

"Not this time, Nell. This time is about you and your family, they need you too, you know. I'll be here when you get back. I'm a patient man."

I smiled at that. He was a very patient man. My mood swings had improved in the two months we'd been dating, but occasionally he still got a version of me I wasn't proud of. It didn't deter him. He'd also been incredibly patient in a physical way. I'd decided to take things slowly, far slower than I ever had before with a man. I knew he was ready for that next step, and I hoped I would be too soon, but in the meantime, he respected my boundaries. I had no doubts he would indeed be here when I got back. That did not worry me. I was more afraid I wouldn't be me when that day came. I was afraid Michigan without Charlie might break me again.

I didn't give voice to my fears, instead, I smiled and lifted my face for a kiss. Afterward, I grabbed my rolling bag and walked into the airport purposely, refusing to look back. I knew instinctively though he had waited until I was safely inside before driving away.

The airport was decked out in holiday flare and Christmas music played cheerfully throughout the terminals. After picking up a latte in a bright holiday cup I hadn't wanted, I found a seat near my gate and awaited boarding. I couldn't help, but people watch.

Families with young children walked by in droves, some decked out in Disney apparel and others almost buried under heavy parkas and winter gear. I tried not to resent their holiday trips, but it was difficult. Every time I saw a parent snap at a small child or ignore their crying infant, I wanted to jump up and tell them to stop being so ungrateful for the blessings they had.

As I scanned the people at my own gate, my gaze was drawn to an older teenage girl wearing earpods and a VCU hoodie. Her long red hair was piled on top of her head in a messy bun, and she was deeply engrossed in her phone screen. I felt a pang of nostalgia, once upon a time, I had been that girl. Weary from finals, exhausted with the city, eager to sleep in my own bed. I knew my parents would spoil me, loading me down with too many gifts to fly back when I returned to campus. Mom would tsk tsk over my thin frame and insist on fattening me up with huge, elaborate meals. There was also the excitement of seeing my old high school friends, most of who had stayed in the state or in neighboring states, but it was a homecoming for each of us and we were eager to show off with stories from our newly discovered independence.

I wished I could summon up those same feelings of excitement and anticipation I knew were in this girl's heart no matter how cool an exterior she portrayed to the strangers in this airport terminal. I wished this visit could be that uncomplicated. My thoughts were interrupted by the boarding announcement, and I inhaled deeply for fortitude, then stood to board the plane.

A short five hours later, I landed on my second plane in Traverse City. I'd specifically told my parents to do a curbside pickup, but I should have known better than to expect they'd comply. As I walked out of the secure area, there was my father holding a Welcome Home mylar balloon. My mother stood beside him and burst into tears at my appearance before running toward me and pulled me into her arms. Whatever awkwardness I'd prepared myself for, my parents greeting me as they had back in my college days hadn't made the list.

"Oh my god, I told you guys I'd call and then meet you at the curb," I said, softening the words with a smile.

"We know, but we're so excited to have you here. We didn't want to miss a minute of your time on the ground!" Mom said cheerily. She had never been easily dissuaded by me.

"All right, let's just get to the car now. I'm sick of airports," I said as I walked toward the door.

The swoosh of frigid air hit me like a freight train. I'd forgotten just how bitter cold northern Michigan was in December. I glanced at my parents; how did they live with this year after year? We walked briskly toward the parking lot, and I tried not to think about the fact the inside of my nostrils seemed to actually be frozen. Why hadn't I suggested they all come down to Richmond for the holiday instead? The entire time, I focused on the weather, on my parents' recently aged faces, on the people walking around us. What I did not focus on were memories of the last time I'd landed here under the golden umbrella of summer with Charlie in hand.

As soon as we entered the relative warmth of the car, my mother talked. She talked for the entire twenty-five-minute drive home. That my father only occasionally grunted an acknowledgement and my own contributions were limited to the rare, "really?" "oh," "huh," to whatever tale she was telling, didn't slow her down. The Hoebarton's son had dropped out of college and didn't have a plan, the skinny one, not the fat one. The fat one was doing great. Dear Miss Candace was in remission again. The whole church had been praying daily, so it wasn't a huge shock, but what was a little shocking was Miss Candace's decision to move down south to live with her daughter. All that prayer had been worthy, but wasn't it just a little strange she'd pack up and leave that fast? Pinners, the local bowling alley, now had its own brewery. The townspeople were excited about it, but Mom thought maybe it was a little unfair to all the brewers that had loyally shipped their stuff in from other parts of the region for decades. Sarah was still dating that electrician; he was nice enough even if he was originally from Detroit. They'd be joining us the following day for dinner.

On and on, she spoke, at a fevered pace, as if she were desperate to say anything to avoid a moment of silence. It struck me that might actually be her motivation. Perhaps she knew the tougher conversations might be forced to surface in awkward silence. Although I preferred quiet to constant noise, I was thankful neither of my parents had asked me the dreaded question. How was I doing?

As we neared the house and rounded that old familiar curb, I suddenly sat more upright and blinked rapidly. My father had always taken time to decorate for the holidays, but the sight before me was a manic display I'd never seen before. Lights seemed to cover every inch of the house; huge deflated blow-up exhibits littered the yard. A large plastic sleigh led by eight reindeer seemingly ran down along the long drive-way.

My mother turned and smiled at me. "Like it? We hoped to surprise you!"

"Uh, yeah, I'm surprised," I stammered.

"We just thought maybe we'd work extra hard this year to get everyone into the season," she said brightly.

Unable to resist, I asked, "Did you consult with Clark Griswold, Dad?"

He sighed and shook his head, then said, "Come on, let's make a run for the house. You're not dressed for this weather."

I burst into the house, eager to escape both the polar vortex that swirled outside and the slightly disconcerting sight of a half dozen deflated figurines littering the snow-covered lawn like carcasses that had been picked clean by buzzards. The smell inside made me stop in my tracks. It was as if an entire pine forest had been vomited within the walls. I turned to my mother who was peeling her boots off, and asked, "Mom, what exactly did you do?"

"Tis the season!" she said cheerily, although I thought I caught a waver of doubt in her words. As I started forward, I saw a small tree bedecked in red, white, and blue patriotic trim. It was odd. We'd never kept a tree in the hallway before. Shrugging, I turned the corner into the living room. There, a huge tree stood, covered with our normal hodgepodge of ornaments, and multi-colored twinkling lights.

"Keep going!" Mom called out from behind me.

Curious, I walked through the living room to the adjoining dining room. Another full-sized tree. This one was a seashore theme, all white and teal and gold. It was rather pretty, the sort of special tree you might see in a gift shop. Still, three trees were very much overboard.

"Nice. Okay, I'm going to go…"

"Oh no, keep going!" she said again.

Bracing myself, I rounded the next corner into the kitchen. Yep. Tree. This one was smaller, sitting on the small curio table in the corner. It was decorated in Red Wings themed ornaments. Since when did my parents like hockey? I turned around and faced my mother, who was still smiling and said, "Let me guess, keep going?"

She motioned ahead and I walked through the kitchen to the stairway leading down to the basement turned family room. At the bottom of the steps, I saw the white lights of another large tree. I walked toward it and my jaw dropped. This tree was decorated entirely in VCU and UM garb, clearly celebrating Sarah and my alma maters. That we had graduated 12 and 11 years ago, respectively, apparently hadn't dampened my mother's efforts.

"Okay, now you can go to your room."

I breathed in the scent of pine for another few seconds and then smiled at her and said, "Really, it's all lovely, Mom," before heading up to my room. Lugging my bag from the first floor up to the second, I skillfully avoided looking at the photos that lined the wall. I already knew what hung there, various shots of Sarah and I at different ages, a few of my parents, and a bunch of Charlie from infancy onward. It wasn't that his picture upset me, I kept him proudly displayed in my own home after all, but it was the context of this wall. The age progress it demonstrated, that had suddenly and forever ended.

As I entered my room and threw the light on, I froze. There was another damned tree, and it was in my bedroom. That alone was a little perturbing, but it was my closer inspection of it that twisted my gut. It was a small tabletop tree placed on my desk. There were two types of ornaments on it. Flat, disc-shaped ceramic plates were each imprinted with a photo of Charlie. Some were of Charlie alone; some had me in them with him. I even found one of Narek holding him as a toddler. The other type of ornament was a clear glass angel with a gold halo. A dozen of them were spaced between the ceramic discs.

I sank onto my bed and put my face in my hands. I couldn't do this. I couldn't fake a wellness I didn't feel, I couldn't continue this holiday ruse, and I definitely couldn't sleep in a room with this…. Angel tree, lit up in the corner. I considered picking it up and putting it in the hallway, but I'd just have to pass it every time I left my room. I could demand my mother remove it, but to what end? She'd meant well, I knew that it would only make her as miserable as me. In the end, I settled for carefully draping an extra sheet I found in the linen closet over it. I'd just have to sleep with the ghostly looking figure staring at me.

When I made my way down for dinner, I avoided my mother's gaze. I waited for her to mention the tree, but surprisingly she didn't seem to be in a rush to discuss it. Instead, she was hyper-focused on sharing the week's agenda. It was as if she was hosting a camp or a resort as she rattled off every holiday observation, ceremony, party, concert and service in town. I glanced at my father, and I saw his lips were pressed tightly together, as if he were suppressing a laugh. Finally, I couldn't take it anymore.

"Mom! What is going on here? This feels a little crazy. Why are we overdosing on Christmas?"

Her cheeks turned pink and she was silent for a moment as if carefully considering her next words. "It's just that, well, I imagine this will be your most difficult Christmas ever and if we can get you into the spirit of things, maybe that will help you turn a corner."

I felt my eyebrows furl with the effort of not responding immediately. One… two... three... I counted silently in my head, willing myself to be as kind as possible.

"It is difficult, but that's part of my process. I'm not supposed to skip the pain, Mom, and that doesn't mean I'm not actually already turning corners."

I had shared some of what MPV was doing, but I realized there was a lot my parents didn't know. I began to fill them in on our initiatives, and in the process, I made it clear just how close I'd become with the other women. My parents clearly needed some confirmation I was doing much better, and I hoped this would give them that peace of mind.

My father cleared his throat and said, "I think this—" he waved his arms around the room, "This is all a little overboard, but I go along with it because, like your mother, I worry about you. Also, maybe we don't make this clear enough, it's not just worry, we miss you too."

He looked pointedly at my mother, who now looked uncharacteristically nervous and finally, she took a deep breath and continued for him.

"Nell, we know you have relished your independence, and we are proud of all your accomplishments in Virginia. But we truly miss you, Sarah misses you too. We aren't getting younger, and I think we can all appreciate how precious time can be. We would really like you to consider moving back here. I talked to Felix Gardenson and there is a position opening next year at the school. You could stay here if you wanted or we could help you find a place to live alone…"

As her words trailed off, I closed my eyes and sighed. What she was suggesting wasn't so outrageous,

I had no blood ties to Richmond anymore and my parents were not getting younger. Here in Traverse City, I still had family, old friends, a history, the comfort of familiarity. I loathed the winters, but the rest of the year wasn't so bad. Still, I'd found purpose in my Richmond tribe. Our weekly meetings were salve on a still not quite mended wound. Then there was Ben; he needed me almost as much as I needed him. And my students, obviously if I did make a move, it wouldn't be until after the school year ended, but I'd lose sight of them as they progressed up through our district. My own classroom efforts under the new program were going well. It was in ink now, so I was reasonably assured it would continue after I left and I could conceivably bring that to Michigan.

For all the pros and cons I immediately thought of, though, the one that reverberated loudest was Morris. I had no clue where it was going. The spark had barely been lit. Maybe our fledgling relationship would simply fizzle and die like a defective firecracker. Still, a future without Morris to turn to made me feel nervous. I'd grown to depend on his solid presence and practical advice. I'd grown to appreciate his quiet ability to ground me when I felt myself slipping off into a pool of self-pity. Could I really get through the day to day, without knowing Morris could be summoned if the need arose?

"I have a pretty full life in Richmond these days, I'll think about what you said, but it's not an easy decision," I admitted.

My half promise seemed enough to keep the smile on my mother's face, and with the elephant now fully discussed, I felt the mood lighten, and finally, I began to truly relax. After dinner and clean up, we settled in with mugs of spiked eggnog and a game of gin rummy and when I finally headed up to bed with a small, but pleasant buzz, I looked at the sheet draped tree and whispered, "Night ghost tree, night, Charlie."

31

I'd braved the cold to head out to Grand Traverse Commons, intent on loading up with Christmas gifts for my parents, sister, and Sarah's new mystery man. Once there, though, the throngs of holiday shoppers and the endless refrains of almost frantic holiday music made me feel twitchy. I ducked into a bakery to escape the madness. Sitting with my cranberry tart and latte at a small table in the corner, I mulled over the previous night's conversation and the expectations for the next few nights. I'd been texting casually with Ronda when a shadow fell over my table and I heard a man clear his throat.

"Hi, Nell, Merry Christmas..." a friendly voice said.

I looked up, surprised, and realized my visitor was Pastor Dave, the lead pastor at my parent's close-knit Lutheran church. In the past, I'd allowed myself and Charlie to be steered to services a few times a summer as a sort of perfunctory duty. When I did so, I tried to melt into the pew and escape as much notice as possible, so people didn't get any crazy expectations that we might show up every Sunday. That wouldn't be quite as possible in this setting, I realized sheepishly.

"Oh hello, same to you," I said with as much faux cheer as I could muster.

"Mind if I join you?" he asked.

Oh, I minded, I minded a lot. I bit back the words and gestured toward the empty chair instead.

"I knew you were in town; your parents have been so excited. I didn't think I'd get to see you before tomorrow, though, so this is a nice surprise," he said.

I fought to contain my grimace. Tomorrow, meaning Christmas Eve. My presence at services was apparently just assumed. I smiled tightly and just gave a small nod, which I hoped could be read as either an affirmation or as regrets. I still hadn't made up my mind about services.

Surprisingly, Pastor Dave turned out to be a pretty good conversationalist as he deftly shifted the conversation to his own recent visit to Virginia and a rather glowing account of the state's place in the nation's history. I found myself relaxing and engaging, and my guard slowly lowered. That was when he struck.

"You know I was so sorry to hear about Charlie. I didn't know him well, but what I did know sure impressed me."

"Mhmm, thank you," I said stiffly.

"I suppose you've had your fill of hearing he's in a better place," he said gently.

Under the table, my hands were clenched into fists, my nails digging into my palms.

"I have," I said quietly.

He stared at me for a moment, and I noticed for the first time just how kind his eyes were. I'm not sure if it was the kindness I saw, or perhaps it was the manic Christmas energy I'd been forced into since arriving, or if maybe it was just time, but before I could stop myself, I blurted out, "Why? Why do you think he's in a better place? He was pretty happy you know, healthy, had plenty of friends, a nice home. I could get it if he'd been very sick or lived in a terrible environment, but he wasn't."

He nodded. "It's a tough pill to swallow. I suppose the best I can offer is even the best life here in this world is imperfect. There will always be pain to be found, and of course, I believe our worldly separation from God always leaves us, even the happiest of us, with an unquenchable yearning that cannot be filled. Only after death can we finally unite with him, and only then can we know absolute, true happiness."

I thought about it for a moment, wondering if I should confess I wasn't sure I believed in God at all, but I suspected it wouldn't change a thing about what he was saying, and I was suddenly curious.

"Do you think God had a plan, and this was part of it?"

He smiled, but it wasn't a joyful smile. Instead, it was tinged with sadness.

"No, no, I don't. I think this is where all that free will comes into play. The boy who did this terrible thing, it was his plan, not God's. But I do believe when it happened, He was there to welcome those children home, and he's still there to bring healing to the hearts of everyone who was so hurt and devastated."

I stared down at my empty plate; I wasn't sure how to respond to him. I didn't feel offended by his words, they were lovely sentiments and part of me wished I could believe them in their entirety. I settled on offering him my own weak smile and saying, "Thank you, that's a nice thought."

We moved to the much lighter topic of weather, something every Michigander became obsessed with this time of year. How bad would winter get, how long would it last, and when would spring actually arrive? I confessed winter weather had set me on a search of Southern colleges. I wasn't built for these days. He mentioned everyone's recent disappointment when an overnight snowfall hadn't even delayed school, and I laughed.

"So, where I live, if we get an inch of snow, school closes down for a week. Once, when Charlie was in fourth grade, they cancelled before a single flake even fell and then the storm bypassed us completely. He spent the next two winters glued to the television during the weather report because he thought if they mentioned snow, school would be cancelled."

Pastor Dave smiled back, and I felt heady and strange, because it hit me this never happened. I never shared stories out loud about Charlie that made me laugh. Until now, I'd either avoided talking about him at all or mentioned him only in reverent, somber ways. I felt lighter, like the feeling you get at the dentist's office when they lift the heavy lead apron off of you after an x-ray.

"Everything okay?" he asked, at the look on my face.

Was everything okay? Not exactly. I felt like that was a word I'd have to work really hard to accept, but everything was… better?

"Yeah, I'm fine. Pastor, I have to confess, I'm not exactly a believer. I appreciate you taking the time to talk about this all with me, but I'm probably just a hair's breadth away from calling myself an atheist."

I thought maybe he'd launch into a sermon at that, but instead, he threw his head back and laughed. "Good, so you're saying there's still a chance." He followed that with a wink. "I hope you make it to Christmas Eve services, Nell; it was so nice bumping into you here."

I smiled back; it had been kind of nice.

32

Christmas Eve was our jam. We'd followed the same traditions my entire life. Mom served up a huge traditional ham dinner, followed by a sideboard full of pies that none of us really had any room for. We would eat too much; my father would complain his gut hurt, my sister would at some point say something caustic and rude that would make my mother's chin quiver and Mom would accuse her of trying to ruin Christmas. Then we'd clean the dishes and everyone would forgive Sarah. Then we'd get dressed up, open our gifts and laugh over the gag gifts and cry over the special ones. Then we'd head to midnight services. This year would be the same, but different. This year was most notable for both who wasn't there and who was there.

I felt Charlie's absence acutely at the table. I'd never been very gifted in the culinary department, so Grandma's made from scratch feast was a highlight for him. She always made a ridiculous amount of mashed potatoes, largely because Charlie insisted on filling half his plate with them. This year, she was apparently unwilling to break with tradition because, as usual, a huge bowl of mashed potatoes sat in the middle of the table. I felt my eyes sting a bit when I saw them, but I successfully reigned in the tears that threatened and, with a deep breath, turned to Sarah's boyfriend, Gus.

"So, Detroit, huh?" I asked amicably. He'd seemed like a nice enough guy, maybe a little too nice for my sister, but he made for a pleasant dinner companion.

"Yep, born and raised and couldn't wait to get away."

"I can understand that!" I replied without thinking.

I glanced at my mother, who was giving me a slightly sour look.

"Honestly, Nelly, I don't know what you wanted to get away from so badly. You love it here. Why you want to be down there with all of that traffic, and those bugs and hurricanes, is beyond me."

I smiled sweetly and said, "Have you stepped outside today, Mom?"

Sarah snorted and offered me a fist bump across the table. Truthfully, I sort of liked this new older, friendlier Sarah. Since the moment she and Gus had walked in the door, she seemed to have gone out of her way to talk to me and she'd already taken my side in one brief argument with Mom.

My mother would not let go of my earlier comment, though, and I knew it was because she was in full "Bring Nell Home" campaign mode.

"Well, have you given more thought to what we discussed the other day?" She turned to Sarah and said,

"Your sister is considering moving back! Tell her how fun that would be; you girls could have so much fun together."

"Mom…" I said.

"I mean, wouldn't it be ideal for everyone? If you and Gus marry, then Nell would already be around for the shower and dress shopping," she continued.

"Mother!" Sarah yelled.

I looked beseechingly at my father, who looked suspiciously like he was trying to hold back a laugh, and he shrugged at me. He would be no help; he didn't dare take sides against my mother and he was probably secretly just as hopeful of my return.

"Mom, I never said I was really considering that. You asked and I said we'd talk later, that doesn't mean I'm actually considering it. I have a life in Virginia."

I really hadn't intended to ruin Christmas Eve; I hadn't intended to discuss this at all on such an evening. I knew she had been building this entire fantasy in her head and would be crushed with the reality of what I wanted and I'd have loved to have a more graceful, private conversation about it. She'd pushed, though, so it was time for the truth to come out.

"I know you have your organization, but you could have those same goals in this state. Think about it, in a way, it's even better because you'd be growing what you already started there."

"And I have friends there, Mom, and don't say I have friends here too because people who knew me when I was 16 don't have a clue who I am now. I've changed; the people who are in my life now are people who know the person I am today."

She frowned. "I don't want you to lose friends, of course, but you could still stay in touch long-distance, the same way you and I do right now. And there are plenty of people in this town you could eventually be close to if you took the time to get to know them. There are also people in this town, men who would like to get to know you. You are still young; you could still meet someone."

"Oh God, Mom, I've already met someone!" I yelled.

Everyone got quiet for a moment. Sarah leaned across the table toward me and cupped the huge smile on her face before poking Gus's arm in glee. My father's eyes were darting to my mother, I knew he was trying to decide what reaction he was supposed to have, and she hadn't given the signal yet. She was just sitting silently, looking at her plate.

Finally, she said, "You met someone? A man?"

"Yes. We've been seeing each other for a few months now."

She took a deep breath and asked in a much calmer voice than I'd expected, "Does he have a name?"

"Morris. Well, Dan. But I call him Morris; it's a long story."

"I see. And what country is Morris from?"

Sarah burst out laughing. "Score one, Mom!"

I rolled my eyes. "This country. He's 42, he's a cop, divorced with no kids, owns his own home, gets along with my friends, and he's a nice guy. A legitimate nice guy."

She finally looked up at me, and I saw tears in her eyes. Oh shit, I'd ruined Christmas. Usually, it was Sarah who did that. She pushed her chair back, stood up, and then, just as I was sure she was about to leave the room, she walked to my end of the table.

"Nelly! I'm so happy for you!" she said as she leaned in to hug me. I looked into her eyes and I realized she was telling the truth; she really was so happy for me.

"Of course, we would love to have you home, but that isn't why we were pushing for it. I can't stand the thought of you alone in that house, coming home day after day to silence. I just can't stand it. This Morris, it's serious?"

I thought about that. I had thought about it a lot, actually, but I hadn't said the words out loud until then.

"It's probably too new to say, but I think it might be," I admitted.

Her smile widened and she hugged me again. Speaking the words out loud gave them power, and I realized I actually might be open to more with him than I'd realized.

Dinner ended on that happy note, too many presents followed, and then our foray to church where I held my candle during Silent Night and, for just a moment, indulged in a few tears. Overall, it was actually a beautiful holiday, far better than I'd expected. I felt reconnected with my parents and sister, and I suspected I might be invited back before too long to a wedding. Maybe on my next visit, Morris would accompany me. I was ready to go home, though. This time, home meant Richmond.

33

It's been almost four months since our first coffee date, and things are changing. Morris respected my need for boundaries and gave me the time I needed to work through my fears of allowing someone else into my heart. He wasn't entirely uncomplicated himself; his ex-wife had left him for another man and he was still a little bruised from that injury. When a few glasses of champagne and a midnight kiss turned into our first walk, hand-in-hand, into his bedroom on New Year's Eve, we'd begun a whole new stage of the relationship.

That I still call him Morris is a frequent source of humor with my tribe.

"Doesn't he have a first name?" Lulu had once asked.

"He's like Madonna or Prince. He only needs one name," I'd quipped back.

He did actually have a first name, but no one called him that at work and for so many years, work had been his entire life, so that was the name he was most comfortable with. I'd first gotten to know him as Morris, and it was impossible now to think of him as anyone else.

My romantic life isn't the only thing that's changed. I've decided I need to move forward by going back, back to the city. I currently have a sale contract pending on my house. It was a bittersweet decision, but it was the right one. Charlie and I made so many happy memories in the little ranch house, but there were also enough darker memories stamped on the walls. I feel the need for change. Charlie will be with me, in my memories, wherever I end up. I don't need to see a daily reminder of an unused bedroom to properly honor him.

Allowing myself to be vulnerable with a man again and planning the sale of my one-time safe haven are just some of the changes. Earlier this morning, I called Ben and asked for a favor. After I explained what needed to be done, he readily agreed. I called my tribe and asked if they'd like to be a part of my moment and without hesitation, each promised to be there. On my way to Powhatan, I stop and pick up the items I seek and then make my way down that long, familiar road to the sanctity of Ben's farm.

I can see Ronda's beaten me here; she's engaged in conversation with Ben in front of his art barn and the two wave. She's ditched her normal footwear for a pair of comfortable boots, I'm happy to see. Sherry, Lulu, and Angela all arrive together a few minutes later. We greet each other, and there's no sadness here today. We're all bundled up against the chill of the late February day, but even Lulu resists complaining about the cold.

Ben leads the way across a field to a cleared spot that houses charred logs and a blanket of old ash. Ronda smiles and hands me the first painting, and I study it for a moment after laying it face up in the pile. The carefree girl on the canvas is a stranger. Her smile is seductive, flirty, and I realize now that it is oh so smug. She doesn't have stretch marks on her belly; her breasts are small and firm, her golden-brown hair is a thick crown cascading behind her shoulder. She is a girl with her whole life in front of her, and she is completely unafraid.

I lay the second painting over it; the girl is a woman now, her belly huge and round, her breasts much fuller, her face slightly rounder, and her smile is different too. It's the smile of someone who is excited, but also a little unsure. She's a woman who knows the endless paths open in the earlier painting, have suddenly and irrevocably narrowed and changed. She is still blessedly naïve about the pain and heartaches that would lie ahead, but it seems there is a hint of trepidation in those eyes.

"Are you sure about this?" Ben asks, interrupting my thoughts.

"I am. These have been sitting in storage for a lot of years now, I just can't imagine a scenario where I'd ever want to actually display them. I feel like I need a clean break. I don't need to hang onto the ghost of Narek anymore, and I don't really even need to hang onto *her* anymore. I'm ready to move on."

Lulu hands me the lighter fluid, and I go about the business of spraying down the top canvas. Sherry hands me the matches, and after I light one, I smile across at Ronda and drop it purposely onto the target.

Smoke rises from the fire, like an offering to the gods of mercy. I follow its progression up toward the docile clouds and feel a sense of peace overtake me as it reaches the heavens. Afterwards, after every bit of wood, and canvas, and paint has disintegrated into the blanket of ash, I hug my tribe and Ben and thank them for being there for me. Finally, I walk purposefully toward my new life.

Once home, I prepare for the special date I'd never dared hope might actually happen. I shower to wash away the smell of smoke, the last of the evidence and then dress casually in jeans and a sweater before heading out again.

This date is a little different. We have a guest joining us. We'd decided to take her to a sushi restaurant, as she'd requested. Sushi is apparently very en vogue for teenagers these days and we wanted to give her the most authentic, Yelp 5-star experience possible. I've arrived first and am led to a discreet corner that's buffeted by a silk screen wall. Traditional Japanese figures are painted on its face, transporting me to another world. The table is low to the ground, chabudai style. I gingerly sit on the gold tapestry of a legless dining chair and await the arrival of Morris and Callie.

I've seen pictures of her, Morris has snuck a few to me even though I know he's not really supposed to, but I haven't spoken to her since the day they saved her. When she walks in the door with Morris, I recognize her from the photos but am still surprised at the changes. Those earlier photos had been of a small, pale girl, with a serious face. Tiny in stature, she'd looked a few years younger than she actually was. She had short blonde hair, green eyes and tiny elfin ears. The girl who walked in the door was all legs and braces. Her slightly longer hair is pulled back and I can tell from the ears she's the same person.

I smile as she approaches and stand to greet her. I yearn for her to be comfortable around me, to wipe away any hint of awkwardness she might feel at knowing I knew her deepest secrets. She smiles back nervously and I can't help it; I move toward her and embrace her in a hug.

"Hi, Callie. I've wanted to meet you for a long time," I confess.

She blushes and admits, "I've wanted to meet you too."

Morris points to a chair and suggests she has a seat. He's much more familiar with her than me, and I can see how at ease she is with him. I understand that trusting men can't come easily to this child, and I know it speaks a lot about Morris and the kind of man he is. I don't really need anyone else to convince me of his decency; I see and feel it every day, but it's still touching to watch.

"Morris tells me you're doing great in school!" I say brightly, hoping she still feels safe with me.

She nods and admits, "I guess I am; I try not to focus too much on grades, my counselor says it's more important I focus on feelings and reactions. But it seems like the more I focus on those feelings and how I react, the better my grades get."

"Smart counselor and smart girl," I observe. "And... your family? I understand there's going to be a change?"

At that, she smiles widely and nods her head. "Yeah, the Polinskis are going to adopt me! We go to the courthouse in two months to make it official, but they say they already consider me to be their real daughter. They said they'd planned to foster kids short term, but ended up with me first and decided they could never get a better one." She laughed. "I know they'd probably have done this with whatever other kid they might have gotten first, but I'm the lucky one, so I will take it."

I prod for details about her new life and smiles as she shares stories about life on the horse farm, what it feels like to suddenly have a little brother, and her funny early attempts at learning to drive the tractor. The child who had texted me, almost a year before, had been a broken porcelain doll. She'd been placed precariously on the edge of a shelf, ready to tumble down into the abyss. The child who sits here now is a confident, healthy girl who sounded eager to wake up each day.

As if she were reading my mind, she spoke frankly. "You know I probably would be dead if it wasn't for you."

"Oh, I don't know, you're stronger than you knew you were. I think you might have managed to pull yourself out, anyway. I'm so glad you turned to me, though, and we could get you out of it."

She glanced at Morris when I said the word 'we' and asks eagerly, "Is he your boyfriend now?"

I chuckle and reply, "I guess you could say that."

She grins at that news. "Really? Yay!"

I smile back at her and it feels awkward to bring this up, but I want her to know how important she is to me. "You know, I just wanted to say, we really saved each other. Talking to you, helping you, that all really helped me too. And it's more than that. That one night, I was in such a dark place. If you hadn't pushed me to call 911, I might not even be here today."

She looks confused for a moment. "911? I don't remember that."

Mom call 911 now. It's not time.
Please...

It's been almost a year, I reason. She's been through a lot since those difficult days. Perhaps if I prod her enough, she will remember. I look at her sweet young face, sun kissed from her hours on horseback. Her eyes are a guileless green, flecked with bits of gold, they'd seen the very worst of humanity, but she hasn't given up. They house no deception. I feel Morris's hand tighten over my own during the momentary silence, and I smile up at him before turning back to her. Maybe she's just forgotten. Or maybe she hadn't texted me. Do I really want to know?

"I don't know, Callie; it's been so long, I'm probably confused. Anyway, tell me all about these horses you love so much."

She breaks into a huge smile and tells us about the first time she rode Lucky Lady, and I looked back over at Morris. He's also smiling widely, nodding along at her story. His joy in reaction to her joy sparks a glow around our entire table. He glances at me, and the smile changes to something else. This smile is softer, and it doesn't quite conceal the hint of desire.

Callie pops another California roll into her mouth and closes her eyes to enjoy the sheer pleasure. After swallowing, she smiles and declares, "Sushi is life!"

Morris throws his head back and laughs deeply, and affirms, it is indeed life. As I watch him, warmth fills my belly and with chopsticks in my hand, I reach for a sushi roll. I stuff the life into my mouth and I look back up at him, covering my mouth with my hand, unable to contain the laugh that emerges. I am struck with certainty. I am in love again. With sushi, with Morris, with life.

#

AFTERWORD

The Richmond School of Art and Design is fictional, as are the K-12 schools named in this novel. Artist Ben Hamilton is also fictional- although I'd like to think his prototype exists out there somewhere. Mabel's in Powhatan is very much real, and I highly recommend the Sprinkled Donut Crazy Shake.

While this story is fictional, the themes of child abuse, bullying, and gun violence in schools are entirely too real. The prevention heroes are the thousands of real teachers and social workers who have answered their calling to serve our children. The difference they make in a child's life and the life of every person that child comes into contact with- isn't fiction.

About The Author

Kristy spent her childhood as a Navy "brat" and her adult years first as a service member and then as a Coast Guard wife. A lifelong wanderer and now empty nester, she's set permanent anchor in Virginia Beach, Virginia with her husband and that most rascally of rascals- her cat Percy. When not plucking away at her keyboard or eagerly devouring every book she can get her hands on; she enjoys theater, beach combing, hiking, wine tasting, and obsessively planning the next journey.

Made in the USA
Middletown, DE
19 February 2021

34026290R10175